I0553842

It's a Long Way Down
by Ian Canon

Other works by Ian Canon

"Before Oblivion," by Ian Canon and Jai Tanninen.
A collaborative work of poetry and painting.

"Madam, in Eden, I'm Adam," by Ian Canon.
A collection of short stories.

Contact Ian Canon

facebook www.facebook.com/thisisallcanon
instagram @thisisallcanon
twitter @thisisallcanon
website www.thisisallcanon.com

Book Cover & Design
Katya Worbets

"There are things you do sometimes, actions
that you take by obeying sudden impulses, without
stopping for even a fraction of a second to think,
and then you spend the rest of your life either
lamenting it or thanking yourself for it.
They are rare, unique, and perfect moments. "

— IRENE GONZALEZ FREI

it's

a

long

way

down

one

OUT ON THE BALCONY of his large master bedroom in Los Angeles, under the silver hue of the moon and the stars, David Emmeret Smith flipped through the mental file folder that contained the last 56 years of his life. By anyone's measure, his life had been a success, was currently a success, and on its present trajectory, would offer more success in the coming weeks. But, instead of drinking in the joy of his achievements, here he sat, staring up at the universe, wondering what it meant to anyone, to everyone, to exist, to be, and to succeed in a world like his.

David was an artist and his art was acting—and that is not to say that all actors are artists, but simply that this one was. The New Yorker once wrote of him "...he was the preeminent actor of a generation. His talent was only exceeded by the admiration of his peers and his ability to connect with an audience." In the last ten years alone, he had won three Golden Globes, each of which coincided with an Academy Award nomination, but as of yet, his coveted 13½ inch golden man had escaped him. Now his fourth—and, he thought, possibly final—nomination was upon him and the word around town was that the prize was his to lose.

One would not have had, upon meeting him, the immediate impression of a great artist. His face was soft and round and worn, but, in the age-soaked lines, there yet remained a comfort—a nostalgia for another time, like the worn out trinket-lined walls of a grandparent. His unkempt hair was a pale blonde, thinning, but appropriately for a man entering into the latter half of his 50s. He had the triumphantly squishy body of an elderly hedonist and an indulgent artist; he wore thin black circular frames and kept his yellow beard short. Often, as was currently the case, a cigarette dangled from his thin lips—a bad habit he paid little attention to, to the dismay of his wife, Alice.

It had been ten years since his first nomination, which meant it had been ten long years spent considering what came next: a revered peer thumbs an envelope, turns over the seal, and calls out a name, his name. He makes his way through the crowd as they rise from their seats and break into deafening applause. What should be a monumental, life-changing event, a world-altering experience that kept him up with excitement, instead filled him with dread. This was his Mount Everest. But what happens when a climber breaches the top and returns home safely? What is he—who is he—after that? Is he still a mountain climber? Or is he a man who once climbed a mountain? When you achieve your life's work, what do you become? These were the thoughts that occupied David's mind every night and every day since the passing of his mother three months ago. Her death brought with it a nihilistic wind sweeping through his life, leaving behind a crater of meaninglessness perpetually expanding and contracting as the day of the awards approached.

The moon now hung low in the sky and a grapefruit globe of light tickled at the edges of the earth. David's wife stumbled out onto the balcony rubbing her eyes.

"Have you been out here all night? It's almost morning."

Alice, her oval face illuminated by the mature moon, leaned against the sliding glass door, scrunching her nose at him. Though she maintained a charming likeness to the girl he had met 25 years ago, both her face and body had rounded with age. Her once rich, deep blonde hair had gone grey, and her face was lined with the contours and folds of time. David, however, perhaps moved by love's ignorance, couldn't detect the signs of sand moving through the eternal hourglass. To him, the bushy brown eyebrows that furrowed in his direction were the same that he had met at an off-broadway production of Death of a Salesman. David was Willy Loman, and Alice, a stage-hand, had recently taken her first job out of college. She was this tiny, rapid-firing mouse in a black turtleneck, which she tucked into high waisted faded blue jeans, poking in and out of where she was needed on short, scurrying legs. He could see it from a distance, the ebullient energy she carried within her small-frame. As he watched her, before he knew her name, he called her "little mouse." Quickly, they were inseparable, then living together, then married. Now she was behind him, disappointed in his apparent insomnia.

"Can't sleep," he said, flicking ashes over the side of the balcony, watching them fall a few feet and simmer in the dewy grass.

"Still?"

"My mind's a mess. Mother, the nomination, the win, my future. Too many things for one man."

"But it's past five, David." She joined him at the ledge, looking out over the horizon. "You have to be up in three hours. You'll be a zombie tomorrow."

He wiped a stiff hand across his forehead. "A few more minutes. I just need to clear my head."

"It's just…" she sighed and walked back inside.

"I love you," he mumbled to the trees. They responded with a waning rustle.

He closed his eyes and let the cool morning air tickle his face. His mind wandered towards his mother, Janet, half-awake on a hospital bed, more bones than body, a phantom of the woman who raised him. Her pale hands extended towards him, beckoning him closer. He took her bony hands in his—they were cold, almost inhuman. She mumbled something unintelligible before closing her eyes, never to open them again. The flatline of the heart monitor still rang in his ears.

A far-off alarm pulled David from the cotton embrace of a dream. He groaned, rolled over, and flopped a loose hand around the side table like a fish out of water. The ringing stopped. His arm went limp beside the bed. He basked in the few seconds of silence allotted to him before opening his eyes: 10:00AM blinked in and out of existence. His eyes sucked into their sockets and he shot out of bed.

"Fuck!"

In a single motion, he was dressed and running down the stairs. At the kitchen table, Alice sat calmly, eating her breakfast, reading the paper, as if unaware of his tardiness.

"What the fuck?" He buttoned the last two buttons of his shirt and slipped the tongue into his pants. "Why didn't you wake me up?"

She folded the newspaper away from her face. "When's the last time you've gotten more than an hour or two of sleep? I did you a favour."

"But now I'm an more than two hours late!"

"Darling, you're Caesar. They can wait for their Caesar."

"God damnit. You know that's not how this works."

Alice shrugged and returned to the paper. He shook his head, grabbed a muffin from the table, and was out the door.

Thirty minutes later, he arrived on set: an elaborate green screen setup surrounding a structure that looked specifically ancient and vaguely Roman. A re-creation of the infamous Theatre of Pompey, the historic site of the assassination of

Julius Caesar. The film was to be a mainstream, heavy-on-CGI epic, detailing (in historically-inaccurate fashion) the popcorn version of Caesar's life, titled "The Rise and Fall of Gaius Julius Caesar." It was a relative departure from David's arthouse roles, but what the hell, he thought, the money would be nice, and it might be a bit of fun to goad the critics into wondering what he was thinking following up his Oscar nominated role in "Goodbye Blue Sky."

The first to recognize his presence on set was the director, James Thomas Reid. By all accounts, he was a man of exceptional averageness with, other than being able to turn a profit from a turd, no distinguishable talents. The only memorable feature he had, in person or character, was his closely cropped beard, which was a hodgepodge mix of red, orange, and brown. He was running towards David, one arm up in the air, steaming from head-to-toe.

"For God's sake! Do you have any idea how late you are?"

"I know, I know. I'm sorry, James," he said, looking through the man. "I haven't been sleeping well and Alice took it upon herself to reset my alarm."

James' expression, all at once, evened out. "Ah, I suppose wives know best, don't they, David?"

"So she tells me."

"Well, get moving. Wardrobe is waiting for you. Today's the day. A once in a lifetime moment to act out the biggest betrayal the Romans ever committed."

"I'm going to be crucified?"

"Alright, so it's the second biggest betrayal. Still, an exciting day!"

"Can't wait," David said, his eyes rolling in their sockets.

He moved past James and into the set. A small crowd of idling actors, stage hands, and extras had gathered around the replica of the Theatre of Pompey, and a familiar voice distinguished itself from the crowd.

"Sleep in again, David?" it said with a forced, English accent.

Standing in the middle of the pseudo-theatre was a sharp featured, wiry man with a frame noticeably smaller than the toga that was draped over it. A rubber short sword hung from his hip and an ear-to-ear grin was painted between structured, gaunt cheeks. His deep black hair was disheveled and curly, sitting atop a strong Roman nose. This was Scott Peterson, playing Marcus Junius Brutus, the man who would bring down the great dictator.

"Need my beauty sleep," David said, without stopping.

"That you do, Caesar." He unsheathed his sword and pointed it at David. "But hurry up. You have a date with destiny."

In the last few months on set, David had taken to Scott, seeking him out when he was bored, enjoying his brash humour and straight-forward manner. Even dimly lit bulbs light the way in total darkness.

David, rounding the length of the set, exited at the back, into an opening between his set's warehouse and the one next door. Parked outside was a massive, double-sided trailer that served as the on-set wardrobe and makeup area. He knocked, then entered the twin on the left. A young woman, the costume supervisor, had her legs up, scrolling through her phone. Startled, she scrambled to her feet.

"Hi, Katherine."

"Oh, hi. You're here. Let me get your toga."

At the back of the trailer hanging from a rolling rack was a family of costumes, all Roman. She pulled one out, which had a large red tag on it: "Caesar, death scene."

"Be careful with that," she said, handing it to him. "You wouldn't want to prematurely burst your blood packs, would you?"

"I suppose not." He took the outfit out of her hands and was surprised by the unnatural weight of the packs hidden within. He donned his Caesar's hair and robe in a change room at the back of the trailer.

He passed Katherine on the way out. "Don't you look to die for," she said, looking up from her phone.

David suspended the word "dying" in the air, before continuing towards the set.

"Alright everyone, it's been a long day. Let's bring this home." James sat back down in his director's chair.

"Scene 41, take 18. Action!"

Caesar strode through the corridor of the Theatre of Pompey and immediately the chatter died down, heads turned, bodies rose, and the attention was on him.

"Caesar!" Tillius Cimber called out, raising his hand to get the attention of the dictator. "My brother! What will become of him? Have you yet reached a decision?"

"The matter is still being contemplated, Tillius. Have patience."

"Patience!" Tillius ran towards Caesar and struck him in the chest with a fist. "You've made promises, Imperator!"

The rest of the senate closed in on the commotion, inching their way towards their dear leader.

The Dictator's pupils bulged and his face tightened. "You dare strike out at your Caesar?" he shouted through clenched teeth.

Their gaze met and the whole room, as if holding their breath in synchronicity, went dead. "You are no Caesar of mine," he whispered.

"Now!' Servilius Casca shouted.

The clang of swords unsheathing wracked off the walls.

The surrounding throng of robed men lashed out at their Caesar. Unsheathing his own sword, he stood his ground bravely. He parried a single blow, then another, before he was struck from behind and staggered to one knee. Another slash came at his face, and another at his shoulder, and another at the spine of his back. He collapsed as the men, like a pack of crazed dogs, crowded over his body. He disappeared among the slashing betrayers.

The men dropped their swords and slowly cleared away, as if they knew not what they had done. Caesar was left alone, covered in his own blood, breathing heavily, and mortally wounded. The cowards watched as he crawled desperately towards the foot of the Statue of Pompey, reaching out for it in his delirium, as if his old friend and enemy could see him now.

Brutus approached the dying dictator, touching him gently on the shoulder, then turning him around, wanting to see, for the last time, his face. As he held the dying man in his arms and unsheathed his dagger, tears welled in both men's eyes.

Realizing the extent of his betrayal, he whispered, "Et tu, Brute?" as Brutus plunged the end into his gut. A single tear rolled down Brutus' face.

A high-pitched "CUT!" broke through the thick emotion in the air. "I think we got it everyone! That's a wrap for the day!"

Scott Peterson, formerly known as Marcus Junius Brutus, even more formerly known as Scott Kaufman from upstate New York, held his hand out for David.

"Thanks."

"Coffee?"

"God yes. I didn't get much sleep." David followed Scott to the craft table.

"Too excited to sleep?" Scott asked, as he poured two coffees.

"Excited?"

"Stop playing coy. You know exactly what I'm talking about. Hell, a stranger could yell the same question at you from across the street and you'd know exactly what they're referring to."

David, his attention waning, blew on his coffee.

"Well, are you?"

"The Academy Awards?"

"Jesus, David. Yes, the Oscars."

"Haven't thought much about it." He popped the top off his coffee and continued to blow.

"Then why haven't you been getting much sleep?"

"Frankly, that's a personal question."

"Fine."

Minutes of silence passed between the two. They sipped their coffees and watched the busy bees dismantle the set.

"Alright, maybe I'm a little nervous," David said. "Maybe I'm really nervous. Hell, I don't know."

"But you're a practical shoo-in at this point. Everyone knows it."

"I guess I'm not everyone. I don't think I have a shot in hell."

"Seriously? Everything I read is stating it as an inevitable fact of life. David Emmeret Smith: Oscar winner and acting legend. God only knows why you decided to join us plebs down in the popcorn flicks."

David took exception to the phrase 'top of your game' as what goes up, will inevitably come down. "Okay. I get the message."

"I'm serious. I would be practicing my Oscar speech every night. Twice a night. Three times a night. It would be the only thing I would be thinking of."

"Alright, I—"

"You're going to own this town for a night, David."

"Right."

"If I was you, I would be over the moon."

"Got it."

"I'd be screaming it from the rafters. A man on a mission."

"Is that all?

"A lifelong dream. Success coming out of my goddamn ears!"

"Jesus," he said, slamming his coffee down on the table. "Can you shut up for a second?"

The scene around the two slowed as heads turned to watch the impending car crash.

"Sorry, David," he said, and the commotion resumed.

"It's alright. I get it." David used napkins to wipe up the small ring of coffee around his cup.

"Maybe I got a bit too excited."

"Maybe I'm just being an asshole."

Scott met David's eyes. "You're definitely being an asshole, David."

The room was still, then a smile broke on David's face, followed by laughter. "Thanks."

"You know what I think you could use?"

"What's that?"

"A drink. On me."

David looked at his watch. "Why not? Where to?"

two

SCOTT PULLED INTO an empty parking lot of a pub. He parked below a red neon sign blinking the letters s, m, t, t, y, s. The i, like the gapped-toothed mouth of a decrepit old man, was missing.

"What kind of place did you bring me to?"

"Not your typical watering hole, is it?"

"It'll do, I guess."

The inside of the bar looked like an outlet window from Craigslist—a mismatched lottery of chairs, tables, stools, paintings, and art. The air was thick with dust, accentuated by the setting sun bleeding in through red-stained church windows. A low hum of rockabilly music played over hidden speakers and it smelled faintly of cigarettes. They, the only two in the room, took a seat at the U-shaped bar.

"Hello?" they asked in unison, looking for a bell to ring.

A man materialized from a backroom door. He had long, thinning hair, a pockmarked face, and the crooked nose of a thief.

"Yeah?" he said, as he cleared his throat, rolling the spit around in his mouth.

"I'll get a scotch. Johnnie Walker if you have it," Scott said.

"We only carry whiskey."

"What labels do you have?"

"It's just whiskey."

"Uh, sure, whiskey then."

The bartender frowned, took out two short glasses and poured. The glass half-full, he slipped his finger over the spout and held it over David's glass. "And for you?"

"Same."

He filled David's cup, stopping half an inch higher than Scott's. "That'll be $20.00."

Scott slid a wrinkled bill across the bar top. The man pocketed it and disappeared.

Staring at the wide assortment of scotch behind the bar, David lifted the glass to his lips. "Tell me about yourself, Scott." It was warm on the way down.

"What do you want to know?"

"Girlfriend?"

"Not right now."

"Have a reason?"

"Should I?"

"You're good looking enough. I would've thought you'd have a woman's attention by now."

Scott grinned, glaring his teeth. "I have more than one woman's attention, actually."

"More than one?"

"Commitment, they say, is for the elderly."

"Are you calling me old?"

"I wouldn't say you're young."

"Oh." David took another, deeper sip. "You don't want a serious relationship?"

"Not really."

"Doesn't it get lonely?"

"Everyone gets lonely, don't they?"

"Then why not have one woman in your life to fill that hole?"

"Do you still get lonely?"

"Sometimes."

"Well, there you go."

"Still."

"I enjoy not having attachments. Lets me focus on what's important."

"What's that?"

"More women, bigger, better gigs. The sky's the limit. I'm not about to settle."

"Settle?"

"I can almost always find a woman that recognizes me when I go out. Why settle for just one when I can have a new one every night?"

"What's that like?"

"Taking a girl home?"

"Using your moderate fame to meet women. I married Alice long before I had any sort of recognition."

"I thought it was cool at first." He tipped back his whiskey and shuddered softly. "But now it can feel sorta, I don't know, cheap, I guess."

"I thought you said you enjoy it."

"I do, but sometimes I don't."

"What do you mean?"

"I sometimes doubt myself. I start to wonder, 'do these girls like me for me, or my fame?'"

"Hate to break it to you, but it's your fame they're attracted to."

"Makes a man feel like he doesn't have any real value in the world."

"Life's who you are and who you are is what you do."

"Easy for you to say. You've done so much."

"And what is that that I've done, exactly?"

"You're being modest."

"Go ahead. Tell me."

"When I found out I was going to be working with you, I was ecstatic. I wanted to learn from you. You're an artist. A real artist, David," he said. "You've proved to the world that

23

acting is a field to be proud of. That we're not all just pretty boys and play models." He emptied his glass. "Every time you walk on screen, every time you're in a movie, people know it, they can feel your presence. It jumps out and screams at the audience, 'David Emmeret Smith is here and he's not fuck-ing around!' People see movies just because you're in them. They'll be seeing me in Caesar just because you're in it. And I'm not, you know, just saying this. 'A generational talent' is what I read in the New Yorker. People like you are rare."

David put a hand on Scott's shoulder. He shrugged it off.

"And you're sitting here asking me some kinda dumb question like 'what have I done that's so great?' Come on, David! Look around you!"

The bar was still empty.

"Look at all these other suckers! They're walking around the world half-drunk and blind. What they wouldn't give to be where you are! To be who you are!"

"Would you keep it down?" the bartender said, returning from the back. "I've got other customers here."

Scott lowered his voice to a whisper. "Sorry." His attention darted to the two empty glasses and back to the bartender. "Two more?"

"It'll be twenty each this time."

"But—"

"I got it." David slid two twenties across the bar. The man refilled their glasses and disappeared.

Scott started again, but in a low whiskey voice. "I'm serious, though. You're amazing."

"I've done some good work."

"Better than good."

"And what do you want to do with your life, other than increase your stock of available women?"

"Haven't given it much thought."

"I don't buy that."

"I've only ever thought about the next gig, the next movie, the next tv spot."

"Well, where do you see yourself in five years?"

"It's a tough question to spring on a guy."

"Take your time."

Scott swirled his drink around, looking for answers in the vortex that formed in the bottom of his glass. "I guess, if I were pressed, I would say I wanted to be a leading man within the next five years, star in a big hit, become a household name, maybe settle down with a beautiful woman, probably a blonde, great body, but kind. She would have to be kind. Someone who loved me for me and not my fame. A real diamond in the sea. I'd buy a house, have some kids, get into more serious roles, make a real art of it and get the recognition I deserve, like you have. Then maybe collect a few awards, even direct. I've always wanted to direct, but I don't have the experience. I don't know. Something like that. Like I said, I haven't really thought about it."

"Sounds like you've done nothing but think about it."

"You pushed me, so I gave it a shot. But five years is a long time. I can't tell the future. I might not ever reach any higher than where I am right now."

"Would you be okay with that?"

"I'm happy where I am."

"Would you be happier at the top?"

"How would I know? Maybe? Probably? Are you happier now?"

"Not really."

Scott motioned for the bartender to drop off two more, then waited for him to leave. "Why aren't you happy?" he said, once the bartender was out of earshot.

"I didn't say I wasn't happy."

"Are you?"

David's impulse was to turn away from the line of questioning, but he hesitated, then, perhaps loose-lipped by the whiskey or emboldened by Scott's clairvoyant look into his next five years, he said, "I don't really know if I'm happy anymore. Every day I feel the future grow darker and I don't know what's waiting for me on the other end."

"The other end of what?"

"I don't know. That's the problem."

"When did you start feeling this way?"

"Shortly after my mother died."

Scott coughed on his whiskey. "I-I didn't know. I'm sorry."

"It wasn't your fault."

"I know it wasn't my fault, it's just—fuck. When did it happen? How did it happen? If you don't mind."

"Cancer. About three months ago."

"Damn. I wish I knew what to say."

"You don't have to say anything."

On cue, they sipped their nameless whiskies, studying the bottles in front of them. As if feeling the tension, the bartender appeared and filled their glasses.

"So," Scott said, breaking the silence, "the Academy Awards don't mean anything to you?"

"It's the culmination of my entire life's work."

"But winning wouldn't make you happier?"

"I'm not sure. If I'm being honest, I'm scared to find out."

"Why?"

"I'm scared it's the chase I loved. That it kept me alive, kept me grounded, kept me working."

"And what if it was?"

"Then I don't know what I'll have left. There's always been these three pillars in my life: my mother, my career and my wife. Suddenly, within the last three months, there's just Alice."

"Isn't she enough?"

"My God, I hope so."

"She's a tough woman."

"I don't know." David rolled the last syllable off his tongue and out into the world, putting a period on both the sentence and the topic.

"You know what," Scott said. "Fuck all that for now. For tonight, let's put it aside and enjoy a couple, just you and me. We can drown out everything else."

David cleaned his glasses on his shirt and pushed out a half-smile. "I think I can manage that."

David woke, gasping for air, fully clothed and above his blankets. The weight of the world crashed down on his forehead. He tried to recollect the events of last night, but his mish mashed brain malfunctioned around the second whiskey. Stale alcohol surrounded his body, creating its own putrid gravitational pull. He needed a shower.

With legs as wobbly as a leaf in a brisk autumn wind, he mustered the energy to get to his feet. His face, noticing it now in bathroom mirror, was creased and puffy, his lips cracked, his eyes blood red and silky. He peeled his tainted clothes off his body and got into the shower. The water was warm and inviting, opening his pores for a final release. His mind cleared as the room fogged and a flurry of questions came to the forefront.

When did he get home last night? What time was it now? Where did he go? Did he say anything stupid? Embarrassing? Did he divulge his deepest secrets? Was Scott going to tell anyone? What would he tell? What could he tell?

While furiously scrubbing himself down to the bone, he tried to put back the pieces of the night. Flashes of shots, close talking, and a finality of brotherly love appeared in his mind's eye, like the photographs of a choppy family album. While certainly out of character, he couldn't dredge up any damning memories, but there yet remained an unnerving sense of embarrassment that he couldn't shake.

Once he was as pale, puffy, and purified as a man as hungover as he could be, he turned off the water. Pulling his housecoat from behind the door, he wrapped it around his still steaming body.

What was he going to do today? Coffee—his body raged for coffee.

David tiptoed down his stairs, peeking his head over the railing with each turn, trying to discover if he was alone—and hoping he was. The house was empty, save for one pruney overweight actor.

The time on his espresso machine read 2:00PM. He listened to the inner-workings of the machine until it shuddered out his liquid revival. He sat at the steel island in the middle of the kitchen and read the front page of yesterday's paper. Halfway through, he turned on the radio, got a glass of water, and returned to the paper. Inch by inch, the shake in his hands, the steady headache, his foggy brain, slowly improved. It had been a while, but he remembered hangovers being much worse. Other than the brief moment of terror after waking up, he could manage this. In fact, he might drink a bit more often. It was pleasurable, perhaps even positive, to let loose for a night.

His thought was interrupted by the distant jingle of keys. The door opened and Alice walked in with bags of groceries in each hand. She saw David and giggled.

"Hey drunkie. How ya feeling?"

"I've been better, but surprisingly, I've been worse."

She put the groceries on the counter. "I figured you'd be on your deathbed right now. What got into you last night?"

David, his joints stiff and slow, helped her put every-thing away. "Brutus, that bastard, took me for a drink."

"The young guy? Scott?"

"That's the one."

"And?"

"I was only planning on having a few with him, but one thing led to another, then another, then another—"

"Suddenly you're showing up here at three in the morning, drunk as a skunk, smelling like you've been dipped into a bottle of bourbon and rolled in tobacco."

"Is that when I got in?"

"You don't remember?"

"It's all a little hazy."

"You were ridiculous."

"Tell me."

"You stormed in, woke me up, mumbling something about being 'too old and too young' before trying to take off my nightgown. You barely got a sock from my foot before you passed out on top of me."

"What a man," he said.

"Was it fun?"

"I hope so. Otherwise this hangover was for nothing."

"I can't remember the last time we were hungover. Or drunk, for that matter."

"New Year's last year."

"What'd we do?"

"Dinner at Mélisse. We finished two bottles of red wine: Clos De Tart, Mommessin, 2008. Hell of a wine."

"I remember now. We went to Justin Tamarind's party after. Got so drunk we had to leave the car there."

"You were the one who got so drunk."

"Still, I remember it being a marvellous night."

"You puked at the party and I had to take you home."

She squeaked out a laugh. "Either way, it was lovely, with

my lovely man." She leaned over and kissed him. "Maybe we can get a little tipsy together next Sunday, after you win your very first Oscar. I even promise not to puke."

"I'd love to get a little tipsy with you, especially if I don't win."

"Are you still on this? I've told you a thousand times: you're going to win. You know it. We all know it. Stop looking for sympathy. You're a bigger man than that."

"I'm stressed, that's all."

"You're probably also hungry. I'll make you something to eat."

As the day progressed and David's hangover faded, what replaced it was an afterglow that he hadn't felt in years. It was a renewal, a complete release of emotions. One of those rare times his legacy didn't matter, his art didn't exist, his mountain was a plain, and he didn't think of his mother. Last night's roaming of the world, blind, deaf and dumb to those things that ailed him, freedom from inhibitions and self-doubts, must have carried over into the day.

That night in bed, Alice found him unusually pressed up against her back, holding her tight, feeling her warmth. To her surprise he had an erection, which he firmly gyrated between her cheeks. She pushed back on it, light enough to leave room for him to doubt it was on purpose, and as a result, turn him on even more. Then she did it again, then again, before turning and reaching down.

For the first time in weeks, David slept easily.

three

DAVID, WHILE FOLDING his tie over itself, a tremor in his fingers, rehearsed the names he hoped to thank. This wouldn't be his first acceptance speech, not by a long shot, but it was different this time. Tonight could determine the trajectory of the rest of his life. He just might find out where he stands in the world, what paths were still open to him, and where this long journey has taken him. It was as if he stood at the precipice of his own retirement—a doorway to his golden years. And besides that, he was still rather hungover from last night, and the night before that, and the night before that. In fact, he had been drunk every night since he and Scott painted the town in ethanol. That night something had clicked in his head. He was chasing, every night since, alone in his office, that same euphoric, carefree forgetfulness he had experienced the first night. But it wouldn't quite come and it was never quite the same. Like the perpetual carrot in front of the horse, it remained a hair's breadth out of reach, sitting on the border of his brain, goading him to consume more, which he dutifully obliged, stretching his limbs, a little harder, a bit more determined, towards his coveted prize, only for it to graze his fingers and slip away.

He picked up the glass in front of him and brought it to his lips, swishing the scotch around his mouth, from side to side, and under his tongue, looking to dowse every inch of it in the purifying liquid, then swallowed.

Alice walked into the room, pinning an earring into

her ear. "God, David. Can you believe it? In less than three hours some hollywood schmuck will be saying the words, 'and the Academy Award goes to... David Emmeret Smith in Goodbye Blue Sky!' leading the room to erupt into a roaring applause. You'll stand up, kiss me, and walk up to accept your award. It'll be magical."

"Hey now, I'm one of those 'hollywood schmucks' you just referred to."

"Yeah but," she helped him put the final loop of his tie in place, "you're my hollywood schmuck."

His eyes glimmered in the light, then he took a step back. "Whaddaya think? How does your schmuck look?"

There were many things that David had an instant talent for, things for which people simply stood back and sighed with awe, but a sense of style was far from one of them. His choice for the biggest night of his life was a slightly wrinkled, ill-fitting black suit, paired with an oversized silver tie. If his thick, greying beard and thinning blonde hair didn't give him away, he would have been mistaken for a preteen attending his middle school grad. But his lack of style never seemed to portray a lack of respect. He didn't give a good goddamn what he put on his body and perhaps people found that carelessness respectable, as if they'd love to have that quiet confidence, or the alluring mystique of the quirky artist, themselves. Either way, he didn't pretend to care and, like most things, neither did the world.

Alice tilted her head sideways. "You look lovely," she said.

He looked for a crack in the armour that lined her face. He knew he looked like he was wearing a suit passed down through generations, but he couldn't detect anything but sincerity in her face or her voice. How lucky he was, he thought, that the woman he loved was the woman he married.

"Tell me again, Alice. I'm going to win, aren't I?"

"You're going to win and the whole city knows it. This is your day."

"I wasn't sure before tonight, before you walked in the door, but there's something in the air. I can taste it. I think you're right. I think the whole city may be right. I'm going to win." He took another celebratory drink. "Holy hell, I'm going to win."

"How's the victory speech coming?"

He hesitated. "I threw it out."

"David! Why would you do that?"

"I was reading it out loud. It felt like an imposter was speaking for me. Some disingenuous fake. Someone occupying my body. The whole room would have known it wasn't me who wrote those false lines. The whole world would have known it."

"I thought it was good when I read it."

"But you didn't hear me saying it out loud, Alice. That changed everything."

"Now what are you going to do, wing it?"

"I know the names I want to thank and that's probably good enough. Once I'm through them, maybe I'll have more to say or maybe I won't."

"You'll rise to the occasion. You always do."

"An actor comes prepared, even when he's not. Besides," he looked at his empty cup, "I'll have the loose-lips of liquid courage to guide me."

"Don't drink too much. The loose-lips of liquid courage, maybe, but not the drunken ramblings of a middle-aged man mid-stupor."

"Not too much." He kissed Alice on the forehead. "Just enough. And speaking of, this glass is looking a bit vacant. Do I have time for another drink?"

"The driver could be here any minute."

"I'll make it quick."

The aged birch liquor cabinet in David's office, once nothing more than a showpiece for visitors, was now a focal point of his afternoons, one which he visited at progressively earlier intervals each day. He took out a bottle of his latest obsession: Johnnie Walker Black Label. He didn't know much about scotch, nor did he ever learn anything but the most basic of lessons on what constituted a good drink, but while in the liquor store last a memory floated to him. It was of a journalist he respected, one who was known for ingesting voracious amounts of tonics, and his drink of choice was Black Label with a small spritz of Perrier water. And as it was once the journalist's drink, it soon became David's. It was, so far, the drink that most successfully skirted him away from the center of his emotional black hole, while still remaining intellectually capable. To him, every drink, every swallow, every swish felt like an ounce of history flowing over his tongue and into his body, followed by the sweet wave of warmth, that melancholy elation, where the edges of his psyche were rounded and smoothed. When three sheets to the wind, the stagnation that marked his present life came into sight and shape and significance. He felt like he'd made a lifelong friend in the bottle, someone to divulge his deepest darkest secrets to, someone to let go of it all with. It was a liquid companion, taking the opposite shape of whatever thoughts ailed him.

He poured himself two finger lengths of tincture, a millimetre of perrier, and took a triumphant gulp. He could see it, the warming liquid, rushing through his extremities, to his spider-webbed capillaries, and intermixing with his thinning blood. He poured himself another finger's length.

"The limo's here," Alice said, entering the room unannounced.

The bottle shook in his hand and almost tumbled to the floor. How long had she been standing there, he wondered.

"Jesus. You scared me." He studied her face, wondering if she could tell how much he was giving himself away to it.

"I'm going to finish getting ready. Try to go easy on that stuff, will you?" She turned to leave.

"Alice," he called out to her. She turned her head back towards him. "I can't believe how lucky I am to have you. I love you."

"I love you too," she said. "It's going to be a magical night."

"It already is," he said, from beneath the weight of the whiskey.

Shortly after she left, David filled up a small eight ounce flask and stuffed it into his jacket's inside breast pocket. Forty four minutes later, and two less ounces in David's flask, the limousine pulled up to the Dolby Theatre, among a warzone of flashing lights. Throngs of reporters, journalists, and cameras were outlined through the tinted windows of the limousine. David hesitated to get out. Despite his long career in show business, and his wide-array of appearances at these events, he hadn't ever escaped the feeling that he didn't belong at award ceremonies. Wherever he looked, he saw talentless hacks waving their hands of approval at whatever film or actor filled their coffers and kissed their rings that year. Unless, of course, their mighty wand wagged in his direction. Today, he was honored to receive it, believing it a testament to his artistic talent and toil, despite what he previously thought of their attention. He was cognizant of the psychological maneuvering, the mental boulder blocks he had to move, to find himself within this line of thinking, but it didn't bother him. This year was his. He would line up like a lame duck to receive his gruel, and perhaps next year, if he found the list of nominees undeserving, he'd go back to snubbing his nose at the awards with a distant, though palpable, disapproval. But before he could drink in tonight's festivities, he had to brave the infamous red carpet, and no matter how much praise or recognition he was awarded, the kangaroo court of the strip wouldn't ever appeal to him. Throughout most of his life he found himself lucky, shielded from the cockroach class of paparazzi. There were a few reasons for this. He was a naturally private man, who had always been too ugly—and now too old—to fall within their camera crosshairs. But, blessed though he was with the lottery looks of a loser, his life was, for the most part, drama-free. There was simply nothing to write about, and, although he acted in films that were critically praised, they were commercially unsuccessful. However, tonight was a big night, and it was the talk of the town, so they would be out in full force, and full force he would receive them. If he had to walk through broken glass barefoot to receive his Academy Award, that's exactly what he would do.

He took a swig from his flask. "Shall we?" he asked Alice.

The flashes of hundreds of cameras left little red Rorschachs all across David's field of vision. He tightened his sweaty grip on Alice's hand, while trying to remain loose and cool as he squirmed inwardly. The internal and external chaos, like a lost boat in a raging sea, caused him to walk slow and deliberate down the carpet, while parrying progressively inane questions about his suit, his shoes, his excitement, if he's going to win, what the role meant to him, the meaning of love, and life, and if there was a God, or the point of existence, with flat, but cordial and concise answers. After barely scratching the surface on the meaning of existence with an E! Reporter, David, his throat dry and his eyes burning, was ushered past the reporters and into the Dolby Theatre.

This was David's fifth time in the Dolby Theatre and his fourth nomination. By now, the theatrics of the show, the mood of it all, no longer held much interest to him. If award ceremonies were work affairs, which they are, the Golden

Globes are your office Christmas Party—fun, loose, and not-so-serious—while the Academy Awards are your yearly review: stiff and formal, but you'll be damned if you don't want your due. His purpose for being there was singularly focused, but still, there he remained and he would have to sit through the show, whether he wanted to or not. He patted his breast pocket and the hard edges of his mickey calmed him. They found their seats and the show began.

The host of the evening was Jerry Siegel, who managed to edge out a few good self-aware one liners, ridiculing the very nature of award shows, but by David's estimation, was too safe and too tempered for a room full of adults. His favourite few minutes of the slow, self-congratulatory show came from Bill Murray, who, after winning an Oscar for Best Supporting Actor, gave a genuinely moving tribute to a deceased friend. He recognized the name of the man, but couldn't place him. He made a mental note, before soon forgetting it, to ask Bill about it later that night.

The rest of the show passed by in rising anticipation, with David sneaking quarter ounces of scotch every 15 minutes, to keep himself occupied during a mostly uneventful night. As usual, there was an out of place and underprepared musical number who stumbled through their performance, stiff well-paid actors who read low-paid writers' fun-for-everyone jokes, and the performances of a lifetime, caught on the big screen, from those whose names didn't appear on a winner's envelope. David Willis presented the nominees for Best Supporting Actress and made a particularly big error, pronouncing "Vanessa Chastain" as "Vanessa Chest-Stain," but she managed to recover her dignity by thanking "David Willy," which resulted in roaring laughter from the audience.

Shortly after David had run dry, as if divinely timed by the heavenly curators of the event, Philip Seymour Hoffman walked on stage to present the award for Best Actor. As the actor stood behind the podium, surveying the crowd, waiting for the applause to die out, the pit in David's stomach opened up, threatening to swallow the room whole. Alice slipped her hand over David's and squeezed, their hands, like fish out of water, equally as clammy. The room darkened. Necks craned in his direction. He couldn't see it, but he could feel the heat of their prying orbs. This was his moment and they all knew it. He was about to receive the highest prize and praise of his profession; the peak of Everest was a mere few steps away and all he had to do was reach out and take it. The applause faded.

"Every year," Hoffman said. "We honour the man who stood out amongst his peers by stepping into a character's skin, real or fictional, and vanishing into a performance of a lifetime, a performance that moved us to our very core, where the man who once was disappears, and what is left is only the character he has become. It is an award, one that I've been lucky enough to have received, that celebrates bringing something wholly unique to the screen, and in fact, all six of the men nominated this year have given us this gift, something that originated deep within their soul, and shared with all of us here."

A billion follicles, all across David's skin, stiffened in their sockets.

"These are the men who prove that the profession of film making and the role of an actor is an art form deserving an artist's respect. And ladies and gentlemen, here are your six nominees, all geniuses in their own right, for this year's Academy Award for Best Actor: David Emmeret Smith for his role as Winston Churchill in Goodbye Blue Sky…."

David, holding steadfast in anticipation, clapping with an easy air, ignoring the cameras circling around him, kept his gaze on the stage.

"Jason Segel for his role as Justin Flanagan in Tears For

Friends. Jeff Daniels for his role as Frank Everest in Just July. Daniel Day-Lewis for his role as Winston Smith in Nineteen Eighty-Four. Thomas McCarthy for his role as Moby in Moby. Joaquin Phoenix for his role as Todd Connelly in You're Not Hearing Me Right."

All through the reading, the boulder pushed ever so slightly up the hill, reaching the apex of the great mountain, right before giving way to the other side. David centred on Hoffman's mouth, blurring out the rest of the world, waiting for those binding, perfect words. The final claps for the last nominee died out and David readied himself for the verdict.

This was it. This was everything.

four

"AND THE ACADEMY AWARD for Best Actor goes to…"

David clenched. Cracks, he imagined, spread across his teeth, a bead of sweat, the lone actor on a journey across his back, rolled on into oblivion, and his lungs, as if an escape hatch had opened up, were devoid of air.

Hoffman turned the envelope over, slipped his thumb into the slit, and opened. "David Emmeret Smith in Goodbye Blue Sky!"

It had happened. He'd won.

The crowd erupted into applause, and, one by one, stood up. His own knees were cement, and, for a moment, he couldn't move.

Alice whispered in his ear, her voice barely audible over the crowd, "I knew you had it. I love you."

The sound of her voice snapped him out of the paralyzing jubilation coursing through his bones, and he inched his way out of his seat. He searched the gaze of the people around him. It was locked on him and him alone. He found Alice's arms and she found his lips. It was the warming embrace of victory. His cement legs, trembling still, broke free, and he moved towards the stage, leaving Alice behind. This, though the air was thin, his muscles aching, was the final leg of the journey. Four steps, long as they were, stood between him and the stage. He ascended the peak until he found level ground.

Hoffman approached David with a straight face and a

handshake, firm and dry, then pulled him in for a half-hug.

"This was your year to lose," Hoffman said, placing the statue in his hands and leaving the stage.

David lifted it in the air, holding it at the base with one hand and another at the back of its head, like a newborn, ready to experience the world for itself. It was heavier than he expected, but the gold—glimmering from the stage lights—was soft and warm in his hands. He brought it down to his side and, from behind the crystal podium, faced the crowd. This was the first time he had seen the theatre from this vantage point and it struck him: the awe of the moment. He was free before his peers.

The clapping died out in waves and the room returned to their seats.

"Thank you," he said, pulling back as his voice boomed through the room. He took a deep breath and began again. "My god. I was in a category with giants, men much better than I, so it's truly an honor to be standing here in front of you all. I have a few names I'd like to thank, if you have the time. First, and always first, the love of my life, my heart, my soul, my beautiful wife, Alice. Through everything, you've been my guiding light, there to steer me back on track when I veer off. You're my partner in life, and my partner forever. Thank you to our director, Alejandro. Where is Alejandro? Stand up!"

He found Alejandro to the right of the stage, clapping on his feet.

"You brought out the best in me, as you did everyone who worked on this wonderful, moving film. And in the last few years, you've cemented yourself as one of the greats living among us. Thank you for letting me be apart of it. Thank you to Janice, Justin, Jody, Margaret, Alfonso, Ian, Tyler, and Q. You great souls make navigating the waters of Hollywood manageable. And thank you to all of you out in the crowd, those who are constantly pushing the envelope. You make me, you make all of us, try a little harder, give a little more to each performance. Keep innovating, keep telling the stories we all want to see and hear and tell. Without you all, we would be nothing. I would be nothing. Finally, I want to thank my mother, Janet." He cleared his throat into an empty hand. "Who I lost this year, and who didn't get a chance to see her little boy stand up here and win it all." He held up the statue again. "This is for you, Mom! We did it!"

The crowd returned to their feet and the roar of the room overwhelmed David. He pulled away in embarrassment, but soon, embarrassment turned to pleasure and he drank deeply in their adoration. He searched the crowd for the eyes he respected, for hands he once shook, and saw them clapping, standing, and watching him. A flip switched in his head and before long, pleasure turned to arrogance. He was above all of this, better than it, deserving of more, and more. Why else, then, was everyone here, but to see him and serve him up his much-deserved prize.

Stepping away from his momentary narcissism, he exited at the back of the stage and, coming out the other side, he was startled by how easy it was to make the daring step from humble appreciation to overbearing arrogance.

"Congratulations Mr. Smith," said a smiling young woman, holding a golden tray of skinny stems. "Would you like a glass of champagne to celebrate?"

Wasting no time, he downed the glass, returned it to the tray, then downed a second.

"And if you'll follow me, Mr. Smith," said another woman, wearing a shimmering silver dress, like small mirrors layered on top of each other, miniature Davids spread out all over her body. "We'll be going to the Loews Hotel for a brief question period."

She led him, arm in arm, down Winner's Walk, the clip

clop of her heels bouncing off the narrow passage. His momentary arrogance, now a far-off dream, as if it happened to some other distant stranger, was replaced with the pure, final exhilaration of victory. They stopped behind a velvet curtain.

She let go of his arm. "They'll call your name when they're ready for you."

"Thanks."

While waiting another tray of golden stems floated by, which he snatched from the thick air. He studied the glass. The small bubbles floated to the top and burst; their tiny lives reaching the highest they'll ever go and ending in the sublime explosion of carbon dioxide.

How fitting it all was, he thought.

"You're up," the woman said, pulling him from his personal revelry. She opened the curtain for him.

He walked into a small room, a circular holding cell, filled with photographers and an 'X' on the ground. He stood in front of them and cycled through three not-so-different poses. After a few thousand photos, and a momentary bout of blindness, he was escorted into another room, with more photographers, journalists, and pretenders. An empty podium stood at the helm of the room.

"Hello," David said. He beamed with a contagious enthusiasm.

A woman's voice called out from a hidden location. "We'll start with 218 on the left, followed by 244."

"Bonjour," said 218, presumably. "Jean from French 24. Bravo on your win, Monsieur Smith."

"Thank you. It's an honor."

"If I am correct, this is your fourth nomination, no? What does this feel like now to get your win?"

"Despite what everyone was telling me, when I woke up this morning I honestly had no idea if I would win. Look at who I was up against. Jeff's almost 60 and he's just starting to get the recognition he deserves. Joaquin's time for an Academy award is way overdue. Like me, this was his fourth nomination, and I thought he was equally as deserving as I was. And Daniel, what an actor. Would anyone be confident going up against him? He's a titan: three wins, six nominations. But here we are." He cut himself off to look at his Oscar. "And as I'm talking to you, it's starting to sink in. I've won an Oscar. Sorry, what was your question?"

The French journalist laughed. "Your Oscar, Monsieur David. How does it feel to win?"

"It's been a journey to get here. And… it feels good. Really really good."

"Merci."

"Thank you."

"224," the voice said.

David searched the room for 224.

"Hello David. Tabby Somersett from TV Guide." Tabby, who David knew for years, was a pleasant woman with black hair.

"Hi, Tabby."

"You mentioned it's been a journey for you. What's next on the journey for David Emmeret Smith?"

"I've been asking myself that a lot lately. Right now, as I'm sure you know, I'm on the tail end of the production of James Thomas Reid's 'The Rise and Fall of Gaius Julius Caesar.' It's been a fun change of pace. After that? Who knows. I might take some time off and wait for the next script that blows my way."

"Thanks."

"Okay. We'll go to 331 now."

"Hi, David. Thomas Atkinson from Entertainment Tonight. Winston Churchill is a larger than life character. How did you prepare for the role?"

"After falling in love with the script, and having a

hunger to know more about the man, I read Max Arthur's "Churchill: The Life," front to back, before shooting started. If you haven't read it, I can't recommend it enough. But beyond that, I had an incredible team around me who filled in the gaps wherever I needed it. Alejandro's direction was flawless and I believe we created the film that we wanted to create—and the one we wanted to see. Oh, and Peter Donville, my voice coach, was incredible. He worked with me for three weeks straight, nine to five, until I mastered Churchill's unique way of speaking."

"Thanks, David. And congrats."

"Thanks."

"Okay, last question. In the front, 128."

"Hi David. Congratulations. Jeff Jameson from—"

"Hi, Jeff."

"Hello. You mentioned earlier that your work on JTR's 'The Rise and Fall of Gaius Julius Caesar' had been a change of pace from your earlier work. This late in your career, what made you want to go for a big Hollywood blockbuster?"

"I thought, 'why not try something new and interesting?' Besides, the two films aren't too different, are they? Winston Churchill and Caesar, two larger than life characters."

"In contrast to the directors you have worked with in the past, what was it like working with JTR?"

"He's refreshingly direct and efficient. We don't spend an entire day doing 100 different takes for a single shot, because he can usually get it the first time. It's fun."

The phantom moderator cut in. "We're going to stop here. Thank you so much, David, and congratulations."

There was a half-hearted clap from the celebrity journalists. The same woman who led him to the room appeared at his side. "Right this way, Mr. Smith." She held her hand out for him. "We'll return you to your seat and your wife."

As they walked through the back, he could hear the presentation for Best Actress, which meant there were two final awards to go: Best Director and Best Picture. His skin was crawling with a celebratory desire to break free from the drole final moments of an award show that had already given up its golden goose, but "Goodbye Blue Sky" was nominated for both of the final categories. It was his professional duty to show his stationary support.

She guided him past tables of his peers, now seemingly unaware of his existence, ignoring the fresh oscar in his hand. He spotted Alice from across the theatre. Even now, while she watched the presentation, he could see her head shift slightly left to right, on the lookout for her newly-crowned husband.

He slipped in beside her. For a few long seconds, the suspense hanging in the air, she didn't notice his presence, before turning towards him. Her face was stretched to its limit in glee, as she tried to contain her excitement in deference to the on-going show. She wrapped her arms around him, stifling a squeal into the nape of his neck.

"How did I do," he whispered, keeping his attention on the show. "Did I sound alright?"

"Your mother would have been proud. You were wonderful. A home run. I'm so proud of you."

They weathered the last two awards hands in hand, vibrating together in synchronicity, anticipating the end of the awards, and the start of the celebratory hour. "Goodbye Blue Sky" failed to register wins in the final two categories, which was bittersweet for David. Then, at last, Jerry Siegel returned to the stage, said a few jokes, received a few laughs, and allowed the theatre to escape towards the after-party at the Governors Ball. David and Alice were taken up by the current of the crowd—a single wave in a river of upper class, a high society of moving flesh—up a set of grandiose golden staircases.

Guarding the entrance of the ballroom, in stalwart fashion, was a nine foot Oscar statue, wrapped in gold LED lights, like some gaudy Christmas tree watching over the celebrities, actors, debutants, and artists. They stopped at the feet of the great gold giant and surveyed the brilliant chitter chatter of the worker ants buzzing around the ballroom, manning their stations for tonight's serving battle. In between, Hollywood's haut monde were greeting each other in quick, fleeting hellos, before moving onto their next target, eager to finish their formal rounds of friendship.

"It's beautiful," Alice said, as she guided David into the scene.

All at once it was as if time slowed down, the chatter died away, and the room looked up, watching David and Alice enter, hand-in-hand, king and queen of the ball, ready to greet their court. And then, as if imagined, voices broke free, the eyes looked away, and they were back to reality, being greeted with glasses of champagne from a solitary server. The ballroom was at once fabulously lit, with thousands of gold lights hanging from the roof, and yet, there remained a sombre aura permeating throughout. The walls were landscaped into a lush dark green, but were top lit, highlighting framed displays of past winners, dead and alive, all over the room. There were randomly placed stations of red wine, chardonnay, champagne, food and cocktails everywhere David looked, each helmed by a dutiful keeper.

As they walked through the room, like the Spartan Hoplites at Thermopylae, they were greeted by wave after wave of congratulations: from actors he once worked with, directors he wanted to work with, musicians he didn't know, and strangers he couldn't place. He parried, he ducked, he shook, and he greeted.

"I need a drink," he said to Alice, between faceless hands.

"Get me one too," she said, returning to her conversation with a California senator.

He b-lined to the nearest open bar, keeping his head down and his hands hidden at his sides, one clutching a 13½ inch golden man. Minutes later, a red-faced bartender slid two glasses of ice and whiskey across the bar with a trembling hand.

"David Emmeret Smith, right?"

"What gave it away?"

"Didn't you just win Best Actor?"

He looked at the Oscar in his hand. "Is that why they gave me this?"

"Well, I just wanted to, uh, say, congratulations." David hadn't done the boy's nerves any favours. "I'm a big fan of your work. I think you're really great."

Other than Alice's, this was the most sincere and authentic congratulations he had so far received, probably because it wasn't originating from a place of calculated self-interest. It was one of the problems of being an actor—you could always tell when one was acting.

"That's nice of you to say." He drained his glass and placed it on the bartender's table."

"Another?"

"That's even nicer of you to say."

With a short wink, he free-poured the next. David pulled out two $100 bills and slipped them into the boy's tip jar, returning the wink. He gathered up the drinks and left to find Alice.

She'd moved on from the senator and was making small talk with a director and his wife, both of whom David had once worked with. Walking closer, pieces of conversation floated his way. They were talking politics. He couldn't stand politics.

"Jim! Margaret!" he said, putting on his best fake smile,

made all the more convincing by his blood-alcohol content.

"David!" Jim was also was donning his actor's smile. "Congratulations are in order, I believe."

"Yes, congrats," Margaret said.

"You're both too kind," David said. "It's been quite the night already, and as you can see," he raised his glass to his audience, "I'm celebrating my victory."

"As you should," Jim said. "A much-deserved celebration."

"Thanks, Jim, but it sounded like I interrupted a particularly heated debate," he said, immediately regretting his steering the conversation back.

"Nonsense," Jim said. "We were discussing this year's election. What kind of man are you, David? Where do your allegiances lie? The Dems or the Republicans. A donkey or an elephant?"

"I vote democrat, but I make it a point to stay out of the discussion. The whole thing seems, for the most part, a bit of a circus."

"But it's the future of our country we're talking about here."

"David doesn't think there's much difference between either party."

"Neither do I," Margaret said, trying to hide the camaraderie on her face from her husband.

Jim frowned in his wife's direction. "Not much of a difference? The Democrats barely understand basic economic policy."

Automatically, David's mind wandered, drowning out Jim's Transatlantic accent.
"Plus, Obama's withdrawal of boots on the ground in Iraq will surely create..."

He became acutely aware of the fullness of his bladder. He wondered how long he would be able to put up with this.

"There's no competition," Jim continued. "Any rational man, if he looked seriously at the issues, would tell you—"

"Sorry, Jim. I hate to be rude." He made an awkward cross-legged gesture. "And I'd love to continue, but I have to use the little boy's room."

"By all means." Jim and Margaret separated, opening a hole in their circle large enough for him to escape the clutches of political theatre.

As David parted the celebrity infested ballroom, and anxiety over his bursting bladder rose, he could hear Jim return to the same stimulating line of argument. He probably shouldn't have left Alice alone with that maniac, but like war, he reasoned, it's every man (and woman) for himself out here in the jungle.

At the far end of the ballroom, head down, with determination in his step, he found the bathroom. It was equipped with two floor-to-ceiling stalls and four empty urinals, their black ceramic glossy in the dim light, as if they'd never been used before. David fumbled with his belt and zipper, then relieved himself into the far urinal, closest to the stalls. The sound of the steady-stream bounced off the walls of the deaf room. He studied the painting above the urinal, an anthropomorphic frog with sunglasses jumping into a pink pool. His brain, free-floating in its own pool of liquor, laboured to think of the possible meaning of the painting, but nothing but fog came from the churning of cogs. He made a mental note to slow down his liquor intake before being interrupted by a violent snort. It flew from one of the sealed stalls, rumbling through the floor, startling David, who was stuffing his shirt back into his pants. He froze, hand down his pants, not wanting to give away his position in the bathroom. There was nothing else but silence. David pictured the mysterious man in the stall equally as frozen as he was. The imagined mutual embarrassment emboldened David and he returned to putting back together his suit, then moved to the sink to wash his hands. There was a click from the door behind him. A second wave of embarrassment ran over him.

What if it was someone he knew, he wondered. How should he act? How could he act? Even if it wasn't someone he knew, it would still remain an awkward confrontation between two strangers, both of whom share the dirty secret of the stall and its occupant. Eyes would meet eyes and something unknown would pass between the two. An unknown knowing, not yet spoken, but just as much said.

"David…?"

He turned and saw Marcus Junius Brutus the Younger, better known as Scott Peterson, his saviour, his corrupter, the match that lit his fire. He had his hands out, face flat and even, but for the slight upturned lips of mischief.

"Congratu-fucking-lations, my man. How does it feel?"

He noted the now-third sincere congratulations of the night. "Scott!"

"Part of the Oscar club now." He took the statue out of David's hands and held it at eye level, then returned it to David. "Are we even allowed to be talking?"

"For you, I'll make an exception."

"How do you feel now that you got this puppy under your belt?"

"Pretty much the same, to be honest, maybe a little drunker."

"I told you you deserved it man. And that was a killer speech. Really lit up the place. I mean it."

"You think so? I thought it might be a bit self-aggrandizing."

"I loved it."

"Thanks." He leaned closer. "But I gotta tell you something."

"What's that?" Scott whispered.

51

He pointed at Scott's nose. "You got a bit of powder there."

"Shit!" He turned to the mirror and tilted his head back. "That's embarrassing." He dusted off the tip of his nostril. "I'm glad it's only you in here."

"What is that stuff?"

"You wouldn't be interested."

"Let me decide if I'm interested or not."

He reached into his inside jacket pocket and pulled out a sandwich bag. The bag was full of smaller baggies each with either brown or white powder. "I've got more than a quarter of coke and a few bags of M. You dabble?"

"Back in my college days, but it's been a while." To say that David used a 'bit' back in college would be like saying there's only a bit of water in the ocean, a couple humans on earth, a few stars in the universe. It was an ever-expanding destructive force in his life that threatened to gobble up everything he held dear for two years straight. It had started off as a casual party pastime, with a shared line here, an augmented conversation there, but by the beginning of his second year, it was all consuming. If he had so much as a single sip of beer, he would be up for days. He no longer attended his classes and what money he had, quickly evaporated. Then, by some miracle of self-control, between the second and third year of college, on the verge of being kicked out of school, with no money, and friends who were slowly abandoning him, he broke free. When, throughout the last 36 years, he thought back to this time, it was as if it had happened to someone else—some distant stranger whom he shared his memories with. And now, at the apex of his life, with himself fully in the driver's seat, the idea of starting again percolated his senses, which, till now, had laid dormant, deep within him, biding their time to be flowered, and watered, and to rise again.

Scott took out a white bag and held it out for him. "Want to get back on that horse?"

"Fuck it. Why not?" he said. "Celebrations are in order." He palmed the bag of fine white columbian powder.

"There's my man."

"I guess I'll be right back," David said, rapidly looking back and forth between Scott and the stall. He wore a poorly-masked, grim smile on his face. "What are you going to do while I'm in there?"

"I'll be on the lookout. We can't have our newly crowned Oscar winner caught doing coke in the washroom. It'd be a PR disaster for both me and you. I'd be tarred and feathered, labelled that coke guy forever."

"My life, our lives, are in your hands." He looked into the stall, the walls appearing caved in and closer than they did on the outside. He squeezed his way in and closed the door behind him.

He closed one eye and held the bag up to the light, inspecting his future, one gram at a time. He dumped a quarter of the bag out onto the top of the toilet paper dispenser. The journey that this small baggie of cocaine took to get to him flashed through his mind. The passing of hands, the bloodshed, the blood money, the blood government, the murders and mothers widowed, the smuggling and the rich men in poor countries, riding atop a monopoly board of money. He organized the pile into a line, rolled up the bill, breathed out, and snorted.

It was that moment, that mild firing of pleasure neurons, which threw his life onto a trajectory of ramifications that were, at the time, incomprehensible.

five

THE RIPCORD SOUND of air and cocaine soaring through the rolled up bill, bouncing violently off the walls of the stall, triggered a wave of slumbering nostalgia from deep within David. It was as if he were dusting an old toy found in an aging attic, only to pile the dust up into an appetizing line and rail it, throwing away the less-than-snortable part of the toy. He tilted his head back, gave a few short sniffs to make sure he'd powdered his cranium, and awaited the kick in the jaw. After ten seconds there was nothing more than a mild burning sensation and an elevated heart rate. Perhaps it was his declining memory, or the current state of consumer cocaine, but he expected more than this. He dumped out the rest of the bag.

"What's taking so long?"

"It's weaker than the stuff I was used to. Going for seconds."

"Trust me, the coke's fine."

He'd be the judge of that. He cleared the white runway in one steady lift-off. The clear-cut Colombian aroma ripped through his nasal cavity, right past his mucous membrane, and into his bloodstream, mingling with his cells, imploring them to work harder and burn brighter.

"You done?"

He wrinkled his nose and dusted away any leftover albinos. The full weight of his win—his own greatness—was coursing through his veins. He exited the stall lighter than when he entered, gliding across the marble floor.

"How was it?" he asked, as David re-appeared.

"Just as I remember it."

"Is that good?"

"It's great."

"Good, but I have to get back. If you need anything else, look for me. I'll be the guy with two beautiful models on either arm."

"Got it." They exited the washroom in opposite directions.

While David scanned the room for his wife, it was as if he were high up on a king's chair, surveying the room from a place of divine authority. The room was his and they all his loyal subjects. He could do or say whatever far-fetched, poorly-reasoned thought crossed his mind, and they would bow on one knee and serve his will. He forgot about this feeling. He liked it.

He spotted Alice and split the room with a measured gravity, which no one dared interrupt. She was chatting with a chef, a pale, mousey fellow, who was in the middle of his take on the modernized mini-burger. She nibbled on the edge of one and smiled.

David slipped in behind her and grazed his fingers across the small of her back. "I just did a little cocaine in the washroom," he whispered into her ear.

When she turned around her pupils were wide and her jaw low. She half looked as if she believed—or hoped—it would be someone else standing behind her.

"What did you say?"

"I was in the washroom," he said, as he looked past her, scanning the room from end to end. "And Scott was there, but I didn't know he was there, but he was, and he came out of the stall. And, you know." He leaned on the edges of his toes, his heels dancing. "Scott's a good guy. Great guy. I like

55

Scott."

"Okay, calm down. Tell me, slowly, what happened."

"I was there, peeing, minding my own business, when I hear him in the stall, snorting away. I didn't know it was him, but I heard him. He comes out. He offers me some, and I take it."

"Why would you do that?"

"Am I talking fast?" He rubbed his nostrils. "I feel like I'm talking fast."

"Yes. Jesus."

"I'll try to slow down."

"You didn't answer me."

"Didn't I?"

"Why would you say yes?"

"It's a celebration tonight, isn't it? I'm celebrating."

"But you're an old man. Why would you start doing that now? What if someone saw you? Imagine the headlines. Use your head."

"We were careful and here I am, not caught."

"Still. I'm not angry, I'm just confused."

"It was only the one time. It's the biggest night of my life. It's the biggest night of our lives." He stooped lower to be eye-to-eye with her. "Can't I have a bit of fun, my little mouse?"

"Fine. If it's just this once."

"Just this once."

"Promise me."

"Promise."

She kissed him on the cheek. "I wish you would have asked me before you did something crazy like this."

"It was unexpected, but I know. It's not like me."

"Well," she said, sliding her hands into his jacket and around his back. "How is it, you idiot? Are you having fun?"

"I feel. I feel. I don't know. It's hard to explain. It's barely there, but it's there, and I feel strong, awake, less drunk. There's an undertone of power whirring behind the curtains, propelling me forward."

"So it's a good thing?"

"It was exactly what I needed. I don't want to look like a drunk baboon in a room full of peers."

"You did a line of blow because you don't want to embarrass yourself?"

"Exactly. Is it working?"

"Other than the fast talking, you seem fine. Drunk, but endearingly so."

"Then should we rejoin the party?"

"After you, my little junkie."

For the first time in years, David found himself genuinely intrigued by the people around him. Instead of cowering in a corner, counting down the minutes until he could excuse himself, he raced from person to person, asking for their ear, and meeting it with a gregarious confidence that was noticeably unlike him. If it wasn't the biggest night of his life, people might have been suspicious that this giddiness was more than a post-prize prowl, but the tainted talk of an elderly hedonist, dipping far beyond his years into a shaky past of youthful debauchery. As the night wore on, not letting a single minute pass without the weight of a drink tugging down his arm, his tolerance dipped. His loose lips became all the looser. They barely registered the signals his brain sent them, struggling to form coherent sentences. It finally struck him that the cocaine, like some omnipotent puppetmaster plucking invisible strings from a yet-unseen location, was what was previously holding him up. Without it, he was a puppet without its master, flopping through the masses with little that resembled coordination. He needed to find more.

He thought, for a brief fleeting moment, of his promise

to Alice. "Just this once," she had told him, but what he chose to remember was "just this one night." Coming to a decision, he snapped out of this inner dialogue in the middle of three other actors.

"How ya liking your representation, Jerry?"

"I've got a small part in Denis Villeneuve's new film. It's not the lead, but the exposure is going to be worth it. Lately, that man can do no wrong."

"Which movie is it?" the third asked.

"It's about a child abduction. I've got a good feeling about it. It has Oscar contention written all over it."

He wobbled back and forth on his heels, nodding along, as he scanned the crowd for Scott. "If you'll excuse me fellas," he said, catching a glimpse of the back of Scott's head on the other side of the room. "I've got to say hi to a friend."

They gave a brief nod and continued on with their conversation. With their permission to exit the small circle, he made his way towards his powdery peddler.

Scott was in a rounded booth with his arms around two women, one with straight blonde hair and the other a dark brunette. His right hand was lightly brushing the bare back of the blonde. David circled the table, coming into Scott's view.

"David!" Scott pulled his hands out from behind the girls' heads and, as if he were trying to air dry them, snapped them at David. "The big winner! Care to join us? Tell us of the night's spoils?"

The blonde on David's left, Scott's right, had pale lips and perfect porcelain skin, which made her thick black eyebrows all the more striking. She was rail thin, sitting a few inches taller than Scott, searching his face for far-away answers. The second woman was significantly shorter than Scott, with golden brown skin, almost-black hair, and azure eyes that were so large they seemed to be in the process of swallowing the rest of her features. Those eyes, a tenth wonder of the world, were now profoundly intent on sizing David, from head to toe, up and down, up and down. He met the gaze and quickly looked away—caught in a shameful act. His cheeks, already crimson, deepened.

Scott, noticing David avert his attention, looked to his right. "This is Vanessa." He looked to his left. "And this is Justine." Then back to David. "They're models."

"Hello," David said, still looking at the floor.

"Are you going to join us, David?" Justine, the brunette, said.

He looked up at her. She was batting her eyelashes in his direction. He thought, for an instant, that he could feel small gusts splashing against his face. He pulled from deep within and produced an imitation of sobriety.

"I'm afraid I need to steal your friend for a moment." Justine did her best faux-pout, which after years in front of a camera, was as good as they came.

"But maybe later," David said, trying to appease the big-eyed stranger.

Scott slipped under the table and re-appeared on the other side.

"Don't take him away from us for too long," Vanessa said.

They walked a few feet from the models before Scott stopped David. "Well, what is it?"

"I forgot how short this stuff lasted." With those words, the ostensible hold on his self-control gave out, and his right eye veered off of its own volition. "I'm so goddamn drunk I couldn't spot a hole in a ladder."

"No kidding," Scott said, following the wandering eye around the room. "But I have plenty enough to put you back on planet earth." Scott's hand disappeared into David's inside breast pocket. "Have two all to yourself. On me." He winked at David.

David tapped the outside of his breast pocket. The small protrusion reassured him. "I owe you."

"Not a chance. It's your night and this is on me. Mi casa su casa, my talented, Academy Award-winning friend."

"Still, if you need anything, just ask."

"Not a thing," he said, waving off the debt. "Now if you'll excuse me, I have a young model to attend to." Scott half-turned, paused, then turned back to David with a wily glint in his eyes. "You know, there is a small thing you could do for me."

"What's that?"

"You might have noticed that I happen to have two women with me tonight, not one."

"I noticed."

"You see, Vanessa brought her friend Justine with her. And don't get me wrong, great girl and all, but a little later I might want some alone time with Vanessa, if you know what I mean. That's where you come in."

"How's that?"

"I'm going to need someone to entertain her, while I, you know, entertain Vanessa."

"I'm a married man, Scott, and I doubt Alice is going to let me go out without her."

"Whoa," Scott said, holding his hands up like David had turned an accusatory gun on him. "I'm not implying anything like that. Just that you, I don't know, keep her company for a bit, at some point in the night."

"I can ask her."

"And if she allows it, come find me, and we'll really have some fun tonight." Scott made a clicking sound with his tongue and turned back to the models.

As if the now-peruvian powder in his pocket was already seeping through his suit and into his skin, he walked through the crowd, chest high and firm, parrying requests for conversation with the flip of a wrist. Slipping into the bathroom, he went directly to the same floor-to-ceiling stall and pulled out one of the two baggies. His stubby fingers fumbled at the seal before being interrupted by a cough from somewhere inside the bathroom. His heart thumped so hard that he worried the intruder might hear it. He undid his pants—loudly—and sat down, trying to feign regular washroom use. After a few seconds of dread, his thumbs returned to the seal on the bag, splitting it open. Using a key, he dug out a giant bump, held it to his right nostril, and waited. A gob of sweat rolled down the arch of his nose, missing the key by a millimeter. David, he imagined, was in some sort of stand off with the anonymous figure. One false move and he would be busted—the whole plan up in smoke. Then it happened. A sucking of air and a vortex of water cut through the bathroom. He heaved his nostril onto the key and sucked half the air out of the room. He greedily dug out another scoop, prepared himself with his right hand, then flushed his own toilet with his left. Again, the toilet masked the sound.

He stifled a cough and cleared his throat. The stall next to him opened and the tapping of dress shoes on marble was heard predominantly in his right ear, then his left. Water came from an out-of-sight tap. He counted slowly to five then stood up, tucking his shirt in and doing up his belt. Right as the door to his drug stall opened, the bathroom door was closing. He was alone again.

David checked his face in the mirror for any evidence of his wrong-doing. He was clear, but he lingered longer than he had to on the man staring back at him.

What was compelling him to take chances like this?

But, within seconds, as his veins bulged and he regained focus, he knew why: he liked it. He liked all of it. He splashed water on his face, flashed his teeth at the man in the mirror, and walked back into the party in search of the one he loved.

Always the life of the party, David found her entertaining a group of women. At the head of the group was Judi Donovan, who last year won Best Actress for her portrayal of Margaret Thatcher in The Iron Lady. Not a stretch, by David's estimation. She was as cold, calculated and shrewd as they come. He edged himself towards the outskirts of their circle, saddling up behind Alice, but not interrupting the roundtable of women.

"When I first walked in," an older woman said, who David did not recognize. "I didn't love the lights, but as the night goes on, they're starting to have something resembling charm."

"I'm still not in love with them," another said.

"I would have went for something a tad more seductive," Judi said. "Like free-hanging bulbs."

David, his ears perking, laughed internally. Alice hated these kinds of conversations.

"I quite like it all," Alice said. "Right from the moment we walked in."

"You don't think the grass walls were a bit tacky?"

"They're comfortable," she said. No one replied, but the looks they gave each other said enough.

Judi, noticing David stalking around the perimeter, snapped her attention away from the group. "David—darling! Congratulations."

The group of women turned their heads towards the intruder.

"Judi," he said. "Thanks. How's everyone's night go—"

"Where have you been?" Alice said. Her voice was tense and stern. "Could I talk to you for a second. Alone?"

"Excuse me, ladies," David said, walking backwards from the group of women.

They stopped behind a grassy pillar a few feet away.

"Oh thank God you're here," she whispered. "I don't know how much longer I could have lasted in that dreadful conversation."

"No kidding."

"But seriously, where were you?"

"Walking around, talking, you know." His words were a rapid fire into Alice's ear. "Small talk. Medium talk. Big talk. You name it."

"But you hate schmoozing."

"Tonight feels different. It's quite the party. There's so many people to talk to."

She covered her face with her palm and yawned. "How much longer do we stay? I'm exhausted."

"Would you hate it if I said I didn't want to go home anytime soon?"

"Would you be mad if I said I wanted to go home soon, even if you don't?"

"Not at all. I think you should do whatever you want."

"Then I wouldn't be mad, either. It's your night. Stay out if you want, but I'm going."

David would never admit it, not to himself, and especially not to Alice, but he was relieved. He felt vigorous and his mind was reeling for more—diving deep into a current of high-pace europhoria, with his heart not far behind. He didn't want this feeling, if it was only going to be for one night, to end. The night was still young and he was still old. He wasn't going to get a night like this again. When you scale Everest, you don't start back down right after; you take a few moments to enjoy the view, to look around, to marvel at the charming absurdity of the human condition. You look back over your journey and savor your time at the top. It's a beautiful thing to behold and not something to so easily cash in.

"I'm going to miss you," he said.

"Walk me to the limo?"

"Of course."

He turned back to the group of women behind him. "Sorry to steal Alice, ladies, but we really must be going."

"Oh no," Judi said. "You can't. You mustn't. It's so soon."

"It's been such a long day Judi," Alice said, as David pulled her away from the group. "I'm practically falling asleep on my feet."

"Lovely to meet you Alice!" one woman said, cupping her mouth with one hand

Their feet moved in unison down the stairs and their hands fell into each other's grooves, forged from decades of intertwined pairing. At the bottom of the stairs they turned back and admired the journey—both long and short, of tonight, of their life, and of their love—that they had taken together.

David took a sharp breath in. "Shall we?"

"After you, darling."

They continued, slow and steady, savoring their final moments together. Outside, a crisp California breeze cut the air and flowed over David's skin. His internal temperature, no doubt raised a few degrees from the narcotic in his bloodstream, was like a protective powdery barrier, shielding him from the night. The sky was a dense black and the stars were out to play. They stopped in front of the limo.

What a night, he thought, as he looked into Alice's hazel irises, like it was the first time he was really, truly seeing them. Who is this woman in front of me? Why did she pick me? Her mouth moved before he registered the sound.

"Thank you for a spectacular night, David Emmeret Smith."

"I've been imaging this moment for my whole life," he said, "and when I was young, before I met you, I wondered who I'd spend it with, who would share in my victory—our victory. The day I laid my eyes on you, I knew it was you, and I wondered what it would feel like, what kind of people we'd become. Now that it's here, I couldn't, wouldn't, have have done it any other way. My life, up to and including this moment, has been perfect." He rubbed his face with his palms. "For weeks now I've been lost, utterly lost. Every night, I stared up at the stars and wondered what would become of me after this. But it's over and I'm still here and you're still with me. All is right in the world. All's right with me. I'm content."

Alice's eyes were wide, red and wet with love. She wrapped her arms around him and cradled her face into the nape of his neck. "I love you," she whispered.

"I love you too."

"Are you sure you don't want to come home?"

David pulled back, creating a smull gulf between them. "I can't stop here. I can't let it end. To rob me of the final, late night glory would be to cut it down in its youth. It would be a tragic ending to the single most perfect day of my life."

"Fine, Shakespeare." She smiled and leaned into him. They kissed long and hard. His lips were dry and she tasted like cherries. "I understand." She opened the door to her limo. "But behave yourself tonight, David. The whole world is watching."

"I will. I love you little mouse."

"Forever and ever." She stepped into the limo and closed the door. The limousine disappeared into the darkness of the sharp night.

Once out of sight, his attention turned inward, and he was acutely aware of the power permeating his limbs, as if each pump, each beat of his heart, spread the powder across his body, making him stronger, smarter, quicker. He adjusted his glasses and slipped a cigarette between his thin lips. The smooth grey death, like a gentle fog on a soft spring mountain morning, filled his lungs.

This was what it was meant to be alive. If only he could bottle this moment up and take from it a sip, again and again, reliving it until he ran dry and dusty and blew away in the wind.

six

Scott, still wedged between the two models, was yammering an inch away from Vanessa's ear, and Justine, with her elbows on the table, resting her chin on the tops of her hands, searched the crowd hungrily. She raised her brows in David's direction.

"Anyone in the mood to celebrate?" he said, sliding his hands across the front of their table.

"David! You've come back to us!"

"Back, alone, and looking for fun."

"That's, like, perfect timing. We were just about to go back to mine," Vanessa said.

"Yeah, just the four of us," Justine said, perking up.

"She's got this giant hot tub. It's incredible. You're going to love it. Plus a ton of booze and..." Scott looked around, then said under his breath, "and blow. We've got a bunch of blow and M left. Ever try M?"

"I'm open to wherever the night takes me."

"Takes us," Scott said. "We're now partners of the night."

"All of us," Justine said. "And we're going to make it the best night of your life." She drooped her head sideways and opened her eyes to his. "Are you ready?"

He had no idea what to be ready for, but at this point, he didn't care. His walls had broken down and water was rushing in. He was going to ride this wave wherever it went.

"Am I ready? Are you guys ready? Why are we still here?"

"Let's go," Scott said. He gave small, forceful pushes to the small of Vanessa's back, forcing her out of the booth. On their feet, Vanessa clung to Scott's arm. Justine slid into the open space beside David.

Acting on instinct, David held his arm out for Justine, but pulled it away before she moved for it. The headline flashed through his mind: "Drunken David Emmeret Smith, high off his Oscar win (and cocaine) locks arms with beautiful young model moments after wife, Alice Smith, leaves his side." It wasn't a risk he was willing to take, so they walked, with some distance between them, behind Scott and Vanessa. Their silence was a gulf, ever-expanding with each step, as they looked on at the couple in front of them, locked in something resembling love.

"Do you want to hold my Oscar?" He held it out for her, trying to break through the awkward air.

"I guess.'

"Who knows, maybe the Oscar will rub off on you, like throwing a bouquet at a wedding. Before you know it, you'll be winning yours and thanking me up there." He moved his voice up an octave or two. "I couldn't have done it without you, David. You believed in me when nobody, and I mean nobody, believed I would be up here. But here I am world!"

"Was that supposed to be me?" she said, as they walked down the stairs of the ballroom. "That sounded nothing like me."

"You might not be aware of this, little lady, but I'm an Academy Award winning actor. My voice acting abilities are some of the best in the business."

"I'd stick to live action roles, if I were you."

"If you were me, you'd have an Academy Award."

"Oh, how easily you forget." She held up the Oscar. "I do have an Academy Award."

"You win this round… Justine, was it?"

She rolled her eyes. "You didn't seriously forget my name, did you?"

"I've never had a great memory. Ever since I started acting, I struggled with my lines. 'The man can act, but he can't remember,' someone once said of me."

"I'll try not to take it to heart."

"I hope so. It could happen again."

The line of limos, short and long, extended four blocks in either direction. David tapped his front pocket, looking for the corner of his cigarette pack. It was a reassuring habit that he picked up in college—some people bit their nails, he tapped his breast pocket, as if to say, in times of worry, at least he had a smoke or two to keep him company. He slipped one out and placed it between his lips. "Where's your limo?" he said to Scott, from the corner of his mouth.

"I didn't arrive in a limo. Where's yours?"

"You didn't come in a limo?"

"Not all of us have been touched by the good graces of the movie industry in quite the same way."

"Should we see if any of these limos are open for business?"

"Girls," Scott said. "Could you find us a limo? We can't have David out here trying to hail his own car on the night of his big win."

Vanessa tugged at Justine's arm, pulling her towards the nearest limo.

"So?" Scott lit his own cigarette. "What do you think?"

David watched the girls go from limo to limo, knocking on each window. "Of?"

"Justine, man. She's totally into you."

"I'm not just a married man, Scott." The ember grew bright in the darkness, washing David's face in a warm glow. He exhaled and flicked the cigarette into the street. "I'm a happily married man."

"All I'm saying is, you know, if you want, it's yours for the taking. I can promise you that."

He wasn't sure whether to be contemptuous over Scott's assumptions about the frivolity of his marriage, or feel sorry for the man. He wasn't the type to understand a relationship like theirs; he was far too young, too dumb, and too inexperienced. Theirs was an understated, total infatuation of another. A love that was on the brink of purity, where you can no longer fathom the touch of another. A relationship that you won't understand until it smacks you right in the chest, leaves you breathless and confused—a lifelong slave to its grasping, far-reaching fingers.

"Look," David said. "I'm looking for a fun time tonight, but not that kind of fun. This is the last time you bring it up."

Sensing the chasm his comment had made between them, Scott slipped his arm over David's shoulder. "Hey sorry, man. I'm just trying to show you a good time, trying to be your arbiter of fun. Consider the matter dropped."

The honk of a limo cut through the thin tension. Justine's head slipped out from a midnight window.

"Let's go you silly boys."

Vanessa's 21st floor apartment was a single circular room with a 12 foot vaulted ceiling and a paint-stained cement floor. It was moderately decorated and mildly separated into clockwise sections, going from the cherry door, to a lifted hot tub, to a long frosted glass bathroom (the only real place of privacy in the apartment), to the glass kitchen, to the living room and its floor-to-ceiling windows, to her minimalist bedroom, then back to the door.

The girls sat on a pin-cushion black leather couch—which looked suspiciously modern, yet antique—while Scott and David frantically opened one cupboard after the next, looking for something to drink.

"It's above the fridge," Vanessa yelled between exchanged gossip.

David opened, as instructed, the cupboard above the fridge. It was spilling over with an assortment of half-filled, barely-filled and full bottles.

"Any preference?" he asked Scott.

"Whiskey." Scott, standing at the island separating the kitchen and the living room, dropped ice cubes into the four idle glasses.

David pulled out a full bottle of rye, unscrewed the cap and filled the glasses until the square cubes raised from the bottom.

"Where's the mirror?" Scott said.

"In the bathroom," Vanessa said.

David held two of the glasses up. "Drinks?"

Scott, as the two girls joined David, returned with a round mirror the diameter of a basketball. He placed it, still fresh with dry white streaks, in the middle of the island. Scott emptied a bag out onto the mirror and started working at it. Like a mouse sniffing out his apparent prize on the tip of a trap, David shuffled towards the windows. The city looked like thousands of candles, let loose at sea, free-floating in the night's darkness.

"Some view," he said, sipping his whiskey.

"Isn't it?" Vanessa said. "I was totally head over heels with it the moment I walked in."

"Do you ever worry that the windows leave you a little exposed?"

"Do they?"

"Look, there's one, two, three, four buildings that are higher up than us. Anyone who wanted to see what we were up to, what you were up to, could look in and see everything we're doing."

"But nobody cares what I'm doing."

"Maybe not yet," he said, turning back to the group. "but they might one day. Besides, I won an Academy Award a few hours ago—who's to say someone isn't interested in what I'm doing?"

"Who knows you're here?" Scott evened out the lines on the mirror.

"Not a soul."

"So tonight, you're just like the rest of us," Justine said, holding out a straw for David. "A nobody."

He squared up to the mirror, with its four runways neatly packed, one by one by one by one. It was the proverbial exit hatch of a plane and he could feel the open air on his face. He considered the jump, wondering how high up he was, if his parachute would open, if it would be enough to break his fall, how much the ground might hurt should it fail, and then decided, against all odds, to jump.

He bent over the table, closed a nostril, and railed a line straight into the gooey centre of his brain. He popped up, snorted a second time, and held the straw up to Scott. Scott pushed the straw back towards David.

"Why don't you double up and take mine? It's why God gave you two nostrils, ain't it?"

"It might be, Scott." He dipped down and cleared another. He shot up, craned his neck back and breathed out. "It might be." He handed the straw back to Scott again and took a step back.

As he drifted out of the conversation, he watched the other three lord over the lines, crush up more coke, and yap and yap and yap. He couldn't imagine feeling more at ease, more apathetic, towards the world and all his problems. In an instant, they had melted away, and there was only now, only here, and nothing else mattered. He was at peace. How could he go back from this, he wondered. Once you knew this kind of power, this kind of peace, it stayed with you. It pushed you out into the world in search of more and more and more, looking to devour whatever came in front of you.

"Now what?" David asked.

If he didn't expel the energy pressing against his skin, bulging against the surface, he would blow like a fire hydrant on a blistering summer day.

"Wait," Scott said.

"What?" Vanessa said.

"Something is missing."

The girls exchanged worried looks.

"Music! Throw on a record, David."

"People still listen to records?"

"Some do," Justine said. "I've always found there to be something intimate—maybe even classier— about a record. It's, I don't know, more tactile, something to connect with."

"I've recently got into them," Vanessa said.

"I could get used to hanging out with you guys. Where are they?"

Vanessa pointed to below the TV. "They're underneath."

"I'll help you look," Scott said.

David knelt at the records, the girls blitzing through topics behind him, and Scott peered from over his shoulder. He thumbed through names he did not recognize and Scott muttered "no" with each unknown he passed over.

"That's the one," Scott said, as David landed on Broken Social Scene's 'You Forgot It In People.' "You'll like it. It's chill."

He slipped the record out of its skin and placed it gently, like someone's newborn babe, on the player. There was a scratch in the air, then the searching chimes, winding in and out, and the light bass, all coming through the low-key nostalgic static of the ancient antique record player.

"Not bad," he said.

At the sound of the first blow of a saxophone, Vanessa's head whipped away from her conversation. "I love this album!" she shrieked.

"A classic," Scott said, walking back to the table. He dumped out another baggy.

David tapped his breast pocket. "Can I smoke inside?"

Vanessa pursed her lips, then smiled. "Can I bum one?"

"Me too please," Justine said.

He held out the open pack to the girls, who both pried out a single cigarette.

"Scott?"

"Sure," he said, scooping out his own smoke.

Vanessa pried the window beside her fridge open and the four of them crowded around it. They passed the lighter around, each spark a break in conversation, a moment to grasp to the small cylinder carcinogen in their hands, a break from their drug-induced bonding.

"I've been smoking for the better half of my life," David said. "And I can honestly say there's nothing quite like the cigarettes I've had tonight. Heavenly, I might even call them."

"It's the only way I can smoke," Justine said.

"It's almost as if I was cheated out of the every cigarette I've had until tonight."

"When I'm sober," Justine said, talking over one another. "Cigarettes make me sick. They burn up my lungs, but I love coke and cigarettes together. I can't smoke without blow and can't do blow without a smoke. It's ironic, really."

"Same. Tres ironic," Vanessa said.

"How's that ironic?" Scott asked.

"I don't know," Justine said. "It just is."

They either paused to reflect on the question, or bask in the glory of their break-time smoke, while the room, and their lungs, filled with the rejuvenating black tar.

David wondered what his lungs looked like by now, and then immediately considered it too late to ask himself a question like that. "So, you're models? Do you like it?"

"I love it," Vanessa said, exhaling.

"It can be boring," Justine said. "But it pays my bills."

"What would you rather be doing?"

"I want to write."

"I didn't know you write," Scott said.

"I don't talk about it a lot."

David leaned against the fridge and crossed his arms, letting his cigarette hand hang away from his body. "What do you write?"

"Poetry, mostly, but I've been thinking about starting my first novel."

"You should read some of her stuff—it's great," Vanessa said.

"What's the novel going to be about?"

She took a step back. "I don't know. The right idea hasn't hit me yet. When it does, I'll let you know."

"And what's your plan for inspiration?" David dropped his cigarette into a flower pot, full of floating buds.

"I don't know that either. I'll know it when I find it."

"You know," David said, surprising himself with how much older and out of place he sounded. "I'm reminded of an old quote by Faulkner. 'I only write when inspiration strikes. Fortunately it strikes at nine every morning.'"

"Exactly," Scott said.

"That's real easy for someone big and famous like Faulkner, or you, to say."

"Is it? Or is it easy for him to say because he sat down and wrote every morning?"

"Maybe."

"When I'm modeling, I usually don't know what pose

I'm going to do until I just like do it," Vanessa said, bridging the two parties. "Haven't you ever felt that way?"

"Sure, I guess," Justine said.

"Exactly," David said. "If you wait for inspiration before you do the work, you might be an adequate poet, maybe even a good one, but you'll never be a great writer."

"Is that what you did to get where you are now?" Justine stepped closer to David.

"I buckled down, did the work, learned to love the process and the result. If you don't love the work, you don't love the art. It's not all glamour."

She 'mhmed' in his direction.

"It's gritting your teeth against concrete. Bite-by-bite you force it out and find the expressions that you want to put out into the world, or at least something close to it. Then you etch away the bad parts, until you have a performance, or in your case, a piece, that's passable, something that resembles what it is you want to say. Then you do it again, and again, and again. At the end, you look over the blood you bled to make that something of a something and you tell yourself, despite every ounce of good sense, that it was worth it."

"Is it worth it?" Justine said, leaning, beside David, against the fridge.

"You bet your ass it is." He held up his Oscar.

"Maybe I'll try it, I mean, what do I have to lose?" She looked up at David, flapping her lashes.

David, caught in her Medusa-like gaze, snapped out of it, and shuffled towards the island. "I could use a refill." He held up his empty glass. "Anyone else?"

"Let me get it," Scott said. He took out a small brown baggie. "I have the secret ingredient, after all."

"What's that?"

Justine put a hand on his shoulder. Her fingertips were cold against his pulsating skin. "It's MDMA. You're going to love it."

"It's like floating on a cloud," Scott said. "There's no better feeling."

"I already feel like I'm in the clouds. If I were to go any higher, I'm bound to run out of air." He opened his mouth slightly, tilted his head, and said. "But whatever. Everything in moderation, right? Even air."

"I like this David," Scott said.

"I'm starting to like him too," David said.

Scott poured a quarter of the bag into each drink and stirred it in with a straw. He handed each glass out, as if performing a ritual, and said "To David!"

They clinked their glasses and repeated after Scott.

"Jesus," David said, coughing. "It tastes like bleach."

"Trust me, it'll be worth it," Scott said.

"What does it look like I'm doing?" He took another sip. "This is me trusting you."

The sound of sips filled the dead air. A period of clarity, wondering how he found himself in this position and in this place, washed over David. But, in moments of debauchery, clarity is fleeting and pleasure is constant. Holding onto those brief glimmers of self-reflection are near impossible. The thought flapped its wings and floated away.

Justine broke the slumbering silence. "How did it feel?"

"I don't feel anything yet," David said, holding his glass, looking around the room.

"I mean when you knew you won. When you heard your name being called out."

"Oh, that." David drained the last of the liquid. "It was almost like dying, or what I imagine dying to feel like.

"What do you mean?" Scott asked.

David held off an answer to light another cigarette by the open window before resetting. "My career flashed before my eyes. In a split second, everything I had done to make it to that point ran through my mind."

"Did anything stand out?" Vanessa said. She slipped in under Scott's arm.

"The first role I tried out for, the one that started this journey, and it is as cliche as it gets: that star-crossed lover, that unfortunate inamorato, paramour in life, and death, with fair Juliet."

"Romeo," Justine said.

"That's right." He flicked a long ash off his cigarette. "I was a freshman in High School, craving any sort of intimate contact with the softer sex, when opportunity to play him struck."

"And with it, a kiss," Scott said.

"I had no interest in acting before then. The kiss, whether real or fake, was all that mattered to me. But to get the part, I had to perform a few lines to the drama teacher in charge of the play. Even now, I can still remember them."

"Can you recite them for us?"

David dropped his newly-lit cigarette into the pot, walked around the island, and into the open space in the middle of the room. "He jests at scars that never felt a wound. But, soft! What light through yonder window breaks? It is the east, and Juliet is the sun! Arise, fair sun, and kill thy envious moon, who is already sick and pale with grief, that thou, her maid, art far more fair than she."

The three of them followed each muscle twitch, each movement of his lips, with a concentration not naturally found in those with blood alcohol levels half theirs.

"Be not her maid, since she is envious; her vestal livery is but sick and green, and none but fools do wear it; cast it off. It is my lady; O! It is my love: O! That she knew she were."

Their jaws were low, their eyebrows high, and pupils wide.

"And there!" He pointed at each of their faces. "Just as

I see it on your faces, I saw it on theirs. How my presence could affect the people around me, how it could command a room and move it in exactly the emotional direction I wanted. While I did that first performance, and while I do every performance, I step outside of myself. I become someone totally distinct, yet, somehow, still me. From that point on I knew what I wanted to do with my life. That's what hit me when I was up there. I could trace it back perfectly—where it all started—as if I were transported in time, then back again. As if I could see, as a boy, where I would go, what I would be, and who I would become. That's why I can't get it out of my head."

"Get what out?" Scott said.

"Because everything was predestined, leading to this one moment, but only to this moment, and I've run out of road. There's nowhere else to go."

"Why don't you get out and enjoy the scenery?" Scott filled David's empty glass. "You've found yourself. It's why you're here with us."

"But I haven't found anything. I'm telling you that you won't find yourself—you won't find shit. You'll see that you're as lost as you were at the start."

"Fuck that, man," Justine said. "It's out there. I'll find my purpose. I know it."

"Or—"

Vanessa jumped forward. "Maybe, like, there isn't anything to find or anything to anything. Maybe the searching is all there totally is. The point of it all. I like searching myself. Like, look at us here. We're in it, right now, and, you know what, I feel spectacular." She raised her hands, craned her neck back, and made little twirls around her apartment. Justine joined her, giggling, along the way, at the drastic change in the air, the absurdity of it all.

"Look at these two," Scott said. "How can anything be

better than just being?"

David could barely hear the words floating to him. His mind was flat and clear, but his body bubbling—a great surge was below his skin, causing his hair to prickle at the back of his neck.

This was the pure pleasure of apathy.

Even during his existential rambling, his words seemed more like the mere motions of past projections. Nothing quite had the same gravity that it did before.

"Is this that brown powder I'm feeling?"

"Isn't it incredible?" Scott said.

"I feel… lighter, like I'm being lifted up by grace itself." He closed his eyes and lifted onto the tips of his feet as a cool auditory breeze crashed through the room and over his body. "It's intense," he said. "I've never heard music quite like this." His knees buckled slightly and he stumbled back, then caught himself.

"Easy David." Scott's voice, a deep timbre, wobbled from inside David's head. "You might have taken too much."

He steadied himself against the couch. "This… is… amazing. I'm amazing. You are all amazing. Everything is amazing!"

He stomped over to Scott and embraced him in a gulping hungry hug. The girls, giggling in the distance, danced their way closer, then fit in on either side of the embracing boys. The four of them, dancing in a circle, arms over shoulders, vibrating back and forth to the music, were a ball of ecstasy. An energy grew from the centre of the four, a mystical purpose, like bees who circle around intruders, dancing, gyrating and vibrating until there's nothing left but the charred core of an intruder.

"I want it to last forever," David said.

"So do I," Vanessa said..

"I love you guys," Scott said.

"I love everyone," Justine said.

They made small steps in line with the music, bending at the knee, the circle twisting a few inches at a time.

"Maybe this is what life is!" David said, breaking from the circle. "It's living in the moment, day by day, without any past or future."

"Man!" Scott said, running his hands through his hair. "That's what I've been trying to tell you!"

There was madness on his face. "I don't need to work another day again."

"You're set for life," Scott said.

"Set for life." The words were a soothing poison in his own ears.

"Today is the first day of the rest of your life," Vanessa said.

"How do you want to spend it?" Justine asked.

"I'm open to ideas."

"I've got just the one."

Justine crossed her arms at her waist and pulled her dress over her head. She had on, under her dress, a delicate white bra, half-cupped over small breasts, and see-through lace panties. The white was made all the whiter by her bronze, oiled skin, untouched by age, and augmented by a blurry eyed David.

She was, to him, a temptress dreamed up by Greek Gods in Olympus, ready to play his fiddle for a fool—and a fool he was.

Vanessa followed lead, her dress quickly up and over her head, with Scott not far behind. David stood alone, dumbfounded, still buttoned and suited.

"What are you waiting for?" She slithered towards him with small, deliberate hip movements.

David focused on a mole directly below her left breast, which somehow made her all the more perfect. The blood drained from his face as she loosened his tie and slipped it over his head. Her fingers tugged at his top button. He realized, at that moment, how much of an intimate activity undoing someone else's buttons was; it always led to the two parties being naked. At the thought of it, this delicate woman, less than half his age, stark naked, her bronze body shimmering in the night, moving her hands down his shirt, reaching the final button, he was stricken by a moment of panic.

He pushed her hand away. "I'll take it from here," he said.

If she had went any lower, no amount of cocaine, no age-related penile suppression, could have stopped the lighting of his torch.

Justine watched him strip down to his underwear with heavy, searching eyes. "Come on now," she said, extending her palm to him.

He took it proudly, and she led the way to the hot tub. He locked in—hypnotized—on her hips. They cut through the air like a pendulum. The cement floor, cold under his feet, felt like it was moving, like the flat escalators you find in airports. She ascended the three small steps to the hot tub, then turned and looked down at him, from atop her pedestal.

"Wait!" he said.

They turned towards him.

"What is it?" Justine tilted her head and squinted.

He ran back, his feet slapping against the floor, and stole the half bottle rye from the counter, holding it close to his chest on his return trip.

"Almost forgot the late night libations."

"Good call," Scott said from the corner, already saddled up next to Vanessa.

David, goosebumps prickling outwards from the point of contact, slid a foot into the water, followed by the rest of his body.

"Isn't the water lovely?" Vanessa made small waves at the surface.

"Marvellous," Scott said.

Justine leaned over. "Don't you just love the way it feels?" Her hand slid across the water's surface, bursting bubbles as it went. She pulled it under and stopped on his knee.

Sirens went off in the distance.

"Feel what?

"The water, silly. Doesn't it feel wonderful on your skin?"

"Oh," he said quietly. He kept his gaze on the water. "I feel like a giant baby in a bath."

"Is that good?" Her hand moved from his knee to his thigh.

"I think so." He swallowed deeply and tried to avoid making eye contact.

Vanessa was now deep in Scott's lap, whispering in his ear. Like a mouse caught in a corner, he was trapped by this charming feline femme fatale.

"What should we talk about?" His voice quaked.

"Why do we have to talk about anything?" Her mouth moved closer and her hand higher up his leg.

How young she was, how naive of the world. Barely half his age, a babe fresh from the womb. This was not the woman he wanted. This sweet woman. So youthful, full of life and energy. Not what he wanted. What he wanted. What he wanted. What he wanted.

"Do you want to kiss me?" He could feel the sweetness of her whisper inches away from his ear.

"I… uh, am not—"

"I want to kiss you."

Her hand moved between his legs. It was like a pleasure punch to the stomach. He tried to form the words to mark his refusal, but the air wasn't there. She climbed onto his body and her face, looking through him, was all he could see. He was trapped on a raft, lost in her oceanic globes, with no land in sight. Dry-mouthed, starving and afraid, the only option left was to drink deeply of the salted water.

seven

LIKE A GREAT gaseous release, the work of millions of years of building pressure, David was awoken by the simultaneous escape of last night's bodily abuse seeping from every pore of his body. He rolled over, his body crinkling in pain, and checked the time through the space between his fingers: 4:07PM. He rolled the cover back over his head and groaned. He was broken. And he couldn't remember how he got home. If only he could drift off to a place where he could stuff his memories down deep, so deep that they were unretrievable, gone to the world. A place and time where he could face his wife.

God damnit, Alice. How was he going to explain what he was doing out so late? How could he explain anything without having it written across his puffy, swollen dumb face? She'd read the confession in everything he did. There would be no escaping it. He would have to come out and tell her. No. He couldn't. He wouldn't. The shame of it would be punishment enough. Every day he would be haunted by his betrayal in his actions.

He sighed, still under the covers, and got another whiff of the alcohol still ever-present in his bloodstream. Dry heaving, he rolled the blanket off himself and exposed his guilt, once again, to the world. The sun splintered through the glass doors on his balcony, as if to shine on his shame and reveal it to all. The space between his eyes ached. He got up, shut the doors, and closed the blinds. Under wobbly knees he stood and surveyed his now-dark room. It stunk of despair, he stunk of despair, his clothes, they stunk of despair. His ragtag mind could only latch onto the smallest improvement, the next miniscule step, to escape the torture of his thoughts. Like a lost beggard in the sahara, he dragged the tops of his feet across the room, to his closet. He undressed with feeble fingers, browned from hours of smoke, and dropped his clothes into a puddle beside him.

Those clothes, touched by the devil, should burn.

From the lower recesses of his stomach, that seventh layer of hell, a growl sprang forth. He couldn't remember the last time he ate, but it couldn't have been in the last 24 hours. His wounded mind, his weak body, couldn't contemplate his next move until it ate.

But what if Alice was downstairs waiting in ambush? Could he face her? Did he have the strength of character—or strength of body—to face his demons?

A small glimmer of perspiration formed on his upper lip from the rage going on inside both his body and mind.

What kind of man couldn't face his own wife? What kind of coward was he?

He slipped a house coat over his broken shell and put one swollen stub of a foot after the other. The stairs creaked beneath the weight of his guilt, but he steadied himself on the railing and moved on. His feet touched the heated floors and his body held in what little breath his body clung to.

"Alice?" His voice quaked.

The house was quiet.

"My little mouse?"

Nothing. He was alone.

He rounded the corner with small hesitant steps into the kitchen. It was eerily empty, but for a note which sat alone on the middle island. A thin line of sweat, half water, half ethanol, instantly caked his body. As he walked across the kitchen, towards the note, the room turned and he felt faint. He picked the note up, shaking as if an invisible wind raged around him, and held it a few centimeters from his face.

"Good morning party animal. How's it feel waking up an Oscar winner? Like a hangover, I bet. I'm out with Jean. We're going to discuss (y)our big night last night. Won't be home till late, but not as late as you were this morning! 8AM! You must have had some night. Can't wait to hear all about it when you're feeling better. I made an omelet and smoothie for you to start the recovery process. I'm sure you're going to need it. Anyway. I can't wait to see you later. Love you, Alice."

There was a small heart over the the 'i' in her name.

A buildup of stale air, something akin to relief, but not unlike dry-aged cigarette smoke, flowed from David. He'd escaped discovery. This would be nothing more than a learning lesson—a great big dumb mistake. After a day or two of rest, rejuvenation, and relaxation, his life would resume and nothing will have changed.

Even the light from the refrigerator burned the back of his bulbs. He winced and looked for the food Alice had made him. At the sight of the eggs, lovingly wrapped, his stomach ached. He pulled it out, along with the smoothie, and placed them on the island beside Alice's note, which he flipped over and scribbled on the other side:

"My love. Woke up and saw the note. It was a sight to see for the eyes of a damaged man. Thank you for being you— and thank you for the smoothie and eggs. You don't know how right you are about fixing me up. I'm in bad shape. I couldn't be more thankful to have you with me, today, and every day. I'm taking one of your Lunestas. Going to check out for the rest of the day. I'll be in the guest room sleeping off this murderous hangover. Hold my calls. See you in the morning. Love you my little mouse. David."

He read his note over, searching the spaces between the lines for an admission of guilt, an unintentional slip up, something that subconsciously spilled out onto the page. Then he read it again, and one last time. It took all the courage he could muster, and half the omelet, before he convinced himself that the note was clear and simple. He finished the food, then popped a single Lunesta. It was dry going down. A shower followed, then the sweet healing embrace of slumber.

eight

"Wake up!"

Her tiny, angry fists, an alternating clop and snap of bone and skin, rained down on David's back, snapping him from his tenth hour of drug-induced slumber.

"What the fuck?" he said, turning on his side and covering his face.

Her knuckles bounced off the corner of his elbow. She hesitated, and he caught her wrist as she sprung forward.

"Jesus," he said, tugging against her struggling wrists. "What is it?"

She broke free of his grip and pulled away. Giant globs welled up in the corners of her eyes. "What is it? What is it? I'll show you." She held up a copy of today's US Weekly. "Everything's a lie." She threw the copy at him and began to sob.

The magazine was fuzzy, but, as he slipped on his glasses, he saw it. On the front page, beneath the headline "David Emmeret Smith wins two trophies on Oscar night" were both his and Justine's naked censored bodies.

"It's not what it looks like. I can explain." He tried to process an explanation, but his brain failed to run, hitting some kind of computing error, and blue boxes of death spread through his field of vision, forcing him to shutdown and restart. "Alice..."

There was nothing to say. He was trapped into a corner of deceit. There was no way out. He had betrayed his wife in front of the world.

"Well?" She searched his face for some chance, some inkling, of a story. Something to soften the crushing weight on her heart. She would have believed anything that sounded halfway reasonable.

"I'm sorry" was all he could think of.

A lifetime of silence passed between them. She blinked rapidly, trying to whisk away the nile of betrayal splitting her cheeks.

"I…."

"You what, David? YOU WHAT!?" The scream was the last gasping breaths of a dying fawn, searching for their mother to save them, for someone, for anyone, to swoop in and rescue them.

She stepped away from the bed and walked in small circles, with her hands in vice-like claws near her face. He could do nothing but watch from the bed. It looked as if a swarm of bees had gotten inside her head and were stinging her brain in succession, over and over and over. Then, without warning, as one of her circles passed near David, she lunged at him again.

"You bastard!"

David, as if caught in a trance of his own betrayal, let her sad fists ricochet off his cheek, and his nose, and his forehead.

She pulled away from him, her chest rising and falling with heavy uneven gasps. "A woman half your age! You're old enough to be her father!"

"I can make this better." He was misty and his face swollen. "Just tell me how I can make it better."

She collapsed onto the floor, into her hands, which muffled her sobs. "Just go," she said, between her fingers. "Please, just get out of here."

"But Alice," he stood, walking around her. "Where

would I go?"

"Get out of here!" She threw the magazine at him. It hit him in the chest and fell to the ground. "I don't want to see you! I don't want to hear from you."

"How long?"

"I don't care."

"Can't I stay in my office for a few days? You won't know I'm there."

Her hands darted away from her face and she was twisted in anger. "I SAID GET THE FUCK OUT OF HERE!" She pointed at the door.

His lips moved in her direction, but no sound came out. He closed the door behind him. On the stillness of the other side, he could hear her smothering her screams into her hands.

There was an ever-expanding sinking at the pit of his belly. He'd betrayed the last 25 years of his life, the greatest friend he'd ever known, the closest, most rock-steady thing that's ever existed. It was all gone in an instant. Damaged beyond repair. A giant fucking mistake. All for one night of pleasure. She would never speak to him again and he deserved it. He deserved to die alone. He deserved whatever misery, whatever weird version of his life, would inevitably follow.

He loaded a suitcase with four pairs of socks, four pairs of underwear, three shirts, and one pair of pants. There was still some far off delusion that he would be back in his house before he ran out of underwear. On his way out, he stopped by his office and stuffed four bottles of whiskey into his suitcase, the weight he carried now a little heavier.

In an attempt to avoid the more-than-usual amount of paparazzi lingering outside his house—he counted three men, compared to the norm: zero—he drove himself to the private parking garage of his driver, then had the driver drive him to a relatively inconspicuous middle-class hotel called The Grand Sea.

It was shaped as if built by individual building blocks, like shipping containers, or legos, stained brown to look like aged brick. He gave a pseudonym to a woman at the front desk whose name, according to the golden tag on her left breast pocket, was Peggy. She looked at him sideways and squinted, trying to place him. He hoped she wouldn't ever quite get it. She handed him a card, 301, and said g'day with a mid-western smile. His room was small and unassuming— the kind of place he imagined a man hiding from the world would find himself in: a double bed, a small bathroom with a stand-up shower, a desk, a phone, a tv, and a balcony (he'd requested a balcony, so that he could smoke without leaving).

Standing in the room now, he looked up and laughed. Popcorn ceilings! Hadn't seen those in years.

After the absurdity of it all faded, the sadness set it. For the next six days, he faded in and out of consciousness, remembering mere moments between drinks, unanswered calls to Alice, and passing out wherever his body gave in.

When he ran out of booze or cigarettes, or on the rare occasions that his body called out for food, he had his driver hand-deliver them to the door. Under no circumstances, but for the grace of his wife, would he re-enter the world. Then, on the sixth day, he searched his bag for his in-case-of-emergency mobile phone—an old brick from an era when having a cellular phone was a luxury, not a requirement. He found Scott under 'R' warmly saved as "Rise and Fall Scott."

It was, he knew, polite to save someone's number after they had asked for yours, whether or not you had any intention of ever calling the number, or even opening your phone, unless it was forced upon you.

He clicked clumsily at the foreign buttons, having to stop and survey the keyboard between each letter, and pinpoint the next spot his thumb should and would go.

"This is David. Can YOU HELP ME?"

Somehow, he'd turned the caps lock on mid-way through the sentence and he didn't care enough to turn it off.

Scott replied within seconds. "Man! I heard what happened. So sorry. U ok?"

"PARTY?"

"We're back on the set tomorrow though."

"WANT TO PARTY."

"I can't."

"Fucking bastard," David whispered to himself. He texted back, "YOU OWE ME!"

"I do owe u. ur right. But I can't party."

"DRUGS?"

"I can give u a #?"

"OK."

"555 413 3168. Tell him u no me."

He wrote the number down on a piece of paper, not knowing that you could simply copy it. The pen wobbled as he wrote. He created a new contact in his phone under "Scott's guy," texted the number, then continued drinking.

When he woke up to the phone buzzing in his pocket, the sun outside had long disappeared. He rubbed his eyes, stretched then picked up the call.

"Yo. Who this?"

After a long career of voice acting, playing with accents, and trying on different ones, David could tell an imitation when he heard one. This was a cheaply forced hispanic accent.

"What? You called me."

"You texted me hours ago. You need something, homie?"

"Oh, right." Flashes of shaky, sad fingers texting a stranger for drugs ran through his mind. "What can I get?"

"What can you get? I don't know you."

"Scott Peterson said you could help me out. He's a friend of yours, isn't he?"

"We ain't friends, but if he gave you my name, you cool."

"Okay, what do we do?"

"Jesus, man. You new?"

"Extremely, but I got a lot of money, and I want to spend it."

"Where you at?"

"The Grand Sea Hotel."

"The fuck is that?"

"It's just outside of downtown. Can you meet me?"

"Hell no, I ain't about to go that far. You know how much heat I got on me?"

"Where can we meet?"

"I'm in Inglewood, homie. There's a liquor store by my place. Nelson's Liquor. Meet me there in a half hour. I'll be driving a red Ford Focus."

David splashed water on his face and under his armpits, gargled complimentary mouthwash, and counted his cash. He stopped to look at himself in the mirror and wonder who he was or what he was doing.

"Fuck it," he said, as he turned the door knob and braced the cold of the outside world.

nine

THIRTY THREE MINUTES later David was smoking a cigarette in his car outside of Nelson's liquor store. Four minutes and one cigarette after that, a 2001 Ford Focus—as if the driver knew exactly who he were going to, or because he was the only other car in the parking lot—parked beside him.

The driver rolled down his passenger side window. He was white, dusty, and bald, save for a few wisps of hair curling around his ears, and looked nothing like the failed accent tried to imply over the phone.

"You meeting someone here homie?"

Where would Scott have met a character like this?

David sat up in his seat, tilted his neck back, and raised his brow. "Yeah?" he said slowly. He repeated the word in his head, investigating the depths of his own failed coolness.

"Hop in," the driver said, reaching over and unlocking the passenger side door.

The interior of the car was an aged ashy brown, far from the original colour, and the seats were sprinkled with burn marks. David's feet shuffled amongst empty burger containers and fast food wrappers, trying to find some way to comfortably nestle in them. The car turned right out of the parking lot.

"Cigarette?" the driver asked, holding out a packet of camels. It was gnarled at the edges, with only two left.

"No thanks."

"Suit yourself." He threw one in his mouth, his accent

having not-so-mysteriously disappeared.

"You have a name? Or are you not supposed to tell me?"   David wasn't sure how this conversation was meant to go, if you were supposed to jump right into it or make some sort of attempt at small talk.

"Sure, I can tell ya." He didn't take his attention off the road. "It's Freddie. What kinda shit you looking for?"

"I don't know."

"Well, fuck. That's a new one. This ain't no candy surprise bag, homie. Ya gotta tell me what you want."

"Well, what do you have? Let's start there."

"I got it all." Freddie let his tongue ride through the last vowel, holding onto it, before letting it out. David wasn't sure if that "all" was ever going to end. "I got uppers, downers, you name it. I even got some shit that'll make you go sideways."

"Let's stick with ups and downs for now."

"Whaddya want? You look like the cocaine and caviar kinda guy."

"How much for just the cocaine?"

"For you? $100.00 a gram, my dude."

"How many is there in an ounce again?"

Like he was, until then, focusing on some far off object, some other worldly idea of David, Freddie's pupils dilated and David came into focus. "An ounce?"

"Sure."

"I ain't got an ounce on me, man."

"How much do you have?"

"Eight grams. That's it."

"I'll take it." David flipped open his wallet and fingered through a wad of cash, counting out $800 in 100s, leaving behind a thumb's thickness of more bills.

"Damn. You ain't playing." He took the next side street, pulled into a back alley, then behind a closed off garage's driveway. They were surrounded by trees and a high fence.

"Let me count it."

"Let me see the coke." He pulled back the fist full of cash.

"Alright. Alright."

Freddie leaned into the backseat and came back with a worn leather knapsack. He undid the zipper and pulled out a bag with eight small ziplocks, then handed them to David, who handed the eight bills to Freddie. He fingered the bills greedily, counting from one to eight under his breath. An impression of a smile, more self-satisfied sneering than grin, appeared on his face. He stuffed the bills into the side pocket of his bag.

"Anything else?"

"What else you got?"

"Like I said, I got it all."

"But not a lot of it."

"Whatever."

David counted the remaining bills in his wallet. $700 was burning a hole in his pocket, itching to get out into the world—but what else did he want? He didn't just want to have fun, he thought. He wanted to let go. He wanted to take whatever life he had left, crumple it up, throw gasoline on it, and light the fire. He wanted to take this life of debauchery to the limit, let go and see where it took him.

"Heroin?"

"Yeah, sure man, how much?"

"How much does it cost?

"I'll give you a deal, since you bought so much yayo $200 a g."

"I'll give you $700 for four."

Freddie's top lip curled upwards, and the tip of his canines poked out on either side. They were brown, rounded nuggets, with thick plaque wedged between the neighbour-

97

ing teeth. "You got it." He produced another bag, full of smaller bags decorated with stars and stripes. Money and drugs once again exchanged hands.

David, as if he knew what he were looking for, held the bags up to eye level, inspecting each one individually. "Looks good," he said, in much the same voice he'd pretend to taste-test wine.

"You ever touch that stuff?"

"Sure. Why?"

"Just don't seem like you have."

David stuffed both sandwich bags into his front pocket. "Any tips?"

"Go easy on it." Freddie sounded concerned, almost parental. "It's hard stuff."

"What's it like?"

"Too good, man. Too fucking good. All your problems," Freddie said, staring off at some far memory, "just seem to fade away." He moved his hand, up-and-down, like it was riding a wave.

"Good."

"That it?"

David nodded. Freddie pulled out of the garage and headed back towards the liquor store. As they drove, Freddie looked over at David every three or four seconds. The stolen looks, the silence, the drugs weighing down his pocket, they all built on each other, one by one. David's skin prickled and his hands, which wouldn't stop moving, were muggy.

"Little hot in here," David said, trying to cut the tension.

"You know what?"

David's heart dropped meters from his body. He tried to swallow, but his tongue was stuck in his throat.

"I know you from somewhere, don't I?"

"Huh?"

"You been on TV or something?"

His heart ricocheted back to his body and he swallowed comfortably. "Might've seen me in a movie or two."

"That's right. Movies. You're some kinda movie star, ain't ya?"

"Wouldn't go that far, but sure."

"David... fuck. Somethin' Smith, right? Three names?"

"David Emmeret Smith."

"Holy fucking shit balls batman. David Emmeret Smith, in my car!" They pulled into the parking lot. "God damn. Wait 'till I tell my friends about this."

"Look, what we just did in here, it isn't something you should be going around and telling people. In fact, you keep your mouth shut and I'll continue to call you. Okay?"

"Got it. Lips are sealed. Not a word."

"Good." David got out of the car.

"David?" Freddie said, before David closed the door.

"Yeah?"

"Next time you call me I can come to you."

"Got it. Talk to you then," David said. "Freddie was it?"

"Yup."

"Thanks."

Freddie chuckled boyishly. "David Emmeret fucking Smith. I can't believe it." He put the car in reverse and backed out. "What are the chances?" he said, shaking his head in David's direction. He put the car into first and peeled out.

David watched the car take a right, then a left, and disappear.

Would Freddie leak today's little meeting to another tabloid? The idea scared him. Then, as quickly as it came, it disappeared. He was already on the road to hell. A push wouldn't hurt.

The stars and stripes baggie laid idly beside three thick lines of blow. It was a menacing beacon to David. He paced back and forth, shuffling through the icons and iconoclasts who had gone under the thumb of the big H, the mexican mud, the white lady, the brown crystal—black tar, smack, scag, nod—whatever you called it, it did them in, buried beneath a layer of dirt. It was the real big bad boogeyman in the night, the star killer, haunting the famous and the talented. Phoenix, Belushi, Joplin, Morrison, Sid, Hedberg, Farley, these people, some he knew, some he met, all were geniuses in their own right.

Would his name be added to the list in the end? Would anyone care? Did he care?

He cleared one of the three lines off the table, stood up, and stared the brown devil in the eye. It was rock bottom in a baggie, staring back at him, but it was the bottom he wanted, the bottom he craved—to come crashing down, full-stop, and put out of his misery. But it's a long way down to the bottom, and it took a certain courage to get there.

He cleared the second line in a single sharp inhale.

Those men, those women, drug users under the spotlight, exposed to the world, scabies, scabs and all. They, those, them—they were the courageous ones. They who wore their abuse like a badge of honour with nowhere to hide. They, those sweet beasts, who live their lives like hungry creatures under the starry sunken night. Those who will screech and pull simply for the bottom dollar of their best friends feeding frenzy. The guts it takes for their day-in and day-out glory. He didn't have the guts. He didn't have the courage. He didn't have what it took to bite down on the pavement and ask for seconds. He was a coward. It was time to admit it. But he was a coward with cocaine, and cocaine cowards are antithetical, oxymorons in the flesh. Their courage may be chemical, but as long as there were chemicals, there was courage.

He cleared the last line.

He shot up and clapped aggressively, like some working man's chimpanzee, the sides of his hands spilling one over the other. There was more power in his body than he was used to, more courage swirling around his mind, a fearlessness bordering on blindness. He didn't recognize the man who thought his thoughts, who occupied his mind, and he liked it.

He dived on the bag, his back arched and deformed, his fingers picking at the seal with a ravenous hunger. He partitioned off a small strip of the brown powder and exhaled. This was it. The final moments of his pre-heroin life. A six-storey leap. A fall that could kill. A single line.

Snnnnnoooorrrrtttttt

And then he waited for... something to hit. But there was nothing—no great uplifting high, no soaring wings of an angel, not even the cold taste of pavement. There was only a drip in the back of his throat, reminiscent of crushed vitamins and disappointment. He shrugged and did another line. Then, for good measure, another.

He wiped the powder from his nose, laid down, and waited. He watched the electric fireworks pulse behind his eyelids until, without warning, the gaps between the bed and his body filled in. He went simultaneously smooth and mushy, caving into himself. A warm glow descended from behind his ears, down through his torso, to the tips of his fingernails, and a little bit beyond, like a protective aura of pleasure, or thousands upon thousands of blissful pin pricks rolling over and over and over his skin. The middle of his back lifted off the bed and his chest raised in the air. Like Dali's clocks, time was suspended in the moment, and everything before it melted away. There was only this. He was alone to float in an infinite black sea of joy, an oarsmen on a river of hedonism. He was free.

He breathed slowly, exploring the way the air filled his aging body, imagining the tiny air sacs filling with oxygen and travelling through his bloodstream, like God's organic version of public transit. He wanted to bury himself in this feeling, wrap himself in it, like a pleasure cocoon, and emerge ready to face the world and his problems, or be free of them altogether.

What a wonder this was, what a gift to mankind. The opiate. Morphine. A little brown powder. How easy it is to destroy all thoughts, all worries, and replace them with indescribable pleasure. The jump was hard but the fall was sweet. How could he have missed this? Why wasn't he here sooner? What was his life before this? Until man leaves earth, until the light of the sun goes out, until entropy plucks every last living creature from the universe, there would be only this. And if the Lord up above made anything better that sonofabitch kept it for himself.

Then, as if a carnival ride was turned on, the room began to tilt and spin. It was slow at first, then, as all carnival rides do, it picked up. David looked for something to hold onto. He stood up, as if to steady himself, but his stomach, leaving his body behind, remained lying down, causing the whole movement of his insides to zip up like a yo-yo. He had to purge. Using everything around him as a means of balance, he stumbled his way to the bathroom, barely making it to the toilet before chemically-infused scotch erupted from his mouth, all over the rim, and on the floor. He surveyed the damage, shocked at the amount of liquid that came from his body, or the amount of liquid that was still remained, and purged again, slumping over as he expelled. Despite the grotesqueness of the scene, there was a tinge of joy to his pain, like he was detached from it, watching from the comfort of a television screen, between buttered popcorn fingers, barely aware that that man on the screen was him. Curled up on the bathroom floor, mostly unaware of who he was or what he was doing, he nodded in and out of pleasure. The only thing he knew for sure was that it felt good.

An unknowable amount of time later, David opened his eyes to two puke-encrusted bolts screwed into a ceramic square. He was wrapped around the toilet bowl, his head squeezed behind the base. Using the lid of the bowl and shower as supports, he strained and staggered to his feet, the pressure pounding on his already swollen head. He scanned the bathroom and laughed.

What a mess. What a stinking mess.

It was as if someone threw a barf grenade into the toilet while David, without a care in the world, opted to sleep in it. He turned the shower on, splashing water around the room, and mopped the puke up with three of the four towels in the bathroom. He then removed his clothes and mopped himself off.

Now this was living.

ten

FOR THE NEXT three days a whirlwind of impulsivity, hedonism, and hangovers was the general theme of David's 13' by 25', door-to-window, hotel room. He was searching for that same jaw-dropping wall clawing high he'd experienced on the first night. But, in much the same way you can't re-pop a balloon, it can never be experienced again. Your cells, forever changed, cannot undergo the same metamorphosis twice. A man chasing a high, however, does what a man chasing a high will do. He'll look for that same high in every crack and crevice his junk-sick bones can muster. On the first of the three days, with seven tenths of the first bag left, he finished it off. It was good, perhaps even great, but not quite the same as the first time. On the second day, he went right through a whole bag, and a small scoop into the third. On the third day, he finished off the open bag, and crushed through the final bag. On the fourth day, Freddie arrived to re-supply, and a new development in the search for an absolute bottom presented itself.

Freddie was wearing a sweat-stained short-sleeve henley and counted out grams of Heroin on David's hotel room desk. The chair creaked as he rocked back and forth.

"One, two, three, four, five."

On five he swiveled to face David, whose eyes were running up and down the length of Freddie's arms. He swerved his gaze as if his company's attention was oncoming traffic. Freddie slipped the five baggies into a sandwich bag and threw it at David, who missed the catch.

He picked the bag up. "Let me ask you a question, Freddie."

"Sure."

"It might be a little personal, but I don't know who else to ask."

"I'm an open book."

"You ever try heroin yourself?"

"A good salesman knows his product." Freddie squeezed from a wink any sign of grace.

"Do you snort it?"

"I bang it." He tapped his ditch, the inside of his elbow, with two fingers.

"How come you don't have any track marks?"

"I'm careful."

"What's it like?"

"Because you're injecting it right into your blood there's no come up time. It's an instant blast off, right to the moon. Shorter, sure, but stronger. Holy hell is it stronger. Better than any other high you're going to get."

The tip of David's cock tingled and shifted at the thought of the high. "Can you show me how? I can pay you."

"You don't have to give me shit. When do you want your lesson?"

"Today? Right now?"

Freddie breathed through his teeth, looked around, and opened his phone. "Fuck."

"Busy?"

"No, it's just—fuck it. Sure. I'll have to go get my kit from my car, though."

"Sure."

He stood up. "Be right back."

David scratched his forehead and looked around the room. He got up and poured himself a drink from the same glass he had been using for the last four days. The once-clear glass had a thin layer of brown tar at the bottom, which he covered in whiskey. It burned the back of his tongue, swollen now for days, on the way down.

Was he taking it too far? He didn't know anything about this guy and now he was putting his life in his hands?

He took another pull of whiskey, enjoying its warmth, despite the burn. He multiplied the feeling of it by a hundred, then multiplied that feeling by a hundred. Its low-level euphoria was dwarfed by the all-seeing pleasure of his first high, and this promised be better than that—better! He wasn't in over his head; he was on his head, on the pavement, splattered into a thousand pieces and ready to do it all over again.

The light on the door flashed from orange to green and Freddie walked in. He was holding a black leather bathroom bag. "Got it," he said.

David, as if to cheers Freddie's return, held his glass up. Freddie sat at the desk, placed the bag on it, and undid the zipper. Like a young apprentice watching a master, David stood eagerly over his shoulder.

He removed two needles. "You want fresh, unused needles. Lotsa junkies can't afford fresh ones, so they try to clean and reuse them. Don't."

"Where do you get them?"

"Any pharmacy, really. But don't go to the same one over and over. They'll catch on and stop selling to you."

He placed a blue plastic pill container beside the needles. "Some dealers give it out in paper folds, dollar bills, tin foil, whatever. Shit doesn't stay easily. If you get one of those, you put it in your pill box." He tipped it upside down and a paper package, the size of a mint, rolled out. "I keep these Silica bags in it so the heroin stays dry."

"Bit a science to it."

"An art," Freddie said. He reached into the bag and took out a spoon. "Spoon," he said, and held it out for David to see. It barely fit into the palm of hand.

"Where did you get that?"

"Man, I actually can't remember where I got this, but you can probably find one like it in an antique store or whatever. But any spoon works, I just like this one." He placed it on the table, the equipment forming a drug kit line up.

"Anyway, alcohol swabs," he said, pulling them out, "are key. Only junkies and druggies don't use 'em."

"Got it."

"A tiny bottle of contact solution."

"For?"

"Cooking."

"Right."

"And cotton balls." He picked them out with his left hand. "Finally, a lighter." Like a moth to a flame, a caveman to a fire, he held it up to eye level and produced a flame.

"What are the cotton balls for?"

"You'll see, homie.."

"What about rubber bands or belts? What if air gets in from the needle?"

Freddie cackled and slapped his knee. "A stupid myth. A junkie uses a belt because a junkie ain't got no water in his body."

"So?"

"It's harder to find a vein when you don't drink water. The belt builds up blood and the veins pop."

"I haven't been drinking much water lately."

"But you ain't a junkie, not yet. I can still spot your veins a mile away."

"So, then, that's it?"

"That's it. You ready?"

"Sure."

Freddie used his hand, the one with the brown finger-nails—not that they didn't both have brown fingernails—to wipe off a corner of the desk. He tapped on the bag and the brown powder billowed out, forming a tiny mountain. "A dose is about .1 of a gram, so each bag has 10 doses in it. It's your first time, so your dose is a little smaller."

"Pour yourself one too," David said—the way down was lonely.

"Aight, but you go first." He tapped out another, slightly larger, pile. "Let's cook."

David was wrinkling onto himself, gyrating with excitement.

"Watch." Freddie scraped the powder onto the spoon, added five drops of water, and stirred it with the end of the needle.

The two swirled and combined in the spoon, while David quietly contained himself.

"Add heat." He held the lighter underneath. "And wait 'till it boils."

How far he'd fallen. If Alice could only see him now, she'd take him back. She'd know what a mess he was without her. How low he sunk, almost immediately, with no one there to catch his fall. To be so vile, it was thrilling.

The chemical concoction bubbled.

"There it is," he said. He held it up to eye level like a young scientist observing a breakthrough in a beaker. "One last step." He set a cotton ball on the solution, which sucked the spoon dry. "You don't need the cotton ball, but who knows how pure the junk is. I buy it, but ain't nobody out here telling the truth, so it helps filter all the shit you might not want in your body."

He pressed the needle point into the middle of the solution and sucked. David, his tongue lolling out of his mouth, followed the chamber as it filled.

"Boom. That's all there is to it." He held out an alcohol swab and the needle for David. "Ready?"

With the needle in hand—which felt like it was made to be held by him—he was salivating with desire. "Okay, where do I shoot it?" He pointed to the inside of his elbow. "Here?"

"Junkies call that their ditch. There's other spots you can shoot, but that's easiest."

David, looking for a vein (it didn't seem as easy as Freddie made it out to be), held his arm up and readied the needle.

"Wait," he said, getting out of his chair. "Lay on the bed, get comfortable, it's going to knock you on your ass."

"I like the sounds of that," he said, lying down on the bed. The old mattress creaked under his weight. "Am I ready?"

"Go for it."

David exhaled, his battle-worn nostrils whistling, and pierced the skin. It was sharp, but manageable. He looked to Freddie for further instruction.

"Push off."

The mixture moved slowly down the length of the needle. It was warm and comforting, like the day's first glass of whiskey. It disappeared beneath his skin. "Pull it back up slowly." Tiny speckles of red shot into the needle.

A crashing ripple of relaxation—which emanated from the back of his knees, unlike snorting, which started behind his shoulders—slackened the sinew between muscle and bone. Before long, they separated altogether, and he seemed to float within himself, a bone body without lines, in the sea-salt chamber of his skin. He was safe here, wrapped in the goblin's glow of depravity, and it was calm and still and right. He leaned back on the wall. His eyelids fluttered, then closed. On the backs of them, a crisscrossing of red-blue-yellow light, a memory formed. He was a child and it was winter. He'd returned home, the wood croaking beneath his feet, from a long day of ice-skating with his mother. Her voice, telling him to wrap up in front of the fire, still rung in his ear. It was a ritual of warmth. The fire, the flames, they nipped at his feet and face, the rest of him protected by a blanket. And in that moment, within the warmth of the cabin, he knew what it was to be safe, from the cold, from life's troubles, from everything.

With the two of them locked in place on the bed, frozen in ecstasy, day became evening and evening became night. All at once, the pleasure dropped and David's senses returned. With it, he became acutely aware of the man beside him, the man whose clammy arm was pressed against his. He shuffled onto his side, then rolled off the bed. He was still stiff and weak at the knees. He found his glass, still a finger of whiskey left, on the corner of the desk, beside Freddie's drug kit. He put back the remaining whiskey, then stumbled into the bathroom. His face was uneven, red and puffy. The whites of his eyes, like a newborn, were glazed over. There was spittle in the corners of his mouth. He tried to spit, but his saliva was an unmoving white molasses. He rinsed his cup out, then drank deeply, refilling the cup until he had his fill. He splashed his face with water, then returned to the room. Freddie's chest rose and fell, a slight whistle bouncing off the walls as he deflated.

David enjoyed the sight of the man, in his own comfort—he didn't have a care in the world. Or, at least, the pains he did have, the worries, came across as insignificant to David, like a child's.

He tapped his left jacket pocket for a cigarette, then walked out onto the balcony. The night air was cold on his junk-warm body. He lit a cigarette and pulled hard, the ember crackling in the quiet night. From the third floor of the balcony the surrounding buildings, their hulking midnight steel, looked menacing.

There was a rustling inside as Freddie stirred awake. David kept his eyes on the outside world.

"Fuck," Freddie said, walking onto the patio. "Did I pass out?"

"Yeah."

"Shit, sorry."

"It's fine." He flicked his cigarette off the balcony and pulled out another one. "Cigarette?"

Freddie, his hands shaking, took a cigarette out of the packet and placed it between his teeth. "I've got something on my mind ever since I met you."

"What's that?" He lit his cigarette, then Freddie's.

Freddie exhaled. "The fuck you doing here?"

"Getting high, Freddie. Same as you."

"I watched a couple of your movies after I met you. You're fucking good homie. Like real fucking good. I don't get it."

Freddie's stare was burning a hole in David's cheek, as David kept looking straight ahead, smoking peacefully.

"Well?"

"Maybe I'm running from something."

"What?"

"You don't read the news, do you?"

"Should I?"

"No."

"What happened?"

"I fucked up."

"How?"

David coughed, then forced another. "I cheated," he said quietly.

"Don't you kinda people do that shit all the time?"

"Famous people, sure. Not me, though. Not us."

"How'd she take it?"

David turned and looked at Freddie. "I'm here aren't I?"

"She ain't likely to forgive you?"

"Would you?"

"Fuck no, but she ain't me."

"She's proud."

"Have you asked her?"

"She needs space. Time to breathe. If I reached out, I'd only dig myself deeper."

"Some plan," Freddie said, flicking his cigarette off the balcony.

"Sorry?"

"I said 'some plan.'"

"Are you being sarcastic?"

"It's just, you get caught cheating, so you run away, hole up in some shit hole, and start pounding smack? The fuck kind of attitude is that?"

David squeezed his eyebrows together and jutted back. "Are you lecturing me right now?"

Freddie shrugged. "Just saying, is all."

"Well don't." He raised his voice. "You're here on my dime. Remember that."

Freddie hunched over the side of balcony. "Aight," he said, his voice flat. "Alright."

David saw the hurt in Freddie's eyes and wanted to reach out and touch him, but said, instead, "Wanna have a drink and do a couple lines?"

"Sure."

eleven

TIME HELD LITTLE meaning between those thin hotel room walls and meaning held little value outside of them. The two of them were mere floating specks in a black universe of smack. All around them, nothing, and inside those walls, everything. The hours, the days, they blended into each other and neither could tell you how much of either had passed. All they knew was the end of the needle and the terrifying, but short, intervals when Freddie had to re-stock. And for brief moments, when David was totally and completely annihilated on the junk, when he was crescendoing on a symphony of black tar, bleeding from the ears on ecstasy, would his mind drift into the nothingness of pure pleasure. Those were the moments he chased. But, inevitably, they would pass, and he would come back to reality, with Freddie, a cold reminder of life on earth, beside him. That's not to say he didn't enjoy his company. While Freddie brought him heroin (and other drugs), which—undoubtedly—produced a conditioned pleasure in David whenever he walked through the door, he was also starting to enjoy having him around. Through the sparse words they shared, which looked not unlike conversation, David began to form an idea of Freddie. He was nearing 40, still lived with his mother—though, with the money David was bringing him, he had plans to change that—occasionally worked in his brother's warehouse, and did not have a girlfriend. And now, at the peak of his life, his best customer was a man who Roger Ebert once said, "is a force to be reckoned with."

He wasn't sure what he liked about him, if anything, but he was sure that he did. Perhaps, he thought, it was the absence of a lifelong human closeness that he was trying to fill, a physical gap in his life, where Alice once stood. Besides, they had a lot in common: smoking, drinking and poking themselves with needles—a match made in oddball heaven.

"David," Freddie whispered. They were nearing 40 hours straight of pure limit-pushing pleasure.

David's eyes were closed and his arms crossed on his chest. He mumbled something unintelligible in response.

"What?" Freddie asked.

"What?" David said, opening his eyes.

"I've been thinking."

"About what?"

"About your old lady."

David sighed. "Whatever you're going to say, please don't."

"Hear me out."

David sat up. "What?"

"When was the last time you talked to her?"

"Two weeks? Three weeks? I don't know. She wouldn't pick up."

"Why were you calling?"

"To explain."

"You think if you'd explained yourself, she'd take your ass back?"

"I know she would."

"How do you know that?"

"Because I know her better than I know myself."

"Why the fuck are you sitting here with my dumb ass then?"

David scratched his head and looked around the room. "What do you mean?"

"Go home. Explain yourself to her face to face."

"You think?" His stomach churned. Happiness now was nothing more than a concept to him. He didn't know if he could stomach going back, but he didn't know if he could stomach all this depravity, either.

"I'm sure of it, man."

"Fuck it," he said, standing up. "You're right. Just go there and talk to her. Not like I have anything to lose."

"I can drive," Freddie said, rolling off the bed.

"You're a mess. I'll drive."

"I'm a mess? Look yourself in the mirror. You could go shopping with the bags you're wearing."

He rushed to the washroom. "Fuck," he said, pressing his hands into his face. The traces of his fingers left a white line on the pink and puffy skin. "I can't go like this."

"We're coming up from a big ass hit. We should give it some time."

"Right. Maybe a couple lines will help freshen us up."

Freddie pulled out his special vial, the one he carried his own coke in. "Wouldn't hurt."

"She wouldn't know the difference anyways," David said, stammering slightly on the soft 's'.

"We can tell because we know." Freddie said, sectioning off a line.

"Cut me up one too."

He clasped a straw between his thumb and index finger. The line disappeared. "Lil' bit of gas in the tank and we'll be good to go."

He passed it to David and the second line disappeared. "One more?" He said, looking up.

Freddie's hands went up as the corners of his lips went down. "Not like a second line of blow ever killed nobody."

They repeated the process.

"Straight?"

David, with what space he had, paced up and down the room. "Straighter than ever. Maybe too straight."

"You seem a little nervous."

"Fuck, wouldn't you be?"

"Relax. Have a drink."

"A drink?" He toyed with the idea. "Yeah, a drink."

Freddie handed a half-full glass to him. "You gotta walk in there with confidence." He held fists in front of his face. "And take back your life!"

"That's right. Take my life back!" He raised his voice. "Another line Freddie!"

That lined turned to two, then three, then four. Before he realized it, he was knee deep in coke and ready—roaring—to go. His face tingled, hot to the touch, and his eyes stung with alertness. Confidence (cocaine) he had.

But, thirty minutes later, as he walked up his driveway, the sight of his house was sobering. His legs were pool noodles and a tremor ran down his left arm and into his fingers. His body cried out for chemical adrenaline, but a drink would have to do. He tiptoed the final few steps to the door. The overhead light turned on and he froze. He listened for footsteps over the sound of his thumping heart. With moist hands, he inserted his key, turned and pushed. The door came open, the key still worked.

A television set echoed through the hall, masking his steps. Alice was home. A quick drink in his study and then he'd face her with the full force of his confidence behind him. He entered the door on the far right of the entrance hall, just before the living room, and silently shut it behind him.

Everything looked exactly as he left it. The memories of this place, which came flooding back, felt like another life, another David. He didn't recognize himself in the familiarity—but he still recognized scotch. Placed neatly on a liquor tray beside his desk, as if past-life David had left current-life David a present from beyond, were two glasses and a decanter of Scotch. He sidled up next to it and poured himself a glass. He brought it halfway to his mouth then, by some miracle of God or devil, dropped it. It came thundering down onto the corner of the tray with a crash, flipping the tray, the decanter, and a second glass with it.

Seconds later, the door spun open. "What the fuck?" she screamed. "What are you doing here?" A thin line of mascara ran down each of her swollen cheeks.

"I live here, don't I?"

"Do you, David? Because I haven't heard from you, haven't seen you, in weeks."

"You weren't answering my calls, my texts, anything. What was I supposed to do?"

"Not show up like this." She stuttered through her words, fighting back tears. "You break into your own house just to have a drink?"

"I didn't break in. I have a key." He held it up to her.

She walked towards him with her palm out. "Give it to me."

"No." He stuffed it back into his pocket.

"Give me the fucking key David."

"It's mine. This house is mine."

"Not anymore."

"Why?"

Her body shuddered, her hands trembled. "How dare you ask me why."

"Would you believe me if I said I was sorry?"

He stepped closer to her, she stepped back.

"What difference would that make? You humiliated me in front of the whole world. You broke my heart."

"I came here to apologize." His words were long and slow, struggling to form the proper vowels. "I want to make this better."

"Look at you! You're a mess!"

"I'm fine."

"You can barely speak."

His lips betrayed him. "I can talk just fine."

"Are you high, too?"

"No."

"Empty your pockets. Let me see what you're holding."

He didn't move.

"Do it."

"Why?" He shrunk away from her.

She stepped closer, towering over him. "If you want me to hear what you have to say, you'll empty your pockets."

He stepped over the spilled liquor and slowly, reluctantly, emptied his pockets onto his old cherry desk: lighter, pack of cigarettes, keys, and wallet. "Happy?" he said, his voice quaking.

"Show me your hands."

He looked her in the face. "What?"

"You heard me. Palms up, hands open."

"You're being ridiculous."

"Do it!"

David, as if cut off from his arms, them, having a life of their own, watched his hands move through the air. In the right were two bags, one white, one brown.

"What is that?"

"Cocaine." He snatched his hands back, putting his things back in his pocket, careful not to look her in the eyes.

"No, the other one. The brown one."

"They're both cocaine."

"Since when is cocaine brown?"

"How would you know?"

The muscles in her jaw tightened. "For a guy who wants to explain you're awfully hesitant to answer my questions."

CHAPTER II

"It's..." he looked down at the floor, "It's heroin."

She bit her cheek and took tiny steps backward. "Oh." Her eyes misted. She breathed through her teeth, then opened her mouth, trying to form sounds that imitated vague approximations of words, but were nothing more than faint fricatives.

"I've been having a hard time with all this."

Tears rolled down her face, travelling along the already made path of mascara. "I don't understand what you're doing here. I don't know who you are."

"I'm David."

She held her hands in a fist near her chest and looked right through him. "It's like years have passed and there's an ocean between us."

"I'm right here." He inched towards her with his right hand extended. He was trying to bridge the gulf that split the tiny room apart.

"I need you to leave," she said, staring at her feet.

Out of misplaced compassion or a desire to put things right, he tried to place a hand on her shoulder. She slapped it away.

Her face was ravaged with anger. "Please don't touch me, don't do anything, just go."

"Alice...."

She pointed to the door. "Leave."

Emboldened by defeat, desperate for victory, he turned to anger. "How could you abandon me like this?"

"Abandon you?"

"You were everything to me."

"I'm abandoning you? Do you fucking hear yourself, David?"

He extended his arms. "Look at me. I need you more than ever."

"You need me?" She walked in circles, pulling at her

hair. "What about when I needed you to not fuck anoth-er woman? Huh? What about then? Where were you then? That's right." She grabbed a book from the shelf and hurled it at him. He ducked under it. "You were fucking another woman, you bastard! Remember this David. Remember it as the night you ruined your life! The night you lost everything! Now," she threw another book at him. "GET OUT!"

She stormed out of the room. As if waiting for his op-erating system to reboot, to process it all, he continued to stare where she'd just stood. The sound of her walking up the steps was faint, but her scream, followed by a door slam-ming, bounced within his ear, entering his brain, and burn-ing a permanent mark on his psyche. He looked to his left, then right, surveying the ruin that was his life, and forced himself to breathe. His legs, slowly, shuffled one after the other, right then left, carrying him out of the house. His arms stayed monotone at his sides.

In the car, Freddie bobbed his head to a vocal heavy house track while taking quick bumps from a key. When he spotted David a few feet from the car, morosely lurching along the driveway, he turned off the radio and unrolled the window.

"How'd it go?" he asked, leaning out of the window.

"Shut up, Freddie," he said. He opened the door to the passenger seat and slid into place. He stared straight ahead. The only movement he made was the result of a clenching jaw.

"Not good?"

Freddie stared at David for a few seconds, hesitated, then started the car. They drove back to the hotel in an ag-onizing silence. In the driveway to David's hotel, Freddie tried to again. "Wanna get high?" he asked, desperately.

"Not with you," he said, as he slammed the door shut.

twelve

IF NOTHING ELSE, the salvation of a powdered tincture would always be there for him—the sweet, sweet toxic embrace of the tar—ready to rub his shoulders into oblivion. It, unlike others, would never leave him high and dry, on the side of the road, thrown out with the trash. It wouldn't lead him down a dark alley, only to let him bleed out like a dog, left to paw his way to help. No, this inanimate pleasure powder, God's gift from the ground, was all he had left. It was what he would turn to in the cold of the morning. It kept his bed warm when he was alone. His intravenous snuggle buddy, his only friend left on earth.

On the rare times that he had any awareness at all (his come downs), he ordered room service, boozed, smoked cigarettes, and watched a select few television reruns, which predominantly included Seinfeld, the odd Curb Your Enthusiasm episode or The Office (American version). At most he saw Freddie once a week, but it was only to restock. Their relationship had subsequently devolved into nothing more than a cold transaction between budding capitalist and hungry consumer. The last time any warmth passed between the two was right before David attempted his reconciliation with Alice. Some men hold grudges, some men get high, and David, as over-indulgent as ever, did both.

But there was a certain comfort in David's new life, an ironic joie de vivre, or non-life. To not have anyone to care for, to let all inhibitions be left at the wayside, and to blissfully sit there, idling, laughing at man hands or the soup nazi. The radical newness of it all, after a lifetime of sweat, was refreshing. And he would have been content to spend the rest of his days in exactly that position, grafting to the bed and engorging himself on life's little—and large—pleasures, but life can sometimes have other plans for you.

One day there was a knock on the door.

He bumbled his way towards the sound, using the wall as a crutch, with no idea who could be on the other side.

"Hello?" he said to the phantom.

He opened the door an inch and peeked out. Nothing. There was only an empty space where he expected a man to be. He looked down and saw a serving cart, with a silver tray on top. He scratched his head and squinted, as if judging the tray's importance in the world. He opened the door wider and, moving the tray to the side, stepped out. Looking side to side, then coming to the odd, yet satisfactory conclusion that he was alone, he shrugged and brought the cart in. He removed the lid and, expecting food, found a rolled up copy of the LA Times. He threw it on the bed and resumed watching an episode of Seinfeld, the one with the cigar store Indian, before shooting up.

Some time after, having rolled around in his bed in a postpartum heroin slumber, he had splayed the newspaper all over the room, the only page left on his bed being the classified section.

Circled, and in purple ink, was an apartment for sale: "The David Thompson." He repeated the name in his head 10, 20, 30 times before moving on to read the rest. It was described as an "arts building" made for—and run by—artists, but the truth was closer to it being inhabited by those who ran peripherally in artist circles, but who had neither a desire nor a talent to create art. According to the ad, it was "modern, yet rustic, perhaps even Victorian, with tall, coffered ceilings, brick walls, a living room gas fireplace, hard-wood floors throughout, a large bathroom with claw bathtub (no shower), marble-lined kitchen, a large master and private balcony. Comes pre-furnished. 1525 sq. ft."

He picked up the room phone and dialed the listed number.

The voice on the other end was squeaky, almost mouse-like. "Hello, Timothy speaking."

"Hi, Tim." His tongue hurt to move, his voice-box shot from days of inactivity. "Is this the David Thompson?"

"Indeed it is, sir."

"I'm looking here at an ad for one of your apartments."

"Sure."

"Is it still available?"

"We have many available suites in many papers, sir. Could you be more specific?"

"It's the LA Times."

"Oh," there was the click-clack of a keyboard, "I wasn't aware we had an ad in the LA Times."

"Okay."

"But ah, yes, here."

David could hear the man smiling.

"701. A fine suite. Would like you like to take a look?"

"I would."

"Could I get your name, sir?"

Timothy listened to David's breath while he waited for an answer.

"Sir?"

"David Emmeret Smith."

"Got it. David Emmeret—oh."

David coughed. "Is there a problem?"

"No, not at all, sir. The David Thompson would make a lovely home for someone of your... stature."

David's voice was sour and biting. "Good."

123

"Would you like to make an appointment to see it, Mr. Smith?"

"How about in an hour?"

"Oh, well, that's uh. One second." Static rich top 40 played over the phone for a minute, then clicked off. "Mr. Smith?"

"Hi."

"Sorry about that. We can make an hour work."

"Is there anything else I should know?"

"Not as of right now, sir."

"See you in an hour."

"I look forward to it."

"Yup," he said, hanging up the phone.

David took a scalding shower, lined up three lines of coke, brushed his teeth, did a line, fixed his hair, did a line, got dressed, took a shot of whiskey, did a line, and, feeling like a fresh-faced teenager with an extra pep in his elderly step, was out the door. Less than an hour after the phone call, he stood at the entrance of the David Thompson, smack-dab in the middle of LA's Art District. The exterior of the building, a century-old relic, was worn and unassuming. The red brick was dusty from a city that grew around it, an antique in a progressively gentrified neighbourhood. David pressed an electric doorbell at the front door and waited, wondering if the buzzer was nothing more than a withering vestige of the building's past life.

A tiny man with wispy, crimson hair—of which he, in a final hurrah, a last-stand against aging, attempted to comb over—appeared in the doorway. "Hello!" the man said, raising his hand in a quasi sieg-heil.

David was tempted to return the salute. "Hello."

The man unlocked the door and extended his hand. "Timothy." They exchanged grips. "Nice to meet you, Mr. Smith."

"Call me David," he said, following the man through a brick archway and into the lobby.

In the small square lobby, across from a teal elevator, was a glass room with a desk and a computer. "This is my office," he said. "And I'm here almost every day, if you need anything."

"Got it," David said.

Timothy pressed the button to call the elevator. "There's seven floors. The apartment we're looking at right now is on the top floor."

David nodded.

"Which also makes the apartments on the top floor the nicest. They have taller ceilings, bigger rooms, exposed brick, newer hardwood. You name it."

The elevator doors stuttered, then opened. The carpet inside was stained, the walls of the elevator dinged and scratched. Chet Baker's "My Funny Valentine" played over an unseen radio.

"I must say," Timothy said, turning to David. "I'm a huge fan of your work. Before Goodbye Blue Sky was over, I knew you had the Oscar in the bag."

"I had a great director," David said, staring at the ground.

"That you did." The light at the top of the elevator moved from 6 to 7 and the doors opened. "Anyway, down to business."

The hallway, a respectable upgrade from the elevator, was narrow, with virgin white walls above glazed hardwood floors. They exited the elevator to the right, stopping at the first door, again, on the left, with 701 sketched below a peephole. On the opposite side of the hallway was apartment 706.

Tim slipped the key into the hole. "Ready?" He looked back at David, slack-jawed and smiling.

"Sure, I guess?"

Timothy opened the door. The apartment was, more than

anything, a modern take on the wide hallway. They stood at the entrance, by the kitchen, and looked down the full distance, all the way to the balcony on the other end. On the left were large wooden windows supplanted on brick walls. On the right were ocean blue walls, with two large sliding glass doors. The ceiling, littered with exposed ventilation, was coffered, a postmodern Victorian mash-up.

"The first door on your right is your bedroom, the second the bathroom."

David crossed his arms and rocked on his heels, taking it all in.

"Take a look around.".

David surveyed the kitchen, sliding his hand across the marble countertops. He opened the glass cabinets, overfull with dishes.

"The apartment comes move-in ready. Everything you see will be yours upon purchase."

The furniture was minimalist, sparse, more attuned to the modern millennial than a baby booming his way down. But, more than anything, he liked that it had furniture. He passed through the apartment, out onto the balcony.

"We'd be willing to furnish the balcony, too, if you'd like, Mr. Smith."

He looked over the edge, towering over the two and three and four storey buildings in the neighbourhood.
He felt big up here. Tall. On top of a small world.

"Can I smoke?"

"Right now?"

"In general."

"It'd be your place to do with it as you wish."

"Got it." He shuffled back through the apartment, one hand on his ribs, the other on his chin. "I'll think about it."

"You don't like it?"

"I like it, I just need to move some things around in my

head, consider some options," he sniffed hard, cleared his throat, "before I get back to you."

"Did you want to take a look at the bedroom or the bathroom?"

"I'm okay." He made for the door, with Timothy close behind.

"Did you have any questions?" Tim said, locking the door.

"If I think of any, I have your number."

"You do."

David called the elevator. He bit his nails to avoid the small talk. The glow moved from one to seven, then the doors opened. Standing before them, in the elevator, was a flat-nosed fiery giant with wavy auburn hair down to his shoulders, extending into an auburn mane. A club-like hand stroked his beard.

Timothy took a step back. "Hi, Theodore."

"Timmy!" The brute, leaping from the elevator, slapped David's companion on the back. "Showing this ol' chap around the building, eh?" He turned to David, holding out a catcher's mitt for a hand. "Name's Theodore. I live on this floor."

David let the hand engulf his. "Hi," David said, understated and hesitant.

The man held on. "Wait a second." He pulled David closer. "Do I know you?" He looked at Timmy. "Don't I know this guy, Timmy?"

"No, I don't think so," David said, pulling his hand away. Like a detective trying to produce a confession, the man, squinting, inspected the right side of David's face, then the left.

"He's an actor," Timmy said, trying to calm the temperamental titan.

"That's right!" He said, broadcasting his enormous chiclet teeth with a smile. "The fancy type, with three names, right?"

"David Emmeret Smith, but if that's too fancy for you, you can call me David. David Smith."

"David. Emmeret. Smith." He rolled his tongue around the name. "Didn't you just win some big honour?"

"An Academy Award."

"Oscar, eh? Congrats are in order, I imagine." He punched David on the shoulder with a ham fist.

Timmy's voice broke, "We should really be going."

"Well, shit. Before ya go, tell me. Am I getting a new neighbour or what?"

"I'm not sure," Timmy said. "Why don't you ask him?"

The big man winked at David. "I ain't about to go doing your work for you, Tim"

"I haven't made up my mind yet," David said. "But I'm considering it."

"Glad to hear it, David… Emmeret… Smith." His laugh betrayed a warmth. "Anyway, gotta run. Don't fuck this up, Timmy my boy. Big fish for you." He walked past them, whistling on his way.

While David was lost in thought, Timothy recalled the elevator. He couldn't place it, but there was an undeniable attraction for David, almost sexual, raw. Something deep inside David moved him towards the red giant. He craved something in the air, wanted to know more.

"Teddy's a well-known face around here. Just about knows everybody on the block."

"That so?"

They got on the elevator.

"Plays a jazz night down the street. He's good, too."

"With those hands?"

"Surprising, isn't it?"

The doors opened to the lobby. Timothy exited. David stopped, hesitating at the edge of the elevator.

Timothy turned around. "Mr. Smith?"

David was a deer in the headlights. "I'll take it," he said.

"Sorry?"

"701. I'll take it."

"Really?" Timmy was incredulous. "What changed?"

"I've just got a good feeling about it."

"So do I, Mr. Smith, so do I."

thirteen

"37 BARS OF XANAX, 100 adderall," Freddie said, sliding a blue see-through pill bottle across the desk. "An ounce of H and two ounces of blow."

David threw a fist full of cash at Freddie. He flipped through it, as if to fan his face, then tossed the wad into his backpack.

"Big score," Freddie said. "Enough uppers to get you to the moon."

"Enough downers to stun a small elephant."

"Any reason?"

"I'm moving."

"Out of the city?"

"The Arts District."

"When?"

"Tonight."

"Why?"

"Why not?"

Freddie zipped up his backpack. "Okay."

"Okay."

There was a bitter air between the two of them, like ex-lovers divvying up their leftover belongings.

"Cya later?"

David nodded.

———————————

David, at an undisclosed time, because his first act of business was to remove the clocks from his apartment, rubbed his eyes, yawned and rolled over in bed. It was his first morning—or early afternoon—in his new apartment. He stood up and, with enthusiasm, stretched, all the way from his toenails to the top of his head. There was vigor yet left in his body, perhaps more than when he began this forced-upon-him journey. It was as if he were undergoing a renewal, a shedding of his old skin, and emerging a drug-riddled butterfly. Like his liver, adapting to the new toxins, took over, shouting "I got this buddy." It knew, he knew, his body knew, that artificial energy was always—always—around the corner.

From below his bed, spilling over with every assortment of uppers and downers, quaaludes and black mamba bombers he could get his hands on, he retrieved a black leather briefcase. To start the day, he swallowed, with some effort, a 30mg adderall. He'd rationalized—a drug addict was always in the business of rationalizing—a number of benefits of his daily adderall: it wasn't as destructive as cocaine, kids (kids!) used it daily, with no overarching side effects, there was a gradual comedown, not a mid-sized collision, it was less treacherous on the heart, he still had—somewhat—of an appetite, it wasn't as addictive, it was cheaper, legal, didn't destroy his nose or make him look like a loose-lipped jaw jacking junkie, and perhaps most importantly, it offered him all the energy he needed in one convenient plastic pill.

The damned things were everything cocaine wished it was—or what others claimed it to be.

He poured himself a morning whiskey. The once present inflammation on his tongue was, like most things, adapting to his new life and all but gone. David guessed, judging from the advance of the sun over his patio, that it was early afternoon—a guess he didn't take seriously, having never payed attention to the sun and its corresponding time. His patio, an additional 300 sq. ft. of apartment, was hot to the touch, but empty. Timothy promised to furnish it within the month. For now, he dragged a white leather chaise onto it and picked up a month-old copy of TIME from an assortment of pre-selected magazines fanned across his coffee table. On the front, it had "UNDERSTANDING PAIN" in thick red letters printed over an emaciated androgynous back. He lit a cigarette and laid down, the leather already warm against his skin. Looking down the length of his body, he noticed that the once prominent hill that was his belly had somewhat straightened—a result of a powder-based diet.

Huh, he thought, warmly. I'm looking great.

He flipped through the pages, scanning through head-lines and paragraphs, as if he were pretending to read for the benefit of some far-off onlooker, intermittently taking drags and drinks. At the end of the magazine, snapping out of his mild morning trance, he re-lit his cigarette and started again. This would have carried on indiscriminately, without cause or reason to change course, if not for the deep down grum-ble within his belly, telling him that his engine was empty. He stubbed out his cigarette, threw TIME to the side, and, after dislodging himself from the chaise, went inside.

A junkie's mouth, no matter the junk, be it booze, hero-in, coke, or adderall, is more akin to the surface of mars—a once plentiful place of water and moisture and life, now dried out and dusty. For a junkie to nourish themselves with anything but liquids would be like throwing dirt in a des-sert and hoping for roses. He poured a blended mixture of fruit and protein into a cup and chugged, trying to down as much as he could before his battle-worn belly resisted. With a quarter left, and actual caloric energy flowing through his body, he now had permission from the control tower for a full-fledged, balls to the walls take-off. Wiping down the counter for any residual wetness, he crushed a bag of coke into a fine powder using an old gym membership, then divided it into even lines. He opened one drawer, then another, then another, looking for a straw, which he found behind a cupboard of cups. He cut the straw in two and blasted off.

"Whew," he said out loud, "there it is."

Another rationalization, which built upon his earlier, dawned on David. Despite the early reviews, adderall wasn't, wouldn't, couldn't, be better than coke. Why? Because cocaine was, well, cocaine. Often imitated, never duplicated, there was nothing like it.

He finished the last quarter of the smoothie and railed another line straight into his cranium. He shuffled, careful not to spill his drink, over to a thin, modern record player. He skimmed the records with his fingers, crawling sideways across the titles, which David was happy to see were anachronistic to the minimalist apartment. He stopped at "Sgt. Pepper's Lonely Hearts Club Band."

He couldn't remember the last time he danced. He set the pin and closed his eyes and moved, imagining the clapping and the cheers were for him, for how smooth and free he was, for how down-to-earth and in the moment he liked to live. The song ended and broke him away from his dream, but not the rhythm. Sliding his feet across the floor, making small circles with his hands, and moving his head from side to side, he danced over to the coke and cleared another.

Inspired by the collection of records, sitting cross legged on the floor, he explored the bookshelf beside the record player, stopping when he recognized an author's name. Amis, Burroughs, Chaucer, Dostoyevsky, Faulkner, Flaubert.

They were alphabetized and he wondered if they'd used one of those book-buying firms who stocked shelves so that upscale manhattan types could impress guests with their faux-sophistication.

Hemingway, Joyce, Kafka, Orwell, Poe, Tolstoy, Twain,

Vonnegut …. He slipped out the soft cover of a name he didn't recognize: John Williams's "Stoner" and opened it to a random page.

"In his extreme youth," he read out loud, "Stoner had thought of love as an absolute state of being to which, if one were lucky, one might find access; in his maturity he had decided it was the heaven of a false religion, toward which one ought to gaze with an amused disbelief, a gently familiar contempt, and an embarrassed nostalgia. Now in his middle age he began to know that it was neither a state of grace nor an illusion; he saw it as a human act of becoming, a condition that was invented and modified moment by moment and day by day, by the will and the intelligence and the heart."

David set the book down.

He was wrong, he thought, this Stoner. Having attained heaven, then lost it, it was now his false religion, and there was no more becoming, only being, followed by non-being. Those were the only two things, pleasure and death, he had to look forward to.

The last line of the row disappeared behind a white and red straw. With veins popping, muscles bursting, and a low hertz humming in his ear, he paced the length of his apartment, up and down, winding between the furniture, and out onto the hot wood of the balcony. He leaned over the brick barrier and studied the teeming life, the bobbing youth, below. The unfamiliar street, its drooping sidewalks, narrow roads, and sondering foot traffic, called his name, asking him to come down and play and explore.

He walked with jittery, hyper-extended movements down the cobbled sidewalk, like someone—or something—had sped him up, but never seeming to outwalk those around him. The street, from behind orange sunglasses, was washed over in a glow. His skinnier frame, mangy beard and unruly hair were an open air disguise, and those that passed by didn't appear to recognize him, or they didn't care. This type of apparent anonymity, being hidden in plain sight, was comforting. It was the junk mask. Another benefit of using, which he noted for a later rationalization.

As he walked he drew a mental map of the block, trying to situate himself in his new home: ATM across the street, a Mexican, Thai, and Ramen restaurant, the last of which he picked up a flyer from, an old Irish pub, the "Painted Rose" and a jazz bar, "The Black Cat," which David assumed was the place his neighbour played at, two coffee shops, one across the street from his apartment, the other on the far corner, filled with angelheaded hipsters, a clothing store, which he was not even close to the target market of, and a dollar pizza joint.

At the light at the end of his block, at an angled cross-roads, he considered his options. Another couple, appearing from behind, laughed. A girl, barely a woman, giggled into a man's shoulder. With one hand, she clasped her fingers between his, while caressing the length of his arm with the other. He could feel his own fingers, interlaced with Alice's, could smell the peach rose of her perfume, could hear the way she snorted while she laughed. The light turned green and he watched the couple stroll into the street, wondering when they, and their love affair, would dry up and turn to sand in their hands.

He turned—wanting out of this world—and walked, slowly at first, then, every few steps a short run, the click clack of his shoes bouncing off the walls of the narrow street. Like a madman on a mission, as if he were looking to revive the recently OD'd with a shot of adrenaline, he burst back into his apartment. The cooking process was swift, an almost scientific precision in his junk ceremony. He cranked it back and released.

When he woke the sun had retreated from his apartment

and the credits of a movie were playing on the television. He picked away the cotton from the corners of his mouth and called "Coast Noodle," the ramen joint across the street.

A good junkie doesn't want to eat, but knows he has to. Their cellular makeup, though no medical professional would, or could, back this up, is vastly different from the cells of a non-addict. They mutate into something that, while similar to a regular cell, can—and at times, must—run on alternate energy sources. The mutation, which at first has aspects of an advantage, allowing the junkie to save money, lose weight, to go without food for long periods of time, quickly shows what it truly is: a disease. The part that runs on junk ultimately takes over every part of the cell, desiring more smack, more junk, more filth. Soon the cells no longer need or want other fuel sources, but scream out for maximum junk. As if, having latched onto every last cell, the junk has formed a symbiotic bond with the host body, and every living moment the host is propelled towards the junk, until the man is more skag than skin.

David was an early patient, a stage 1 addict, with cells that, for the most part, still ran on organic sources of energy. But it was undeniable: his appetite was shrinking, and those rotten spots on his cells would, at some point, overtake the rest.

His front buzzer rang. "Coast Noodle," a man said through a thick Eastern accent.

He buzzed him in, paid, and swallowed two Xanax. His dinner table, the faux divider between his living room and kitchen, was aged mahogany cased in metal. He sat at the head, slowly forcing the noodles down his throat, slurping viciously as he went. By the time the bowl was empty, his eyelids drooped across his sockets. He collapsed over top of the blankets and didn't move until morning.

For a while no day looked different than the rest. If one

did, he couldn't distinguish the blending from the bizarre. The only thing he was aware of, from one day to the next, was the ever-moving hour before he tapped into the needle. While each day the hour he surrendered himself to it was earlier, the time that passed in-between each session stretched out into misery. On the day that he ran out of his first order, he spent an entire—agonizing—hour smoking cigarettes on the balcony, resisting an itch he couldn't see, waiting for Freddie to arrive.

"God damn. Now this is more your style," Freddie said, opening the record cabinet, winding through furniture, sliding the bedroom door open.

David, sitting on a stool in the kitchen, his arms crossed at his chest, watched him like a predator.

"So," he said, strolling back. "You went through it all already?"

David nodded.

"Might want to slow down on that shit. You ain't young."

"Where is it?"

Freddie rolled his eyes, took off his backpack, and threw it across the room. David pulled from the backpack a sandwich bag with two smaller bags inside of it.

"Two ounces of H," Freddie said. "I got them Lunestas too."

David stuck his head back in the backpack. At the bottom was a pill bottle. He took it out and threw the bag back at Freddie.

"Cash?"

David handed Freddie a thick envelope.

"Anything else?"

"No."

"Okay," Freddie said. "You know where to find me."

David, turning his back to Freddie, not watching him go, unfurled the ziplock on the sandwich bag.

Twenty seconds after Freddie closed the door behind him, David was holding a lighter up to a spoon. Suddenly, there was a knock at the door.

fourteen

DAVID, MUMBLING obscenities under his breath, wondering what could possibly have driven Freddie, that idiot, to return, whipped the door open.

"What do you—"

There, standing in his doorway, was his neighbour, the flat-nosed giant, holding out his brick of a hand. "Hiya, neighbour."

David didn't take his hand. "May I help you?"

The man wore a black button down shirt, spread open two buttons too low, tucked into stiff black jeans. "We met a few weeks ago. Theodore Burrows." He looked down at his own hand. "But you can call me Teddy."

"I remember," David said, unmoved.

He leaned into David's apartment. "Don't seem like you leave your place much, friend."

David narrowed the view into his apartment, leaving only enough room between the frame and the door for his head. "If you don't mind, I was taking a nap."

He raised an eyebrow. "That's interesting, because it seems to me you just had company over."

"Are you spying on me?"

He had a giant's laugh. "Sure, sure. But only from the comfort of my own home."

"Why?"

He moved his shoulders up and down. "I like to know what's happening around me."

"I'd prefer if you didn't spy on me."

"I'm not exactly going out of my way here, am I, David? It's David, right?"

"I don't like it."

"Look, what you do inside your own home is your business, but when you're in eyesight of my peephole, a man's going to take a gander."

"You still haven't told me what you want."

"Just being friendly, is all."

"I don't need more friends. If you'll excuse—"

The door, lodged against the man's foot, wouldn't move.

"Tell me, friend," he said, closing the distance, "what was this visitor of yours dropping off?"

"What?"

"Shall I repeat the question?"

David's cheeks burned. "Work stuff." He regretted the answer the moment it left his lips.

"That's funny," Theodore said, through the side of his mouth.

"Why?"

The man, with every word, seemed to David to grow larger, more imposing. Every alarm in his head was going off—this man was a danger to his way of life, an alpha predator on the hunt. "Don't know many people who can work after taking the stuff you're taking."

"Are you accusing me of something?"

"I think you know perfectly well what I'm saying."

David, feeling like a kettle about to blow, wobbled at the knees. He was cornered prey. The only thing left was to be torn apart, then exposed, for the vermin he was.

"Whoa, easy pal." The neighbour stepped back from the door. "You're shaking. I come as a friend."

"You aren't being very friendly."

"I'm only here to offer you a present, a housewarming

gift, you could call it."

"A present?"

"The same sort of present your little friend—your dealer, I presume—dropped off a few minutes earlier."

Competing forces from deep within his body vied for control. One faction wanted him to slam the door in Teddy's face, to avoid him at all costs, and never think of this moment again. The other faction, which originated from the slow symbiosis in his cells, that same faction that drew David to Theodore when they first met in the hall, was intrigued.

"That so?"

Theodore looked around the hall, then once again came closer. "In fact," he whispered, "I have a bit kicking around my apartment. Shall we share a taste, neighbour?" He grinned. They could recreate stonehenge from those teeth.

"Right now?" His face betrayed his eagerness.

"If you're ready."

Teddy's apartment was a mirror image of David's, but with low-lighting, black drapes over the windows, a black sheet across his balcony window, and smelled like burning plastic. At the far corner, closer to the balcony, Teddy had laid a single mattress. The rest of the furniture, a black leather couch with no legs, an old blue lazy boy, a beanbag, a large green chest, and a stained sofa bed, was picked, seemingly at random, then dumped in place. It was as if he had asked for it to be left "for now," but never got around to moving it to its rightful spot. The only thing that looked remotely purposeful was a saxophone, in front of the balcony window, sitting in its stand next to a chair. The rest of the apartment was lined with shelves, which held books, antiques, and trinkets. A junkie, without fail, is a collector by nature. Like moths to a flame, things accumulated in their apartments—things that would remain there until one of three things occurred: a drug-induced cleaning fit, they got clean, or they went clean,

141

by way of the grave.

Theodore put on a record, which was in the exactly the same position, but mirrored, that David's was in. The slow plucking of a guitar, followed up by a lead saxophone, filled the apartment.

"I'll go get the supplies," Teddy said. "Make yourself comfortable." He disappeared into the bedroom.

David flopped into the blue lazy boy. It was soft, but worn, like wearing someone else's fitted leather shoes. There was a clang, then the door to the bedroom slid open, and Teddy was standing over David.

"What do you think?"

"About your apartment?"

"The music man." He mimic'd the sound of a saxophone while the real thing played over the speakers. "That's me on the sax!"

"It's okay."

"You don't like it?"

David crossed, then uncrossed, his legs. "I just don't really listen to all that much jazz."

"Then you ain't living, but you'll learn."

"Learn what?"

"Why do ya think almost all the great jazz musicians were heroin junkies?"

"Why?"

"When you're swimming knee deep in scag, and you hear it, you'll know. It'll light a fire in your soul and you'll think of nothing else for at least 24 hours."

"I'll keep that in mind."

Teddy, startling David, threw a small bag of white powder onto his lap. The bag was marked by a black and red four leaf clover.

"Any idea what that is, neighbour?"

"No, but I'm sure you're going to tell me."

"The best goddamn H you're going to find in LA. Hell, probably the best you can find in all of California."

"Where do you get it?"

"Where do you get it?" He raised his left brow. "Or where do I get it?"

"Where do I get it, I guess," David said, expressionless.

Teddy held his bowling pin of a thumb out, then pointed it back at himself.

"You?"

"A cool five feet away, neighbour."

David muffled a laugh. "That sounds, I don't know, almost too convenient."

The music faded out, leaving only the static of an empty needle. "You see that four leaf clover?"

David turned it over, as if he were seeing it for the first time. "Sure."

"See it before?" Teddy asked, replacing the old record with a new. Miles Davis' Blue in Green filled the room.

"Can't say I have."

"That's surprising. Popular brand for your kind."

"What kind am I?"

"You know, the fancy high society type."

For a time, only the sound of the music passed through the room. David stood. "So, was that it?"

"What more could there be?" Teddy said, eyes smiling. "Just wanted to give you a lil' housewarming present, that's all."

"Appreciate it." David started for the door, then turned. "Let me ask you something."

"What's that?"

"How'd you know?"

"Know what?"

"That I'd be interested."

"Hah," he said, with more words than laughter. "All

junkies wear hats."

David cocked his head to the side and looked up and to the left, as if an explanation was hidden on the ceiling. Finding nothing, he blinked a few times and went home.

fifteen

THE ONLY SOUND in David's apartment was a light whistle of air moving through his nostrils as he was taking his first nod of the day.

Bang bang bang.

David sprouted up, his head above the couch, looking at the door.

Bang bang bang.

He rubbed his face and stood up.

"David! Open up!" Teddy said, slamming his first into the door again.

"Okay!" he yelled back. "Relax!"

He opened the door, yawning as Teddy rushed past him.

"You're not going to believe what I just saw on television!" He wore cargo shorts, a cut off white tee shirt, and brown uggs.

"What?"

Above and beyond the daily drop-offs, Teddy was making ever-more frequent stops to tell David increasingly inane things. But, as long as he kept bringing him drugs, David didn't care what he did. In fact, he often looked forward to Teddy's quick visits. Once, he even caught himself wanting to go over to Teddy's to see what he was up to, but he was quick to remind himself what happened with the last drug dealer he let into his life.

Teddy plopped himself down on the couch. "This fucking zombie fungus, brother. Even if I told you, you're not going to believe it!" He dumped a bag of blow on the coffee table.

Accepting his new waking reality, David followed him back to the couch. "Zombie fungus?"

"On Planet Earth, with that English fucker, Attenburger or whatever. He starts talking about parasitic spores." He violently cleared each nostril, one after the other. "So I'm hooked. I love me some freaky nature shit." He passed David a straw.

David cleared the line and passed it back. "What happened?"

"The camera closes in on the ant, dramatic music starts playing, and then, suddenly, a giant fucking spore bursts out of the ant's head! I thought I was watching Alien." Teddy cleared his own line. "That's not even the craziest part, though."

"No?"

"Brother," he said, leaning closer to David. "This fungus is smart. It makes the ant do things out of its control, things the ant doesn't understand."

"Huh? A zombie ant?"

"That's what I'm sayin'! It makes the thing attach itself somewhere high up so that it can explode from its head and infect more ants."

"How does it do that?"

"Who fucking knows! But it got me thinking." He poured out more blow. "What if there are things around us, everywhere, that are making us do things beyond our control? What if we're just like those ants, infected with a fungus?"

"If that were the case, some scientist would have named the disease after himself already."

"You ever feel like your actions aren't your own?" Teddy finished another line.

"I look back at things I've done and wonder how I could've done them." He waved off another line. "That's close, I guess."

"Like what?"

"I don't know," David said, retreating to the back of the seat.

"Don't want to tell me?"

"We don't really know each other that well, do we?"

Teddy stood up. "You know what, you're fucking right."

"I am?"

"How long have I been coming over?"

"A few weeks, I think."

"And how much do you know about me?"

"Almost nothing."

"Okay, here's what we're going to do: you're going to come over, we're going to do a boatload of coke, and get to know each other. I mean, really get to know each other."

"That sounds—actually—awful."

Teddy half laughed, half coughed. "Fuck off."

"I'm serious."

"Let me rephrase then, asshole. How about you come over, I give you all the free drugs you want, and you can get to know me better."

"I can check my schedule."

"After you check it, you know where to find me." Teddy stormed out, leaving the blow.

David cut a line for himself. "Seems clear enough.".

Teddy, sitting in a chair David hadn't seen before, a brown leather pin cushion, was fast-forwarding through Planet Earth.

"I cleared my schedule," David said, walking into the apartment. "Just for you."

Teddy swiveled in his chair. "Isn't that just neighbourly of you." He held his hand out to the blue lazyboy. "Take a

147

seat." Teddy turned off the TV. He pushed the antique chest between the two chairs. "Beer, whiskey?"

"Beer."

Teddy returned with a beer and Mount Kilimanjaro. "What do you want to know about me?" he asked, sitting down.

"You tell me. You're the one who called this neighbourhood block party."

"Come on! Think of something!"

"Ugh, I guess, how'd you end up selling?"

"Want the whole story?"

"It's why I'm here, isn't it?"

"I thought you were here for that." He pointed at the plate.

"Might as well get a good story out of it, while I'm here."

"It started while I was on the road in the '80s and '90s—ya go ahead, dip in—anyway, I was a fill in musician for a jazz band. I could play anything, pretty much. Whatever they needed that night, I did: flute, saxophone, piano, whatever. I got to know a lot of people in a lot of different cities. Musicians you know, a lot you don't, dealers, party people, celebrities, from all around. It was an easy gig, fun, but easy. And at shows and after parties, I became known as the guy— "

"Mind if I smoke?"

"Sure. But yeah, whether it was coke, heroin, meth, or pretty much anything I could get these baseball mitts on, I always had a lil' something on me. And so, people knew where to find it, if they wanted it. I wasn't selling yet, just using. I liked to party—still do, as you can see. But pretty soon, after visiting a city three, four, five times, I got sick of it. I was making all these dealers, all these hungry jackals, a ton of money, but I wasn't getting a penny of it. 'Why the fuck am I hooking these people up?' I thought. Naturally, I started to take a cut. After a while, the gigs dried up, and I moved to LA. From there, starting up was easy."

"Ever worry about getting busted?"

"I only sell to people I know."

"You didn't know me."

"I have a keen eye. Could spot the sole user out of any lineup."

"What about the danger?"

"I'm an addict, brother. Danger doesn't bother me. My whole life is a balancing act. I'm teetering on the edge at every moment."

"I guess."

"Another beer?" Teddy shook his empty bottle.

"Sure."

Returning with a beer, he said, "besides, look at me. Do you think some punk is just going to come crashing in and rob me?"

"Good point." David took a sip from his beer. "What about your future?"

"What about it?"

"Ever think about it?"

"Here and now, friend. It's all there's ever been. The rest ain't for me."

"You think you can keep doing this forever?"

"Forever? A man's gotta die. But I've been doing it for this long. I'll do it until I can't. Simple as that."

David held a beer up to his lips. "I like that," he said before sipping.

"And how long do you plan to keep this up, old man?"

"Until I run out of money or die."

"You're what, in your 60s?"

"56."

"And you've been in film most of your life?"

"Better half of it, sure."

"Probably racked up quite the bank balance."

"Lots of zeros," David said.

"Don't imagine you'll be running out anytime soon, then?"

"I'm comfortable."

Teddy, drumming his fingers on his bottle, leaned back into his chair. His lip curled up. "What are you doing later tonight?"

"You're looking at it."

"You ever get out?"

"I'm not into crowds."

"Why not?"

"I like to forget that other people exist."

"Perfect. I'm playing at the Black Cat tonight. The whole crowd, when we're up there, forgets the world around them exists. It's H in the form of music."

"I somehow doubt that," he said, cutting another line.

"Brother, you won't know unless you try it."

His lower lip trembling, David ran both hands through his hair. "I probably won't stay that long."

"Yes!" Teddy said, shaking a fist in the air. "And, just to show my appreciation, everything is on the house tonight." He tossed a bag onto David's lap. "Holy hell. Is that a smile I see, brother?"

David held out his beer, still smiling. "Here's to a future-less future."

"To right now." Teddy clanked his glass. "May it never be anything but."

———————————————

David, his legs like molasses, an ebbing tingle, the whispers of an angel, moving outwards from his neck, followed Teddy down the back alley beside the Black Cat. There was a short line waiting at the back door. Teddy walked past the line, their necks turning in his direction, David a mere shadow at Teddy's side, and knocked. With each thud, crumbs of peeling red paint tumbled off the door. As it opened, the door howled like twisted metal. The man who opened it, a bald headed bouncer wearing a sleeveless black shirt, was snarling.

His face cleared when he saw who was at the door. "Teddy," the doorman said, holding out a fist lined with rings. They bumped knuckles, Teddy's making the man's hand look like a child's.

"I've brought a friend," Teddy said, moving to the side. "This is David. He's an actor. David, this is John. He's our bouncer here."

"Hello," David said, holding his hand out, open-fisted. They shook.

"Actor hey? Anything I would know?"

"Probably not," David said, following Teddy through the door, past the man, and down the stairs. They slowed at a window, manned by a woman who looked up from her phone, smiling, and waved them through. The hallway ceiling was low, forcing Teddy to crook his neck the final few feet before the hallway opened up to the Black Cat, or the Under Cat, as it was locally known. To David's delight, instead of stale beer, it smelled of whiskey, the long-linger of perforated barrels, the wooden cellar having once been used to store home-grown bourbon. The oak walls, in dim light, had an orange glow. It was a full-house, round tables circled by bodies, eager ears directed at the stage.

"Brother!" a smoker's voice said, materializing out of nowhere, whose body, shortly after, slid in next to David, their shoulders touching. The skin on the man's his face, as if it were pinned back at his neck, was stretched thin, barely holding in his bulbous eyes.

"Janko," Teddy said, lording over the o. Their hand slap,

which morphed into a half-hug, was quick and cool.

Janko's attention turned to David, his eyes moving like the stutter step saccades you'd see on Planet Earth.

"This is David," Teddy said. "Janko owns this place."

He smirked, his teeth black at the edges, his gums grey. "Big fan of your work," he said, offering a hand.

"Quaint place," David said, looking around the room.

"What's a man like you drink?"

"Whiskey," he said, the words tripping over the cotton pebbles in his mouth.

"And you, Teddy?"

"The same."

Janko waved over a man from behind the bar. "Two bourbons, Kyle," he shouted. "So David. What brings you into a place like this, with a scumbag like Teddy?"

Teddy sneered.

"Moved in next door a couple weeks ago. He's showing me around."

"That Thompson building right?"

"That's the one," Teddy said.

"Quaint place," Janko said, clicking his tongue.

"Temporary," David said.

"Oh?" The skin wrinkled around Janko's eyes.

Before David could answer, the bartender returned with two bourbons, neat. He gave them both to David.

"Anyway," Janko said, checking his watch. "Teddy's on in a few minutes. We have some things to discuss backstage."

"Right," Teddy said. "Is Cassius here yet?"

"Right there." He pointed to the right of the stage, to the only table with a single man.

Teddy leaned into David's ear. "Cassius is a friend of mine. If you want, sit with him, and if you don't, whatever. Your call." He stepped backwards. "I gotta get prepared, though. Enjoy!"

Teddy followed Janko through a door behind the bar. Like a child left alone on his first day of school, David looked around the room, still holding both bourbons. The air was soft and cool, layered with a low rumble of laughter and conversation. He poured one drink into the other and navigated through the staggered tables.

He approached Teddy's friend, a few feet from the stage. "Cassius?"

The man turned towards David, raising a brow in his direction."Yeah?" His features were sharp, but his limbs long and loose. The sides of his head were shaved at the side, crowning into an exaggerated pompadour.

"I'm a friend of Teddy's."

"The actor?"

"David."

"I saved this spot for you." He pushed a chair out with his foot. "Best seat in the house."

David sat, his legs sighing with relief. A breeze danced on the back of his neck, getting stronger with each millimeter his eyelids drooped. He snapped them open and took a sip of whiskey.

"How do you know Teddy?" David asked, trying to hold off the nod.

"Originally, from here. I was a fan."

"You play?"

"A bit of sax, but nothing quite like our friend."

"You two good friends?"

Cassius tapped his nose. "More like business partners."

"Oh?"

"Sure."

David let that comment pass by, joining the thousands of other vowels and syllables and sounds that floated by his head. It bounced off the walls and disappeared. He sipped his bourbon. "Here every Tuesday?"

"Like I said, I started off as a fan."

"That good?"

"Even without a sax in his hand, Teddy has an energy that can guide a room, but when you put music to the man, there's no one he can't win over."

"No one?"

"Especially when that person is nodding." He winked at David.

Before David could reply, Teddy walked on stage with three men, all wearing the same black button down, following close behind him. He tapped the microphone.

"Testing. Testing. Testing." Teddy pointed up. "Testing." Then thumbed the air. "Glad to see you all survived another week on planet earth," he said. "I'm Theodore Burrows. Behind me is James T on drums, Donald Davy on bass, and Ezra Thomas on keyboard. We are Sisyphus."

They started and the room was pregnant with the melody of a saxophone—a wandering sigh of sound—and David's hair hardened in its root. He shut his eyes and let the music blanket him. The warm embrace transported him to another moment in time, another place, at once unknown, yet familiar—melancholy, yet pleasurable. The bittersweet tears of a clown. The tragicomedy of a lost man. The saxophone ceased, faltering to the slow crescendo of drums, the boom boom tiss—ever faster—approaching happiness. Then, as if to pluck any remaining terror from the air, absolving the room, and everything in it, of all its guilt, the bass joined the drums. They were two forces searching for a purpose, battling in harmony, good and evil, there and then. And that was it, a fire in his soul—jazz and heroin, David and Teddy. Perfection in the moment.

sixteen

A GOOD ADDICT isn't built overnight. He (or she) isn't built in a week, or two weeks, or a month. An addict, much like a well-deserved discipline, a martial art, a painting, or a poem, takes time to build—and a fair bit of money—and David had as much of either of those as any junkie ever had. However, within him still remained a last quality that, in order to be a full-fledged card carrying member of team tar, to wear, not his heart on his sleeve, but junk in his veins, had to be expunged: his pride.

A junkie's pride—once the junk has embedded itself into the cellular structure, once it has forced itself into every nodule and nook and nether region, once it is a necessary part of the the human biome, a cellular symbiosis, a partnership baked in the intertwining facets of pleasure and pain, when you would do anything, everything, for one more taste, one stretched dollar, a soul for a spoon, a prick for a prick— is always the last to go, the final stage in a metamorphosis that no man should undertake. David, naive to the state of his body's new chemical makeup, had to learn this the hard way. He had, as the proud do, decided that he wasn't a man who bent the knee to any drug. He had to show himself that every decision he made was a conscious one, that he had a will of his own, was a man with agency. But, sooner or later, pride leaves the body, and what is left is the junk and a man must come to terms with a solitary truth: knees were made to bend.

The idea didn't occur to him suddenly, but was rather the progressive accumulation, or the nagging result, of the symptoms found in your addict—food no longer held an interest to him, but was merely a prerequisite of pre-junk David, not yet built to run on junk alone. Sex, while far from an option, anyway, still was without the reverence that a man living in a 21st century consumer culture generally held for it. Money, consumption, was something he only thought of in terms of heroin (and other drugs). Time became a thing less esoteric, no longer the philosophical conundrum that plagued a much younger man, but was merely what existed between two points (not in time) of a needle.

For the first few hours, despite the hum in his ears and a nagging eye-twitch, the day went smoothly. He filled his thoughts with Seinfeld reruns, cigarettes and booze (legal drugs were allowed).

It's only one day, he repeated to himself, whenever his thoughts turned to the needle.

He had a relative idea, based on how many episodes he'd watched, of how much time had passed: episode six, two hours, episode nine, three, episode sixteen, four, and halfway through episode twenty two, "The Library," something from deep within him began to lurch and shift. He got up and ran for the bathroom, his blanket at his shoulders, trailing behind him like some junk-sick superhero. His vomit, like a broken fire hydrant on a New York City street, was a dark black tar. It was as if, having taken a break from the junk, his body now recognized the foreign invader cuddling up to its cells and was making a last ditch effort to expel it.

The stream turned to spray, and the spray to a drizzle, until there was nothing left but a quivering stomach, wreaking havoc on a weak body, looking for new ways to expel the junk.

Like the light in his heart went out, a chill filled the bathroom air. He wrapped himself in his blanket, shivering, pulling it over his head, sweat running down the bridge of his nose, and, like a caterpillar returning to his cocoon, drooped to the floor. From within the blanket the outer layer of his skin burned, hot to the touch, reaching temperatures he didn't know the human body could go, while just below the surface, his organs were being replaced with ice. He pulled the blanket tighter. His muscles twitched sporadically, pushing against the outer layer of his wrap, but never breaking the barrier. A layer of sweat and grime and grease, the product of the junk trying to break free from his skin, to find a body more worthy to feed on, adhered himself to the thin cotton of the blanket, forming a kind of second skin. He buried himself further into it, pressing hard against its outer rim, trying to break free of the envelope, but too weak to make any real progress. Before long, he was lost within it, breaking down at the seams, losing exactly where body stopped and blanket began, folding and re-emerging from within its great hunger—each agonizing second, layered on top of each agonizing minute, building upon itself until he was less a man, more of a disease. Then, for a while, he had no place to go, no temporal position, only the life-long waiting of the junk sick.

A foot kicked at his thigh. "What the fuck are you doing?"

David pawed at the blanket, emerging from the top, covered in a postpartum membrane. "How'd you get in here?"

"What's wrong with you?" Teddy asked, shaking his head, arms crossed at the chest.

"I was cold."

"You're drenched in sweat."

"I'm fine now."

"The hell you are." He pulled the blanket off of David,

157

who feebly tried to hold on to it.

"Stop it! I'm taking the day off."

"Off what?"

He shifted onto his butt, sitting up. "All of it."

"Now why would you go and do a thing like that?"

"To prove I can."

"Look at you," he chuckled. "You can't!"

David let his head fall back, jaw agape, resting it on the side of the tub. "I'm fine," he said, shivering. "I'm fine."

"You're sick and getting sicker."

"I've almost made it."

"You ain't gonna make shit, brother. I'm gonna cook ya up a hit."

"NO!"

"You need it."

"I don't—" he dry-heaved and fell over, curling up into a ball.

"I'll leave it here for you. It's your decision."

David groaned, but didn't move.

In under a minute, Teddy returned with a full needle. "Break in case of emergency," he said, placing it gently on the bathroom sink.

Teddy walked back into kitchen and cracked a beer. As if Teddy's throat was inches from his ear, David could hear his long gurgling gulps. Teddy returned to the living room and unpaused David's episode of Seinfeld (The Library). In that time, as if he'd been shocked by a defibrillator, David was brought back from the dead. He stumbled out of the bathroom, his hands low, his body dragged by his head, the sound of his feet muffled by Teddy's roaring laughter, and into the kitchen. He cracked a beer, the psssst a welcome salvation, the sound of water to a wandering desert madman, and slammed it in one ravenous gulp. He cracked another and joined Teddy in the living room.

"There he is! An angel reborn!"

David's voice was low and hoarse. "I could have made it." His vision was unfocused, as if he were talking to some far off ghost, some unseen judge, ready to slam his gavel and speak the sentence.

"Of course."

"I don't need rescuing."

"Who does?"

"People."

"People not unlike you?"

"People without the type of money I have. People who spend most of their days sick and broke and hungry."

"Hell ain't it?"

"I don't ever want to feel like that again," he said, his eyelids low. "And should I?"

"You shouldn't."

"I have all the money I could ever want. I could keep this up for as long as I want."

Teddy turned off the TV and squared up to David. "Tell me something."

A silence, somewhere between a second and a thousand years, passed between them.

"David?" Teddy snapped his fingers, breaking David from his far-off reverie.

"What?"

"Let me ask you a question."

"Sure."

"You have all this money. You had success. A wife, though I read about what happened. You had it all."

"So?" David leaned over and picked his pack of cigarettes off of the coffee table. He slipped one between his rapidly rosing lips.

"So why are you here?" Teddy motioned for the pack of cigarettes.

"Not intentionally."

"What happened?"

"My wife—"

"Brother, I read all that shit in the paper. You cheated. She threw your ass to the curb. I'm asking why." He lit his cigarette and threw David the lighter. "Why are you here, doing this, right now?"

"I'm not really sure, it just, sort of, happened."

"You're telling me it was just series of misfortunate events?"

"No, it was more, well, because." He took a long, slow drag, regrouping his thoughts. "Because success can be suffocating. Because happiness is hard. Because making everything work, keeping it all together, working towards a lifetime of achievement—it was a lifetime of effort. I had it all, but once I had it all, I wanted none of it. I wanted to escape. I wanted to have fun. I wanted to stop caring."

"And here you are."

"And here I am! What you saw in there, the state I was in, I don't have to do that again. Ever again." He held his arms out, looking around the room of his apartment. "But this, this is fun. All of this hedonistic nihilism. This fuck everything bullshit. Who cares, I say. Who cares about it all! God is dead. Fuck meaning. Fuck it all. Let's get high before we die. The end."

"Some plan."

"You got a better one?"

"No," Teddy said, chuckling softly. "I guess I don't."

In his confession, David glimpsed an opening where he might confess to more shameful thoughts, less noble visions of what it meant to be a man, to love, and to be loved. But he stuffed them deep into his psyche, below the depths of his reach.

"Besides, I couldn't go back if I wanted to."

"Why?"

"The man I was before, the man who lived that life, he doesn't exist anymore. When I look in the mirror, I see someone completely different, someone who wouldn't know what to do with that life if it came back to him."

What followed from that day was a short period of relative happiness. David was a man reborn, baptized by the junk water coursing through his veins, and his tour guide through this new life was Theodore Burrows, resident of the David Thompson, occupant of 702, neighbour to David Emmeret Smith, bohemian giant, and exuberant addict. They went everywhere together, everywhere that was anywhere to them, which was no more than the one block radius around their apartment, and included little more than shooting up, eating (but barely), sleeping (but barely), and weekly visits to the wooden cellar beneath the Black Cat, where David enjoyed living in the giant shadow of Teddy, shaking hands with people he couldn't—and didn't care to—remember, exchanging minor sentences with Janko and Cassius, and watching Teddy play. For a brief flickering moment his life had a certain comfort, something approaching meaning, but resembling non-meaning, again.

seventeen

A NEWBORN SUN poked through the holes of the torn black bed sheets. David and Teddy, their damned eyes bleeding happiness, shoveling like coal miners an unequal amount of uppers and downers into their body, running on the smoke fumes, burning dime-sized holes in their brains, chattering like loose-lipped ventriloquists, not to one another, but through each other, were still awake. Jazz played softly in the background.

"This Gil-Scot Heron?" David said, sitting sideways in the big blue lazy boy, his legs draped over an arm, nursing a beer.

Teddy stood, holding a plate of coke in front of his face with one hand, a rolled up bill in the other. "You're getting good."

"Why?"

"Haven't even shown you this one yet."

"You have."

"Coulda swore I didn't."

"Winter in New York?"

"You mean Winter in America?"

"Do I?"

"I think so, but this isn't that."

"What is it?"

"Winter in America is Gil-Scot Heron."

"I thought you said this was Gil-Scot Heron?"

"I did, but this isn't 'Winter in America'."

"So what is it then?"

"It's new."

"Called?"

"Only a year old."

David swivelled in the chair, taking the plate from Teddy. "What's it called?"

"I can't remember."

"Go check."

Teddy's feet dragged, his body leaning on a slant, as if he were pulled by a hook in his chest, towards the record collection. A foot away from the record Teddy stopped and turned. "You hear that?"

"What?"

Teddy's buzzer rang.

"For fuck's sake," he said, walking towards it like a man determined to get eight extra minutes of early morning sleep. "It's ten in the goddamn morning." He stopped in front of the buzzer. "Should I see who it is?"

"Fuck 'em," David said. "Probably have the wrong apartment."

"Nah," he held his finger over the button, "I should check."

"Your call."

He pushed the talk button. "The building better be on fire."

It was a man, though his voice cracked like a child's. "I was told you could help me out."

Teddy took his finger off the intercom and, using the same hand, ran it through his hair. "Junkies man. Fucking junkies."

"Tell them to leave," David said.

He thumbed the button. "Do you know what time it is?"

"Come on man, buzz us up. We came all the way from Hyde Park."

163

"Sorry fellas," Teddy said, smiling into wall speaker. "Ain't gonna happen."

"But Cassius said you would. It's why we came."

"Motherfucker," Teddy said, shaking his head at David. "I gotta let 'em in."

"Why?"

"Because an employee of mine said it was okay."

"So? They're junkies."

"I've got principles." He buzzed them in. "Besides, money's money."

"You're creating a dangerous precedent."

"Thanks for worrying," Teddy said, sitting down, motioning to David to hand him the plate. "But I could use the money." He cut the entirety of the pile, a slight tremor in his hand, into two lines. Like a magician, he made one disappear. "I need to wake up for this."

There was a heavy knock at the door.

Teddy stood up. "How do I look?"

"Sober."

"Perfect," he said, as he walked towards the door.

There was another heavy knock on the door.

"I'm coming, ladies," Teddy said.

He twisted the knob and pulled, the door flying open with a thwack, shattering Teddy in the face.

David sprung to his feet, almost lifting off the ground. Two men in balaclavas, one yellow, one black, brandishing shotguns, stormed into the apartment, shutting the door behind them.

"What the fuck, man!" Blood poured between Teddy's fingers. "Do you know who the fuck I am?"

The black balaclava'd intruder swung his shotgun around, pointing it in Teddy's face, the barrel shaking. "A guy with a gun in his face." His breath was heavy.

The yellow headed intruder, wider than his black balaclava'd partner, shotgun raised, charged David. "Sit down!" His eyes were blue and bloodshot. Perspiration collected in the bags under them.

His teeth chattering, David dutifully followed the instruction.

"Anyone else in the apartment?" The man in black asked.

"Just us two," Teddy said, through rapidly swelling lips.

"Good," he said, looking at Teddy. "This your apartment?"

He spit blood on the floor. "Yeah."

"While my associate watches your friend, you're going to give me every last dollar you have here, plus the drugs."

"It isn't mine to give."

The man shoved the barrel of the shotgun into the apple of Teddy's neck, smearing the blood running down his face. "I don't care whose it is to give, it's mine to take. I have the gun, I get the money."

"You have a point," Teddy said, grimacing.

"Start walking." He removed the gun from Teddy's neck and backed up. He waved his barrel, as if he were sweeping away a mouse.

David turned at the neck, watching Teddy walk, at gunpoint, to his room. It was odd to see Teddy, a king among the thieves of this block, hunched over, bruised and bloodied.

"Don't fucking try anything," The man in front of David said, shifting his weight, trying to dispel the nervous energy that overtook one side of his body, then the next, from foot to foot.

David snapped back to the gun in front of him, holding his hands out, palms up. The man's gaze was twitching between David and the room his partner disappeared into.

"Get his wallet." The man in black said, coming out of the room, a pillowcase draped over one shoulder, still holding the shotgun. Teddy, purple rings around his eyes, the definition between cheek and nose evaporating, followed close behind.

"Hand it over" The man in yellow flicked the tip of his gun as he talked.

David reached into his pocket and pulled it out using two fingers. The man snatched it from the air.

"Let's go," his partner said, backing up towards the entrance.

As the man walked backwards, he pointed his gun to David, then to Teddy, then to David, then to Teddy. The man in yellow, directly in front of David, followed his lead, backing up, until they closed the door behind him. The only sound in the room was Teddy's hoarse and labored breathing. The only thing David could hear, so jumbled that nothing got through but noise, was the rapid fire of his thoughts.

"Fuck!" Teddy repeated over and over, walking in small circles.

"It's not that bad," David said, rubbing sweat from his forehead with the back of his hand.

"I'm a dead man," Teddy said. "I'm ruined." He got two beers from the fridge, opened one, took a swig, and pressed it against his cheek. "How am I going to pay back Matteo?"

"Who's Matteo?"

"My supplier," he said, handing David the other beer.

"How much did they take?"

"I was already in the hole. I'm beyond fucked." He rubbed the back of his neck.

"Do you owe a lot?"

Teddy stared at the ground, defeated. "I needed to push that dope to catch up."

"Look at me."

Teddy looked up.

"How much do you owe?"

He looked through David, his pupils bouncing through

the numbers, adding it up. "A little under $40,000, with what those rat bastards stole from me."

"If you can't come up with the money?"

"You can kiss your good buddy Teddy goodbye."

"Fuck," David said.

"These guys don't fuck around."

David clenched his jaw, then said, "why don't I lend you the money?"

"You'd do that for me?"

"I have more money than I know what to do with."

"You don't have to."

"I know I don't."

"I could figure out some other way."

"I want to help."

Teddy closed his swollen eyes and sighed. "I do really need the money, brother."

"And I have it."

"I'll pay you back the minute I can."

"I know."

"Honest."

"Don't worry about it."

"Now, about my throbbing head. They took all my H. You got any, Davey-Boy?"

"Always."

"What are you waiting for?"

After their next hit, David nodded off and on on Teddy's couch, his existence teetering on the edge of a dream, the brief moments of wakefulness like plucking heaven from air. The final awakening, when the sun dipped low in the sky, the empty sunlight trickling its last rays into the dusty apartment, a Teddy sized shadow appeared on David's face.

"David?" His voice was low, concerning.

"Ya?" he said, breaking the crust that sealed his war-torn lids.

"When you wake up tomorrow, can you spot me that cash?"

The memory of the early morning flooded in. "Right. How much?"

"$80,000 should be enough to cover my debt, pay for what I lost, and re-supply."

"$80,000?"

"Is that okay?"

David sat up and crossed his arms. "I guess."

"Look," Teddy said, putting his hands in the air, "you don't have to."

David looked up at Teddy and smiled. "What kind of friend would I be if I didn't help you when you needed it most?"

eighteen

THE NEXT MORNING, during the exchange of cash, there was a matter-of-factness, a cold, unrecognizable disposition to Teddy that unsettled David. For a brief moment he wondered if he knew anything about the imposing figure who stood before him. If, in the last few months, during flashes of pseudo-sincerity, when the mask of intoxication flayed back, what was left was simply the infinite layers of more masks, more illusions, stacked upon one another, propelled forward by free-flowing junk in his veins.

"I'm still in shock from yesterday," Teddy said, a tremble in his voice, the hand that held the bag of cash shaking. "But you're saving a life here brother. My supplier already got word of the robbery and he's been breathing down my neck all morning."

"When are you going to pay him back?"

"He's not a man you keep waiting."

"Right now?"

"Don't have much choice," Teddy said, heading towards his door.

"Better get going then," David said.

"We'll celebrate later tonight," Teddy said, opening the door. "On me." The door closed behind him.

"Sure," David said, to himself, alone in Teddy's empty apartment.

He looked around at this familiar, yet strange place, the murky depths of his surroundings, the knowing unknowable, and wondered, as all addicts do, perpetually, and often forever, how he ended up here. Then he went home, shot up and dreamed of a past life.

When he woke, plastered to his couch, the skin on his back tugging towards the leather, his lips a swollen pink mass, it was mid-day next day. He walked through his silent apartment, feeling like there was something missing, like someone, in the middle of the night, had moved every piece of furniture, or switched everything out with a new colour. He opened his fridge and chugged orange juice from a gallon jug. Sometimes, he realized, orange juice was the only type of nutrients his body would receive in a day. He shook it off and shot up. Feeling light, warm, and fed, he crossed the chasm of the hallway and knocked on Teddy's door, as had become custom. Steps from the other side of the door, lighter than David was used to, approached.

"Hey David," Cassius said, yawning. "Teddy's not here."

"Oh."

"Did you need anything?"

"Where is he?"

"Said he's got some heat on him. Has to lay low for a while."

"Oh," he said again, as if Cassius's words had shot from his mouth and slammed him in the stomach. "Did he say how long"

"Nope."

"Did he say anything about me?"

"He just told me to hold the fort while he was gone. That's all I know."

"Is there a number I can reach him?"

"Why?"

The words slipped over his swollen tongue. "We have business together."

"I'm handling all his business right now."

"So you don't have a number I can reach him?"

"Not for you," he said, trying to stand a little taller.

There was a ringing in David's ear. "Thanks," he said, chewing his cheek. He turned back to his apartment.

"Let me know if you need anything!" Cassius called after him.

David slammed the door behind him. Leaning his back against the door, he slid down onto the floor. If every inch of his body wasn't blunted by the point of a needle, he thought he might cry.

He wasn't so much hurt by the financial hit—like most addicts his reality wasn't one that found much consideration in the future; even with the loss, he was, he thought, secure into the near term—what he was most concerned about, which surprised him, was the loss of Teddy. He had thought, now recognizing the silliness of it, that they were friends. He closed his eyes and curled over, nestling his forehead into the angle of his arm.

"We were friends," he imagined Teddy telling him. "But brother, $80,000 is still eighty fucking thousand. A man's gotta have his principles and mine just happen to be me."

"But why leave?" he whispered, the words flying across the backs of his eyelids, speckled by an inner eye galaxy, like a spaceship at warp speed, planets and moons and stars zipping by, an explorer of space and time, a man of the new frontier, strong and capable, an idol of the people, risking friends and family for the good of the human race, to be remembered for ages, the man who saved the world by conquering the universe, who battled loneliness and the fear of the unknown, who knew not where he was going, but what he would do when he got there.

He woke up, his cheek an island in a pool of spit, still curled up on the floor. His apartment was dark, the sun down. He pushed himself off the floor, sitting up and surveying the emptiness. This apartment, this was all he knew now, all he had in the world, the only place he was safe, his hovel of hell. He'd burn in here for an eternity—an eternity alone—until he escaped the earth on a one way ticket.

It was Tuesday night, David remembered. Teddy would be playing at the Black Cat. He could catch him in the act, plead his case, tell him to forget about the money, because it didn't matter to him, he had plenty. He stood up, puffing his chest out, trying to feel proud and straight and put together, and walked through his dim apartment, to his bathroom. He splashed water on his face, patted down the matted stray hairs, and put a brush to his black teeth, raw and bleeding.

I should brush them more.

He spit into the sink, a pool of blood swirling down the drain. He cooked up a small shot, just enough to take the edge off, keep the jitters away, and left his apartment.

Smoke swirled from the cigarettes of heavy handed hipsters, their red cherries dancing in the dark cellar of the Black Cat as they laughed and leaned back and laughed some more. David, sitting at the bar, his mouth too dry for anything heavier, ordered a beer.

"Surprised to see you here without Teddy," Nathan, the bartender, said. He was a wide-eyed man in his late 20s, who looked like he was perpetually caught in the headlights of oncoming traffic.

"Is Teddy playing tonight?" David said, tasting hope as the words passed through his mouth.

"Nope."

"Any idea why not?"

"Alls I know is that Tuesdays are going to be poetry night for a while." Nathan's attention bounced from cherry to cherry. "Hence the new crowd." A man's voice, barely deepened by the virtues of puberty, called Nathan's name.

David sipped his beer in silence, looking for answers at

the bottom of the glass. It was an old lesson, he thought. Unless you're prepared to lose a friend, to have them dodge your calls, to never see them again, to have them disappear off the face of the earth, to have them change their name, dye their hair, go into witness protection, you never lend them money. It's as good as gone, and, quite often, so are they. A death sentence for friendship. And he wondered, if that were the case, why more people didn't borrow money strategically when they felt like a friendship had cause for an end.

A damp hand slid over his back. "David!" whispered a hoarse voice.

"Janko," David said, washing down the hard cotton balls forming on his tongue, staring at himself, and Janko, through the mirrored back bar.

"Glad to see you're still coming around, even with Teddy gone." His foul breath curled around David's cheek and into his nostrils.

"He's gone?"

"You didn't know?"

"No?"

"He's ran for the hills. Taken off. New shores. That sort of thing."

"You know where?"

"He told me, but I can't remember. Barbados or Colombia or Cuba or the Dominican. I don't know. We were pretty out of it, but it was a celebration. Said he won big. Hit the jackpot."

"A jackpot?" The outer layer of skin on the back of his legs prickled.

"He wouldn't say what, exactly, but—"

David got up to leave.

"Where ya going?"

There was an irony in it all, he supposed, as he walked back to his apartment, his steps slow, aimless, kicking out oddly, as if an empty can bounced in front of him. For a while, before Teddy came along, he was content to spend the rest of his short tattered life shooting up alone, quietly, with nothing but a hedonist's will to propel him forward, until he collapsed into a pile of his own filth. Then, one fateful day, Teddy knocked on the door to his life and invited himself in. He showed him, if only for a brief flickering moment, that the addict's life was still filled with a certain comfort, that you could squeeze from it something resembling meaning, and that all life, however wretched, was still life. The man, through sheer force of will, had managed to cram himself into the Alice sized hole that was left inside him, and fill it, wherever it didn't quite match, with his heavenly black tar. Now, abandoned at all sides, the hole inside him was mis-shapen, stretched at it its edges, and in pain.

He asked himself: how could he go back to the man he was, the one who came before Teddy, the one after Alice?

What was done could never be undone, history could never be re-written, and the hole inside him couldn't be filled by another. And even if he could go back to being that man, he didn't know who that man was; he didn't even know who this man was. He never quite knew any man who called himself David, whatever temporal position, and what-ever quasi-David-like body that man turned out to be. He was now lost and alone—again—and there was nothing left to remind himself that he was human. From this point on, he resolved to commit himself fully to the junk, to become more heroin than human, and let his dark passenger, the symbiotic parasite inside him, break free.

nineteen

DAVID, WITH SCABBED HANDS, their boney protrusions like rope bridges under his skin, shuddering beneath the weight of themselves, checked his wallet: an empty bag of cocaine, a credit card, the indented numbers on the backside filled with old coke, a debit card, and his California-issued ID. He tore the bag open and snorted the hard-to-get remnants in the corners, then popped it in his mouth and swished it around. Cassius would be knocking on his door soon to drop off his order. David slipped on his jacket, now a few sizes too large, the hand-me-downs of a past life, and left his apartment.

The air was thick and cool, almost damp, grey clouds hanging low in the sky. A junkie's fever raged below David's skin, calling out in its hunger. He imagined steam rising from his body then lit a cigarette, the nicotine a momentary substitute to his cells. His body shook as he breathed out, seeing the distance of the ATM down the street. Through sheer force of will—a will determined towards one thing alone, a desire that kept all junkies alive, the miracle of the junk, if you will—he stepped forward. Inch by swollen inch, blessed by a dope-fiend delirium, out of breath and near broken, he reached the machine.

He pushed the quick cash button for a hundred and the machine spit out five twenties. There was a final whirring, the spinning module of paper, which would print his doom— the perpetual rude awakening of his diminishing funds. But, instead of an awakening, he was only propelled further into a neverending nightmare, one long series of fuck yous from the world.

"No. No. No. No."

Eighty dollars was the remaining balance of his bank account. He held it near to his face, then far, hoping some distance would make it seem less real, then close again, to square himself with reality. It was all he had left in the world. An end of an era, he thought. A lifetime of monetary value built up and burned to the ground. Enough left for one final, glorious hit until—until what? He still received royalty cheques, but how those came in, and from what, or when, or whom, he had no idea. Could he start working again? Who would have him?

Until he could figure it out, he'd be Hector, blind, deaf and dumb, scouring the underworld for a hit, while letting the vultures nip at his heels, looking for their own fallen breadcrumbs. And yet, he reminded himself, he still had a pocket full of twenties, and to a junkie, beyond a single hit was a far-off future, an eternity of ecstasy stretching out between then and now. First the hit, then the future, the hit, then the future. A convenient word, the future, forever out of your grasp. If it's always the hit first, then the future, and the future is always one step ahead, then it is always the hit first, and only the hit. The future. Something we tell ourselves to feel better about the impending hit—the sweet, inevitable hit. He needed to get back to Cassius. One last hit. Then he'd be done.

David looked back at his apartment, a half a block away, and his heart raced. His vision, moving in and out of focus, stopped halfway, on the blinking red and white sign of the Painted Rose. His body wouldn't survive the trip back on the mere force of a quickly evaporating junkie's will. It needed something more substantial, however little, to force his body into action. With a bottle of scotch held firmly in his mind, he made his slow move towards the the Painted Rose.

The man behind the bar, looking up from his glass drying, his hands slowing, then pausing in place, eyed David with suspicion."You alright, ol' timer?"

In a futile attempt to wipe the sweat from his brow, David repeatedly paw'd at his forehead with the top of his hand, leaving sweat-on-sweat lines behind. "Whiskey," he said, as he sat on a barstool, the edge of the cushion daggering into his sore thighs.

Either the place smelled like piss or he did.

"Any in particular?"

"Whatever's cheapest."

"Are you sure you're alright? You're breathing pretty hard." The man reminded him of Scott—young, nosey, a snake in the grass.

As if he were suddenly without glasses, his vision was hazy at the edges. He felt like he was in a far-off dream, like he was late for work, in bed with Alice, in the same bed they always shared together, and he could smell her. His sweet Alice. Where was she now? What was she doing? Why was he here, without her?

"Whose life is this?" he said out loud.

"What?" the bartender asked, looking around.

"No—nothing, I'm alright." David coughed into his hand. "Need a drink, is all."

The man sighed. He free-poured half a glass of whiskey. "You need anything to eat?"

David held the glass with the claw like dexterity of an infant. He brought the whiskey to his lips. The man, seeing the dry spittle at the corners of his mouth crack as he opened up, watched with horror. He filled a glass of water and slid it over the bar top.

"Drink some water man," he said.

A warmth had returned to David's face and the pale

spectre of death, for the moment, had left him. "I'm fine," he said, and pulled out a twenty. It waved in the air like a flag on a windy day, attached to unstable ground. "Keep the change." He swiveled off the chair and took a step, the fibers of his muscles, the inner-workings of his cells, renewed, however minutely, through the aged-ethanol beneath his skin.

Outside, the sky had started to fall. Watching the clip-clop of the raindrops close to his feet, shielded by the awning, he fingered for a cigarette, but was tugged by despair. He'd already smoked his last. He clenched down on the spot on his lip where the cigarette would go, rolling it against his browned teeth, feeling for the groove, as if he could suck out thirty years worth of worn-down nicotine.

There is a breaking point, right before the next hit, that all junkies feel.

"This is the last one," they tell themselves. "I can't do this again. I'm not strong enough. One last big hurrah, and I'll be done with it. I'll get myself back together. I'll figure it out. I know I will," they repeat, but deep down inside, in the recesses of their minds, they know they won't. They know, as soon as they scrape together enough money, they'll be back out there on the streets, looking for their next score. It was in their DNA, speaking to them, at every waking moment. They carried it with them wherever they went.

Feeling all this simultaneously and at once David wanted nothing more than to stop here, dead in his tracks, abandoning Cassius' drop off. He extended his hand beyond the awning, turning it over in the rain, watching the droplets splash off into nothing.

One more hit, the long short goodbye, he reasoned, then he'd be strong enough to quit, strong enough to come up with a plan.

Weakly, he made a fist, clenching, as if to squeeze the

water out of his hand. He needed it, the sickness told him, one last time. He stepped forward into the rain, and his body, in slow motion, with nothing left to give, began to crumple under its own weight. There was no pain, just the progressive darkening of the world around him. And then, as if an angel called out, he heard her voice. Alice, he wanted to say, but nothing came out—no noise—only the clip clop of the rain all around him.

twenty

THE AIR WAS LIGHT and soft and sweet, like the morning after a night of rain. David held his hand up to a lightsource. All around him was a blur of misty white. He felt the dewy green beneath his feet, the sharp blades of grass between his toes. A wind whistled gently from the north, or east, or it came from no direction, because there was nothing in any direction except the grassy knoll he stood on, as if it floated on air, itself a miniature planet in this white infinite universe.

Am I dead?

A familiar voice filled the ivory void, the long expanse of nothingness. "David!"

His head snapped in its direction, but he saw only mist, fast encroaching.

"David!" the voice said again, a woman's voice, now coming from the opposite direction.

As he turned, the voice, like some phantom whack-a-mole, sprung up behind him, then to the side, then behind him, then above him, and all around. As the mist got closer, taking over the entirety of his field of vision, the island of green shrinking before him, the voice got closer, following the mist.

"David," it whispered, stepping out from the mist. Her features were indistinct, yet warm, inviting him to come closer. "I've been looking for you, waiting for you."

He hesitated, a thumping in his chest, his veins filling with blood, the terror of happiness, then stepped forward-

His foot found no solid ground and he clawed at the air.

"Alice!" he yelled, her name bouncing off rapidly passing earth. He expected to hit some type of ground, but the fall continued, and the earth turned from green to grey to black to red.

How far could he fall?

Corporeal figures, spectres from a past life, a future timeline, a life not yet lived, swarmed around him. They were his friends, his mother, and Alice, children he hadn't conceived, yet recognized, their grandchildren, the product of a seed not yet extinguished, a host of ghosts from the what-could-have-been clan. As he reached out for them, desperately stretching every fibre in his body, trying to will himself closer, they waved goodbye, fading out of existence. Tears streamed up off his cheeks and upwards, into the void. Then, as if it had moved up to him, and not him to it, the ground appeared.

He slammed into it, a wasteland of needles, millions of them, breaking his fall. Everywhere birds, frightened by the crash, sprung upwards, away from David. They disappeared into the giant cavern. He scrambled to his feet, the small lances up to his knees, and pulled out one after the other from his already pockmarked body. At the far end of the cavern, there was a tunnel of light, a beacon of hope. He moved slowly, wading through the delicious daggers as they shred his legs, each prick a small burst of ecstasy. Crouching on bloody knees, he reached the tunnel. He could see the light at the end of the tunnel, could feel the open air. His limbs moved desperately, like an excited toddler crawling to his parents.

"David!" A voice boomed from behind him, sick with anger.

David looked back and the air left his lungs, the strength from his limbs. Behind him was a giant needle, walking on

181

arms and legs, the top spraying black tar like the busted vein of an oil well.

"Take pin to skin and push that needle David!" It roared, its voice a conglomeration of terror.

An invisible glue lagged his movements.

"Take pin to skin and push that needle!"

It was inevitable, David thought, turning his head, but still he pushed on.

"Take pin to skin and push that needle!" the voice said, a few feet behind him.

The weight of his body, the torpor in his bones, overcame him. He rolled onto his back, the monster standing above him.

It knelt over him, slowly moving the tip of its needle closer, the black tar spraying all over David. "Take… pin… to… skin….."

David desperately wiped at his face, trying to clear his sight.

"And… push… that… NEEDLE!"

David's eyes opened a sliver, but the light flooding in burned, causing them to flutter. He raised his arm and strings or cords came with it. He covered himself with his forearm. There was a steady beep nearby, muffled chatter and it smelled sterile, flat. He adjusted to the overbearing light and the edges of a room took shape, fuzzy then sharp. It was a white room—a hospital room—and he was laying down, alive. He reeled with excitement.

Alive!

The door opened and a white blurry figure walked in.

"Hello?" His throat was coarse and dry.

The figure gasped, dropping something. "Mr. Smith!" It was a woman's voice—a nurse standing over him. "You're awake!"

"What?"

The woman stepped a foot out of the door, "Dr. Hassem! Dr. Hassem! He's awake!" She looked back at David, her mouth ajar. She stepped aside, holding the door open.

A tall man with broad shoulders, close shaven and Middle Eastern, walked through the door. "Mr. Smith," he said, his American accent tickled by a foreign-born childhood.

"What happened?" He tried to sit up, but his arms buckled at the elbows.

"Easy," the doctor said. "Your body's been through a lot."

"How'd I get here?"

"You were found unconscious in the street, vastly under nourished, with acute kidney failure and dehydration."

"You're lucky to be alive," the nurse said.

"How long ago?"

"About five days ago."

"Am I going to be okay?"

The doctor fingered through David's chart, squinting at the words on the page. "Your vitals are stable, your kidneys are recovering, we've rehydrated and fed you. You're probably going to be fine."

David was surprised by his own relief. When faced with the reality of death, on the verge of expiring in the street, and now given the choice of life, he wanted to live, he wanted to grow, he wanted to get better. Here was his chance.

"That is, as long as you quit the underlying cause."

"What do you mean?"

"The narcotics, Mr. David."

"I don't do drugs."

"Your blood work would disagree. When we picked you up you tested positive for adderall, cocaine, heroin, and had a blood alcohol level of .223. You have injection marks all over your body."

David broke contact, studying the dirt under his fingernails, wondering how it got there.

"I'm here to help, Mr. David. My concern is your health and improving it. I'm not here to judge."

David drummed his fingers on his chin, then caught the doctor's eyes.

"I dabbled," he mumbled.

"You what?" Dr. Hassem leaned in.

"I used a little."

"A little?"

"A lot."

"How much?"

"Every day."

"When?"

"All day."

"All of it?"

"Heroin, mostly."

"Mostly?"

"I liked it all."

"And now?"

"I want to stop. I need to stop, but I'm still a junkie."

"You're right, you need to stop, Mr. David. You're not a young man. If you'd passed out anywhere but the street, we wouldn't be having this conversation."

"I don't want to die," he said, welling up, a prickle in his nose.

"You don't have to."

"I want to be sober." David looked past the doctor. "I want to see my wife again."

"She wants to see you," the nurse said.

"What?"

"Your wife, Alice, she's been to see you."

"Here? She's been here?"

"Every day, so far. She left a few hours ago."

"How? Why?"

"She was your emergency contact," Dr. Hassem said. "We called her shortly after you came in."

A tear, leaving a streak behind, rolled off his chin.

"Would you like to call her?" the nurse asked.

"Call my wife?" he repeated, not believing the reality of the words, trying to force them into existence, hoping to hold on to this dream, hoping that if he repeated the words long enough, hard enough, he could will this life, his old life, into being. "When?"

"Now," Dr. Hassem said, pointing to a small beige phone on the bed side table. "If you want."

Biting his thumb's nail, he examined the phone. Her voice, the close approximation of an angel, gentle and soft, ringed between his ears.

"We'll give you some privacy," the nurse said.

His voice wobbled. "Thanks."

He lifted the receiver off its eternal resting place. It felt heavy in his sweaty palms. He reached out to dial, then hesitated. He was standing at the edge of an old life, a different David, who looked not unsimilar to this David, but, he feared, no longer had anything in common with him.

Would he know what to do with it, when he got it back? Would it only end in ruin? Would he run to the end of a needle? The needle. The sweet embrace of the tar. A quick lick would get him right, help him brave this phone call. If only there was some around here. Where could he get it?

The dial tone snapped him back to earth. He took a deep, wheezing breath in. His index finger, shaking in its socket, moved like a worm bursting through the dirt, from button to button: 5, press and move, 3, press and move, 8 press and move, 2 press and move, 6 press and move, 9, press and move, 1 press and move. The first ring was thunder in his ears. The bed creaked and cawed beneath his shaking legs. The air caught in his throat, choking him. A second ring. He fumbled for his first words, finding only the soft repetition of "Hello. Hello. Hello. Hello. Hello." A third ring.

She knew it was him and she was never going to answer. She could be here while he was in a coma, but she couldn't bear to talk to him again. He was lost to her. He was lost to the world.

The fourth ring sounded whiney, defeated, like the dying hoots of a baby owl. There was a click, then the sound of her voice.

"You've reached Alice Smith. I'm sorry I missed your call, but leave a message and I'll get back to you."

It was auditory heaven—sugar of the ears—and he'd forgotten the delicate intricacies layered within her voice, the soft timbre, as if she would break into song at any moment. He hung up before he heard the beep. That was his shot, and he didn't think he'd have enough strength, or the courage, to try again.

Then the phone rang and his heart monitor quickened.

twenty one

As if the heat from the friction would kick start a fire, propelling him to action, David rubbed his thighs while building up the courage to pick up the phone. He needed that single word, that perfect sentence, that would sweep her off her feet and make her fall in love again—a magic series of words that could erase more than a year of abandonment, that could turn back time and make them whole again. Then, before his brain knew what his body was doing, he pounced on the phone.

"Hello," he said, bringing it to his ear.

"David?"

The sound of his name coming from her lips was sweeter than any drug he'd ever encountered. It was as if, having taken so long away from his one true love, the only drug that truly mattered, every ounce of tolerance that he had built up had washed away, and it was more potent than ever. A mist returned to the corners of his eyes.

"Hello Alice."

"I thought I lost you," she said, choking.

"I thought I lost myself, but here I am, still here."

For a long moment, they talked only in tears, letting the salty streams cascade down their cheeks, listening to one another's love leave their body in quarter gram increments.

"Can I come see you?"

"Nothing," he said, stumbling through the thickened spit in his mouth, "would make me happier."

"I can be there in half an hour."

"Okay."

"David?"

"Yeah?"

"I still love you. I've never stopped loving you."

"I love you too, my little mouse."

"See you soon." There was a click, then the line went dead.

The phone, still shaking in his hand, remained at David's ear. He breathed heavy and searched the room for answers, as if they were hidden somewhere on the sterile walls, outside the window, written in the clouds, found within the beeps of his heart monitor—like he had woken up from some far-reaching nightmare, or an alternate reality, where he stumbled and fell right through the ground, and woke up here, with this life. As though another David was still out there, one who deserved this life, but by some luck of the Gods, that almighty thing called fate, he'd been given it instead.

And yet, even now, his cells, still burning the last remaining particles that fed their internal engines, leaving behind the misshapen traces of an overworked symbiosis, yearned like lost puzzle pieces, searching for their eternal opposite. The desire for a needle pulsated from the back of his neck, pushed through his brain, and pressed against the back of his skull. It stormed through his thoughts like a wildfire, yelling at him to run and take shelter from his life. The voice, however, was no longer alone. Like a sun bursting through the clouds, an angel spreading its wings, it now had to compete with Alice's thundering resonance.

With her by his side, he would not be intimidated into submission, or yield any ground to the big boogeyman in the night, the fear of sobriety. He would beat this. Together, they would beat this.

Over the next three days, while he was closely watched for stability, enduring the hourly physicals, the pricks of pins without a heavenly release that followed, the psychological examinations, the plastic cups full of, surprisingly, normal coloured urine, the interweaving waves of brain scans, Alice stood by his side, her eyes fiercely alight with the sight of him. For the first few hours of those three days, where they towed between a desperate longing to be together and an unsteadiness in their own skin, it was difficult to the find the right things to say. Neither knew how deep to push, where the line of don't-ask-me-that-quite-yet was, and who would be the first to give ground. Then, little by little, as long-lost best friends do, those who know the other better than they know themselves, who can tell you from memory every freckle, dimple and hair on the other's body, who were molded by the hands of god to fit together in a world where nothing ever seemed quite right, they slipped into each other's grooves, rediscovering a love that never left them. Alice, she admitted, took a while to recover from his betrayal, but when she did, she discovered that she was no true little mouse, running for shelter from life's long list of predators. And as David hid from the world—and from himself—she was independent and strong and free, starting her own online blog on love and loss, which was quickly recycled into other magazines, newspaper columns, online forums, blogs, tabloids, late night news, and more. It spread like wildfire, her story. She was praised for her sincerity, her fierce strength in the face of loss, and for her steadfast dedication, despite it all, to David. If only he would have read one of her articles, he would have seen that his love was not lost.

David, on the other hand, not wanting to begin again on a bed of lies, and without the wide-eyed optimism that Alice's sharing had, laid bare all his secrets for her. He told her about the depths of despair and the dark alleys of depression he found himself in. He explained the height of his addiction, the mental weakness that came with it, the loss of self, the shadowy break down of his ego, how, for a long while, he didn't recognize the man who stood before him, like he was a passenger in someone else's body, a slave to the skag, a piece of himself replaced and flushed out with each push of the needle until he was running on junk alone. He explained the outer limits of physical exertion, what the body could take under duress, as long as it was fueled by that same thing that hurt it, an intermixing of pleasure and pain and powder. Short of pie charts and bar graphs, annotated research papers and eye witness accounts, he gave it all, including the apartment shakedown with Teddy, the loss of $80,000, who drove him to see her that mistaken night, what happened the night of the Academy Awards, line by literal line, he gave it all. He even told her the good times, the sky high times, the this-is-really-fucking-great times, the freedom of it all, to be allowed to die in your own filth, to ride off on a rainbow of pleasure, a bucket of never-ending black tar at the end. He told her about his new found love of jazz, the weekly visits to the Black Cat, the late night chatterbox sessions with Teddy. And when it was all said and done, he told her about what really mattered: her.

She listened and cried, was shocked and sad, but then she laughed and mocked, and finally, with a heavy embrace, she forgave—goddamnit, she forgave. As if he had risen from the dead, which in many ways he had, she had her David back. They were together again. Everything, in time, would move forward, and life would resume as it always had—the only life she could remember living—with the two of them together.

And on the fourth day, with David healed, their love restored, a phantom figure back from the dead, they got to go home.

"It feels like our wedding night," she said on the drive home. "We can finally be alone, just the two of us, away from the world."

"I hope it's exactly like our wedding night," he said, a stupid grin painted on his face, salivating at the thought, his sex drive no longer the stunted beat up pinto it was while on the skag.

"Almost like it's our first time again."

"Might have to go a little further back than our wedding night to recapture that moment." He wheezed, his new approximation of a laugh, a souvenir he still carried from his broken body.

"All the way back to your apartment in Kensington."

David forgot how her right canine slipped over her bottom lip as she laughed.

"I hated that squeaky bed," she said. "Eeee! Eeee! Eeee! Eeee!"

Another wheeze. He couldn't believe the ray of sunlight he had before him, the laughter he could share with her.

Later that night, alone in their bed, and between the sheets, a second honeymoon they had. He was high with her—her smell, her voice, her skin—and it crippled his senses. Aged now, and in their maturity, they knew each other's bodies, had studied them for years, and it was better than the first, better than all that came before it. The build up, almost worth the sorrow, almost worth the separation, was a lifetime accumulation of energy for a single solitary orgasm.

Was there anything better?

When David woke the next morning, out from one dream and into the next, he didn't wake Alice. Instead, he rolled out of bed, careful to corner around the well-known creaks, and tiptoed down the stairs. The floor was warm between his toes and his house was bigger than he remembered. He felt small in it, as if he didn't belong between the good graces of the walls, as if they judged his past transgressions.

There was a dull ring, the distant sound of alarm bells, that persisted in his ears. He poured himself a coffee, the automated timer, an old relic, still set to go off for when he woke up. He walked out onto the cold wood of his backyard patio, resting his cup on the edge of the barrier, and surveyed the morning sky. The pink and blue hues swirled on God's pallette, meticulously tapped here and there by puffy white. It was a crisp scene, tempting him to reach out and touch, to pocket and take with him wherever he went, to pull out in times of sorrow.

"Like a patient etherized upon a table," he said, remembering some far-off college poem, the words imprinted onto his memory, but no clue from where, or from whom. He shivered once, a full body convulsion, then walked back in. Alice was standing at the island, her eyes on the prowl, from above her own morning coffee.

"It's still surreal to see you in front of me, to see you here," she said.

"I don't ever want to leave," he said, walking towards her. "You've cured me." He kissed her long and hard.

It was perfect for a while, the two of them holed up in their home, exploring each other, sometimes not leaving their bedroom for whole days, rediscovering what it meant to be them, as a pair, as a unit, in love, throwing coal on a furnace of passion, feasting on it all, a new kind of hedonism, paired and shared, it was pure organic pleasure. Then one day, not long after, it wasn't perfect. Without warning, as if he caught the flu, the spontaneous phenomenon of extreme human boredom hit him. He no longer wanted to get out of bed, talk about the little things, or the big things, feel her body, laugh, or love. Everything was blunted and bitter, like ashes in his mouth.

This crippling boredom of the post-addict is common. They see their sex drive go full tilt, foods explode on their tongue, pleasure returns to things that had long grown stale, and everything ostensibly shifts to the relative normalcy of your pre-addict life, whatever that normal was. But something happens, a trigger, you catch yourself daydreaming about the end of the needle, a conversation reminds you of a time when you surrendered yourself to nothing but the overwhelming pleasure of the tincture, and you hit a snare. Soon, all you can think about is returning to that life, the ease of which time passed and events occurred, an inability to remember the agony that accompanied the time between each shot, the struggle that came with the release.

David was right there, caught, snared in a trap. It was an odd awakening of the ennui, boredom that couldn't be satiated with anything but the pointed prick of a needle, but the needle he would not submit to, could not submit to. His choice, instead, was to lay in bed, to pull the blankets over his head and hide from the world, to rebuff it for its many wide-ranging opportunities to sink back into the old David. Even Alice, in all her glory, was only a reminder of all he could lose, all he stood to abandon, if he gave in. To see her was to see terror, to talk to her was to quake in the idea of a monumental loss.

"Why won't you talk to me?" Her voice cracked with alarm, the possibility of a second betrayal. "Was it something I've done?"

"I think I need professional help," he said.

"Are you depressed?"

"I'm an addict."

"But you were doing so well."

"I need to learn how to deal with this. The nagging. The itch. It's there and I don't know how to scratch it."

"If that's what you need."

"It is."

"How can I help?"

"Help me find a place. Help me look."

They spent that entire day searching, cross-referencing, and calling. David moved with a renewed energy that he lacked during the last few days, a purpose with an endpoint. It was the light at the end of the tunnel, somewhere to go, somewhere to be, something to look forward to: help! Alice, for her part, was right beside him, declaring that no expense should be spared, no stone left unturned—she wanted the best help that money could buy. She would not take any chances, not this time.

"At that price?" he asked. "We can't afford that. I bled us dry."

She looked at David, wide-eyed and devilish. "We both bled you dry."

"What?"

She let him in on her secret: while he was away, she had been siphoning money out of his account. It was slow at first, a hundred here, two hundred there, but she was trying to send a message, to bleed him dry and get him to reach out to her, or to cut her off all together, whichever came first. But he didn't say anything, didn't cut her off, so she kept upping the amount, hoping he'd take notice, ask for the money back, do something. Nothing happened, and she continued until he had nothing left. That's when he showed up in the hospital.

"How much did you take?"

"Over $200,000."

He gagged on her words, wheezing in laughter. "Holy shit."

"I'm sorry I didn't tell you sooner."

He beamed. "You're a guardian angel."

"I had to do something."

After creating a pro and con chart of the top contenders, they settled on a residential, no in-person contact, in-house treatment program at a centre in Malibu called Broken Chains. It was an intensive 16 week program, segregated from the main population, surrounded by trees and the ocean. Every day was governed by a schedule, which began at the break of dawn all the way up to lights out.

"I don't know if I could do it without seeing you," he said.

"It's your journey to take," she said. "You have to do this alone."

"Still."

"You know where I'll be when you get out."

They registered online and paid the deposit. The following Sunday, feeling like he was going off to boarding school, wondering if he would return a man, David packed.

twenty two

LIKE THE BROAD brush strokes of a painter, deep shades of orange streaked by their car. David, pressed against the steering wheel, his neck turning every few seconds, followed the tree line. Stems of redwoods, magnificent in their grandeur, were peaked by a lush green. The inescapable fecundity of it all, away from the robot world of LA, the salt smell of ocean in the air—there was safety here, rejuvenation.

"It's just down the road," Alice said, her nose in her phone.

"I can't tell if I'm nervous or excited."

She put a hand on his knee. "A little bit of both."

He sat back in his seat. "Will people know who I am?"

"Probably."

He focused on a point down the road, a nowhere spot unrecognizable from one to the next. "I hope they don't."

"Why?"

"It's embarrassing."

"They're all addicts in there, David. You have nothing to be ashamed of."

"Right," he said.

"Besides, it's a supportive environment. You'll be able to learn about other people with the same problems you have."

"How many are in the program again?"

"Twelve lonely lost souls, including you."

"I'm not so lonely anymore," he said, squinting at her, smiling without teeth.

She squeezed his knee, but didn't reply.

The road veered right for a few minutes, almost in a circle, before turning into a small cobblestone embankment surrounded by fuller larger redwoods. Unlike their public road cousins, these were meticulously groomed to block out the outside world, to seclude them within their getaway paradise. The car bumped down the road, masking the tremor in David's hand. In the distance, through the bucolic setting, was a statue of a man breaking free from handcuffs, the heavy-handed symbolic destiny that everyone hoped to achieve here. A babbling stream sprouted from its head and rolled down into a small pond. The road wrapped around the statue, whose view, once obscuring, now gave way to the white mansion, more Bel Air than Malibu.

Everything looked new, as if every few months, right before a new cast and crew of addicts arrive, they tear it all down and rebuild. The lawn in front the house was unnaturally maintained, perfect in its simplicity, decorated by circular rose bushes at its edges. The front porch jutted out, with a rooftop deck extending beyond it, which four pillars held up. The rest of the facility stretched on equal sides away from the front porch, forming a two floored rectangle.

"Looks peaceful," David said.

"It will be peaceful."

"Almost too nice."

"You're not going to prison. You should be comfortable."

David turned the key—the short gasps of the engine dying—but didn't move. He was locked on the house as if it were supposed to do something to greet him, to invite him in, to make the first move.

"You okay?"

He cleared his throat and squeezed the muscles in his jaw, then looked through Alice. "Is it going to work?"

"It will if you want it to."

Her words registered a few seconds later, the data noise among the traffic jam in his mind. "I do."

"Then it will."

"Promise?" He sounded hopeful, childlike.

"I promise you'll get better. I promise you'll come back to me."

"I'll come back a better man. You deserve it."

"You need to do this for you, not for me. Remember that."

"I know."

She tilted her head. "You're late."

"I don't want to leave you again." He looked away from her.

She put a hand on his shoulder. "The time I spent without you was the loneliest I've ever felt, but to get you back, to really get you back, I can do a few more months."

He looked back at her, his orbs red and glossy. He removed his glasses and rubbed the back of hands against each eye. "Okay."

"Now, before I change my mind, get lost."

He sighed, popped the trunk, and got out of the car. Alice joined him at the trunk.

"The next 120 days are packed away in here," he said, his hands on his hips, looking down at his suitcase.

Alice put a hand on his lower back. "You'll be fine."

Like he was pulling a sword from stone, his battered arms struggled beneath the weight of his future. Alice laughed through heavy tears. She held her arms open, waiting for him to pull out his destiny.

"At least I get to say goodbye to you this time."

He stepped into her arms and kissed her, salt and sorrow intermixing. "Was the least I could do."

"I can't let go," she said.

"Five more seconds," he said.

"Five more seconds."

He tightened his grip and felt the weight of her beneath his fingers. Every day was a lesson in love, a grand testimony, that no matter how much he thought he loved her, there was always room for more. He loosened the pressure, then let her go.

"Call me the first chance you get," she said, her legs trembling, knees touching, hands clasped over her stomach.

"I will." He rolled his suitcase down the cobblestone drive away—the clatter of the rocks against his wheels the only thing he could hear—and into the house.

The entrance smelled of sage and vanilla. It was painted yellow and sprinkled with motivational quotes like "keep going," "your only limit is you," and "will it be easy? nope!"

A woman sitting at a receptionist desk at the end of the entrance hall looked up. Her features were warm, but unremarkable. "You must be David," she said.

"I am." He approached her desk.

"You're late." She stood up and held out a clipboard. "Sign this, please."

He scanned the list of other names. His was the open space four down, where he sealed his commitment and the process began.

"Right this way," she said, opening her palm to the hallway on the left.

He followed her. The clapping of their shoes, one high and off rhythm, the other a low monotone shuffle, echoed through the house. On each side of the hall there were six doors, the left numbering one to six and the right seven to twelve. She stopped at the last door on the left, number six.

"This is your room." she said, unlocking the door and placing the key in his hand. "Drop off your stuff and then I'll take you to the sharing room."

"Got it."

The room was half hospital, like a doctor had ripped it off at the seam, a fresh version each time a new patient came in, and half dorm room—small, serene, and studious. It had a single bed flush with the wall, a window across from the door, a desk with a fresh stack of pens and a notepad. He dropped his bag by the bed and closed the door behind him.

The nameless woman, holding her clipboard close to her chest, tapped her foot. "Ready to go, Mr. Smith?" Before he could nod, she turned on her heels.

They walked passed the reception hall, around a bend in the house, to a hall on the opposite side. They stopped at a door with "sharing" laser etched into the wood panelling. David stepped back and she knocked, then opened. She motioned, like he were a child, for him to go in. Like a magnetic charge vibrating through the air, his sudden appearance forced to attention the twelve faces sitting in a circle. There was an open spot on the far end of the group.

A man, the skinnier, tanned version of Mr. Clean, looking down at his own clipboard, said, "You must be David Smith!" He waved his clipboard at the open seat. "Please, sit down. We're just getting started."

Every bulb in the room followed his slow shuffle to the open seat, which fell between a middle-aged man with head to toe tattoos and a brunette woman, who was scratching at her forearms, wearing a spotted sunflower dress.

"Now that we're all here," the man said standing up. "Let's get to know each other, shall we?" He looked around the room, searching for the few eyes that were on him. "It is, after all, the sharing room, isn't it?" He wheezed, his laugh reminding David of his own failed approximation. "Look around at the faces you see in this room." He walked into the middle of the circle, closed his eyes, and held his hands in a triangle at his chest, like he were leading a mock conference at Apple. His eyes snapped open and he spread his hands, shifting in a circle. "For the next four months, these are your companions, your comrades in arms. And me? You can call me Jamie. You're staying in my home. It's my garden, my sanctuary, and I welcome you with open arms to it. Here, and if you ever need it, out there, I will forever be your coach, your guardian, and, if I have to be, your drill sergeant." He lowered his voice and continued. "I was once where you all are now, and worse—coke, heroin, meth, uppers, downers, you name it, I wanted it, and I didn't care how I got it. My addiction—as I'm sure some of, if not all, can relate—was an unrelenting force. So trust me when I say I get it. But what I want you all to know is this: what you are all feeling right now, the emotions that are going through your heads, the voices telling you to run and flee and hide, you're all feeling them simultaneously, with one another, which makes you all a team. And as a team I am your captain, and we are going to win this game as a unit, as a single group, together."

All eyes followed Jamie as he wandered around the sharing circle.

"Broken Chains has one of the highest success rates in the country, maybe the world. Heck, I've never heard of a clinic that beats us. Why? Because we know that recovery is a team sport, and knowing you're not alone in this is half the battle. This group, and I don't know why, maybe it's something in the air, an energy flowing out of you all, but this group, will have a success rate of 100%." He angled forward and squeezed his fists into his chest. "I can feel it!" He walked back to his seat and sat down. "Now let's get to know one another." He looked to his left. "And you? Who are you and what is your vice?"

In patient order, the twelve revealed their names, who they were within their lives, and what drug had brought them here—alcohol, heroin, marijuana, housewives, athletes, and thespians. David, during the reflection, looked for judgement on their faces, but he saw only a reflection of his own shame, his own hard-to-admit defeat, and in that, he took comfort.

After the ceremonial sharing, the coaxed words of the damned, Jamie, the captain of this squad of ragtag everyday misfits, stood up and addressed the group. "Now that we've all been properly introduced, one of the best ways to get to know one another is over a meal. Let's eat." He flapped his hands up and down, waving everyone out of their seats and, like school children awaiting the recess bell, formed a line at the door. "Follow me," Jamie said, leaving the room.

In many ways the people in that room were beginning again, like blank slates, children on a journey of discovery, learning to live amongst adults, to not grasp at every sugary powder that came across their plates, to learn the meaning of delayed gratification in a society that sucks from you every last penny in exchange for unrepentant sensory overload. They followed Jamie down the hallway bend, which led into an open room with six tables. The room was abuzz with nameless workers setting the stage, laying down the last bits of cutlery, filling cups with multi-coloured fruit juice, and preparing the lambs for slaughter. On the far wall, opposite of David, were glass doors, opening up into the backyard. Beyond the glass doors was a crystal pool encircled by concrete, accented by a small step ladder and diving board, with the globe of a midday sun free-floating in its shallow waves.

"Breakfast, lunch and dinner will be had here," Jamie said. "And I'm not kidding when I say this is one of the best restaurants in California—we've spared no expense. Good nutrition and positive food choices are a cornerstone of a healthy individual. Any questions?"

The room was silent.

"Great. Find a seat." Jamie moved aside.

Winding through the tables, not wanting to go through the awkward song and dance of asking someone to sit down, David found a seat closest to the glass doors, farthest from the group. Mike, an NFL linebacker who also had an affinity for heroin, was right on David's heels. He was a massive, smooth man with almost no definition, as if, inch by inch, his muscles had been replaced by fat.

He pulled out a chair. "Mind if I sit?"

"Go ahead."

He sat down. The chair creaked under his weight, and his oversized body hung over the edges of the seat. "What was your name again?"

"David Emmeret Smith."

"Actor, right?"

"I was," David said, lingering, "an actor."

"Not anymore?"

"Probably not, but who knows."

"One step at a time."

"Right," David said. "You played basketball?"

"Football."

"And now?"

"Drugs, man. What else?"

David shrugged his shoulders, the blood rushing to his cheeks, moving uncomfortably in his chair, as if he were swimming in its oversized arms.

"Want to hear what happened?" Mike asked.

"What?"

"Man said we should share. Want to hear how I got into it all?"

"I guess," David said, still looking down.

"I was a special teams cornerback in my fourth year. Nothing exciting. I put my head down, played hard, and trained. I broke—"

A bone-thin woman approached the table. Her skin

looked like the last layer of defense, the insides of her body on the cusp of breaking free. "Am I interrupting?"

"Not at all," David said. "Mike was about to tell me how he wound up here."

"Sounds exciting," she said, sitting down. "I love these kind of stories. They make me feel human."

"It was Mia, right?"

"That's me." She fell back into her chair, smiling. "Mike and…" she looked at David., "David!"

"Yup," David said. "Anyway, Mike, your story."

"Well," Mike resumed, "I broke my collarbone in a late tackle. Guy comes flying over like a bat out of hell and t-bones me right in the shoulder. Whole thing basically caves in. Hurt like a mother fucker. To help with the pain, the doctor prescribed me these white devil pills."

"Oxys?" Mia asked.

"Them's the ones. Lovely little fuckers. But before them, I hadn't even used drugs. Hadn't ever been high. I saw what it did to some of my friends in high school. I didn't want to be that guy. I had a life and a career ahead of me."

"Do you still have a career?" she asked.

"Maybe not, but I hope so." Mike looked over David's shoulder and out into the back yard. He clenched his teeth and pursed his lips, then looked back at his table companions. "It was instant. I was hooked. Each time I took one of those little guys, a lifetime of focus, dedication, and hard work, and all the stress that came with it, the hopes and dreams of everyone, all riding on you, it all melted away. For hours I enjoyed life, enjoyed feeling good, without any regret or responsibility, but suddenly I was out, and I found myself lying to the doctor, asking for more time off practice, and it worked. He gave me stronger stuff, more of it, no questions asked. Stronger stuff led to stronger stuff, stuff on the side, seeking out new stuff, similar stuff, shady dudes recommending shadier dudes, weird places, weirder places, needles, tar, track marks, hiding, holding myself up, and if I kept on that direction, probably, I don't know, death."

"Nobody realizes," Mia said, "how quickly it can take off on you. It normalizes and then you move on to the next once abnormal, now normal, thing. It's totally crazy."

"It damn near pulled the carpet out from under me. You think you're under control, then all of a sudden you're not."

"When I look back," David said, talking slowly, his fingers tapping against the top of the table. "It almost feels like there was a second me there—a second me who's probably still here, somewhere deep down inside me trying to break free—who took over. That second you sounds, looks, and talks just like you, but it isn't you, not if you look closely."

"But we're here to shut that loser up," Mia said.

"Even now he's chirping in my ear, trying to convince me I could do this on my own."

"Same," David said.

"Then he's already lost," Mia said.

"Why?"

"Look around you. You're not doing this on your own."

David did as he was told. Each table, each with their own group of addicts, deep in conversation, with bits of words and syllables floating to David's ears, was a mishmash of addicts sharing the only thing they had in common: their addiction. Then, while he was studying the room, a conga line of servers—dressed from head to toe in white—burst through a door, likely a kitchen, each holding three plates, and the chatter died down. Each server found a guest and stood beside them.

Standing at the front of the room, his back to the probable kitchen, Jamie clanked a glass. "As I said, a good diet is the cornerstone of health, the building blocks of the body and the mind. The foods you eat here will all be nutritionally dense, low in calories, high in protein, rich in antioxidants, and curated to rinse the body, and the soul, of the toxic gunk that is ever present in your organs. So, with this first meal, I want to propose a toast. Everyone, raise your glasses."

Twelve reluctant hands raised their glasses.

"To healthy choices. Salut."

A server—a bald-headed man, closely shaven, and smelling like pine—placed the three plates in front of David. In front of him was a small quinoa salad, a bowl of sliced almonds, raspberries, blackberries, strawberries, and blueberries, and an avocado arugula salad. All three had the same meal, but with slightly different portions. Mike dug in first.

Mia moved her quinoa around the plate with her fork, then picked up a berry and popped it into her mouth. "Can I share my story?" she asked, breaking away from the trappings of extra calories.

Mike, racing through the food on the table, didn't look up from his plate.

"I guess," David said. "I mean, why not?"

"Okay. It started," she said, counting on her fingers, "three years ago, right after graduating university. I was a lost child, bright eyed and naive, and wasn't ready for the adult world, didn't know where I fit in it. I knew, like most people my age who have been told this all their lives, that I wanted to change the world, but, with a degree in English, and no idea where to start, the search for meaning felt hopeless. And, like, in reality, when I really think about it, I didn't want to grow up." She slipped a strawberry through her lips. "Life, a career, a family, whatever else you do when you grow up, it didn't feel real, didn't feel like a real possibility. Almost like, I don't know." She bit at her nails. "Like whatever I was going to do, I was going to fail at, anyway, so why even try? Instead I didn't commit to anything. Just kept working my dead-end barista job that I had in university, while day-dreaming about what ifs and partying on my days off."

"Someone once borrowed me Burroughs book 'Junky' and," she said. "A line stuck out to me, 'you become an addict because you don't have strong motivations to be anything else.' And, for me, that's what happened. I honestly didn't have anything better to do, and it just sort of, like, happened. One day you do a little bit of coke, and it's innocent fun, and all your friends are doing it, and before you know it, before I knew it, I was staying up all night, whole weekends, not sleeping, keeping the party going, often a party of one, looking for more, searching for more, stealing, lying, and hiding. The worst part, maybe, was that no one even noticed it. Everyone was out having fun, doing similar things, all the while a monster had grown inside of me, taken me over."

"The second you," David said.

"Exactly."

"Our own personal demon," Mike said, polishing off the last of his food."But how did you stop? How did you end up here?"

"When I had no more money and nothing left to pawn, nothing left to steal, I broke down, and came clean to my parents. I don't know what I would have done without them. I would have been totally lost. My mom, at first, was hysterical, blaming herself, but my dad stepped up big time, and brought us all together. He found this place and now here I am."

Mia scooped a spoonful of quinoa, the small grains rolling over the side of the spoon as she brought it to her mouth. The way she chewed, the quick short rotations of her jaw, reminded David of a rabbit. He studied her features, the sharp jaw, the small nose, and realized he liked this girl, found her interesting and kind and open.

"Think there's going to be seconds?"

"I doubt it," David said, looking to Mike. He was a gentle giant, and David guessed the man would surprise him, would move beyond the one-dimensional cliche of an athlete.

Both of his table companions were fellow lost souls—not that David believed in that sort of thing, never had—looking to regain their lives and regain themselves. There was a comfort, a companion's warmth, in knowing that he wasn't the only one looking for answers. He was glad to be where he was, in this place, with these two people, sharing what he thought only he carried around with him. There was strength in numbers, he thought, and, for the first time in his life, he realized the power of other people, the power of opening up and sharing. Other than Alice, he hadn't really had any other friends, any surrounding companions. There was only ever one at a time, and, until Teddy, that was Alice, but here were two that he wanted to know, to share, and to bond with. He wanted to find his old life here, to try to find the person who could succeed again, out there, and not merely move through the motions. This was going to be work, and he was willing to sweat.

twenty three

AFTER THE MEAL they were ushered upstairs into an open room—the game room, as Jamie called it. Here, he said, they would get free time to play, and relax, and get to know one another while each patient underwent a one on one psychological examination in a nearby room. The space overlooked the front reception area, a wooden railing in a half circle at one side of the room, the top of the still nameless reception worker's head visible to David, the two other walls covered in books and board games, with reading chairs placed between each shelf. The last wall had three easels with blank painter's paper on them, and connected to the space was a cramped room with the words "phone" written on the wall. In the middle of the room, with patients crowding around it, was a ping-pong table, and surrounding the ping pong table were square tables, with pens and notebooks on them.

"Wait for your name to be called," Jamie said, looking down at his clipboard. "First up: Donna."

Donna was over tanned and under worked. A rich man's wife, David guessed. She was there on a court order, the result of her third DUI, and the only way she was going to avoid jail time. After she left, following close behind Jamie, everyone slowly gravitated to their own part of the room. David wandered towards the bookshelves and fingered through the titles. The old book smell produced a melancholy effect within him, a nostalgia for a time when he was just a boy, a time where he enjoyed the quiet serenity of the pages, the ability to get lost in another land, another mind, another world.

His fingers ran over a familiar spine: "Stoner, John Williams." He remembered, while high, reading a passage in it, something about love, or fate, or life, and finding them to fall on false ears. He sifted through the book again, running his hands down the words on the page, scanning for the same familiar phrase or quote. He couldn't place it, couldn't see the words, but he remembered the feeling, and thought he would recognize it when he saw it.

Then, about two thirds of the way through, he saw this passage underlined:

"In his extreme youth Stoner had thought of love as an absolute state of being to which, if one were lucky, one might find access; in his maturity he had decided it was the heaven of a false religion, toward which one ought to gaze with an amused disbelief, a gently familiar contempt, and an embarrassed nostalgia. Now in his middle age he began to know that it was neither a state of grace nor an illusion; he saw it as a human act of becoming, a condition that was invented and modified moment by moment and day by day, by the will and the intelligence and the heart."

As a child, he remembered, he looked to the future as a state of being of which, once attained, would come with all of life's secrets, but as he grew older, he felt it was all a false religion, one where the secrets are never quite revealed, where the truth is always one step away, but now, in that room, feeling the weight of the book in his hand, the dull pain in his abused body, it struck him; all of life was simply an act of becoming, which, if you could love that, if you could find bliss in the ever-changing series of events that constituted your life, you would be happy. Otherwise, if you're out there in the world, searching for truth, or perfection, in life or love or whatever guides you, you'll live in a perpetual state of disappointment, a series of false religions waiting to let you down.

"David?" A voice said, through the chatter of the room. He looked over his shoulder and saw Jamie.

"You're up," he said.

David looked back at the book, creased the corner of the page, and slipped it into his back pocket. Everyone in the room, as if he were a dead man walking, watched him exit the "games" room. Mike, holding a paddle and ball in hand, nodded at him from the ping pong table. David followed close behind Jamie, the skin on the back of the man's neck taut so tight he wondered if plucking it would produce music.

Jamie knocked on a door just down the hall, then turned the handle.

"Enjoy," he said, smiling. His teeth, the likely result of a lifetime of drug abuse, were unmistakably artificial.

The room—its large windows gleaming in the afternoon sun, the light blue and white panel walls anachronistic to the rest of the house—was surprisingly small and smelled of cinnamon.

"Hello," a woman said, rushing, notepad in hand, across the short distance of the room to greet him. She had a smooth but age-worn face, like the wrinkles that did form had absorbed the aging for the rest of her, leaving it untouched and youthful where unbroken.

She was older than David but not so far ahead that it made him feel young. Rather, he looked at her and felt old, the lines in his own face deeper, more troubling.

"Tabitha Brimage." Her voice was light and airy. She extended a hand to him.

David's hand smothered hers, which was cold and silky.

"Sit down. Sit down," she said, walking back to her brown wicker chair. She pointed towards a black bubbled leather love seat.

David sat down, his knees together, the sides of them brushing up and down, his hands, small fists, pushing against each other in his lap.

"Okay," she said, her grey eyes wide and cheerful. "Let me just confirm a few things here: David Smith. Actor." She moved her pen down the length of her clipboard. "57 years of age. Heroin. Wife Alice." She looked up. "Anything else?"

"That's pretty much the gist of it."

"Why don't you tell me why you're here?"

"I'm an addict."

"There are addicts all over the world, David. Millions of people around the world who don't seek help. You're not here because you're an addict; you're here because you want to be here. Why do you want to be here?"

"I couldn't continue living the way I was."

"That's better. How were you living?"

"Without a care in the world."

She crossed one leg over the other. "Can you be more specific?"

"High all the time. Barely eating. On the verge of dying."

"What changed?"

"My body shut down and I almost died in the street."

"And then?"

"And then there she was, back by my side."

"Who?"

"Alice. My wife."

"Is that why you're here? Your wife?"

"I think so."

"What about yourself?"

"I owe it to her to get better. She came back. I can't let her down."

"What about letting yourself down?"

"I'm used to doing that."

"Later tonight, as an exercise, I'd like you to write out ten reasons you want to get better, without mentioning Alice. Can you do that for me?"

"Ten?" he said, shaking his head.

"If you can."

"I don't know."

"Don't worry about it for now. Sit down and see what you come up with. You might find there's more within you worth saving."

He stared at the floor and nodded.

"Let's get back to you, so I can better understand who you are"

"Anything specific?"

"Mom? Dad?"

"Both dead."

"How do, or how did, you feel about that, when it happened?"

"Don't remember my dad."

"And your mom?"

David rested his lips on his knuckles and looked out the window. The ocean, its waves calm but teeming with untapped power, tinged with a late afternoon fire.

"David?"

"It affected me a lot, I guess."

"How did she die?"

"Breast cancer."

"Was it long?"

"It had spread to the rest of her organs when we found out. From diagnosis to death, it was, maybe, two months?"

"And how did it affect you?

"I was lucky at first, I thought. Everything happened so fast. I didn't have to see her whither over years. She was here one day, and then she wasn't."

"So—"

213

"But maybe, I don't know, if it had taken a bit longer, if I had been able to deal with her death while she was alive, it wouldn't have hit me so hard. I wasn't sad; I was numb, or confused, even, looking for answers."

"What kind of answers?"

"It felt like a part of me was missing, like I couldn't find my glasses, but I could still feel them on the bridge of my nose. Do you know the feeling?"

"I do."

"I kept expecting to see her in a crowd, to call, to show up somewhere unannounced, but it didn't happen, and I felt cheated, as if I were owed an answer I was never going to get."

"What was the question?"

"When I think of my mother, when I wonder about her life, about any life, about life in general—I mean, she didn't add anything to the world, no great meaning, no world-changing event, nothing. She lived, she died, the end. Why?"

"She created you. That's something, isn't it?"

"And look at me now."

"Would she have been proud of you, before all this?"

"The win—it would have meant a lot to her."

"The Academy Award?"

"Yes."

"Does it mean anything to you?"

"It meant everything to me at the time."

"And now?"

"Fuck." David scraped his thinning hair with dull fingernails. "Come to think of it, I'm not even sure where it is right now."

"So not a lot."

"I guess not." David chuckled, his laugh scratchy, but gaining body since being comatose.

"What did you mean when you said 'it meant everything'?"

"It was the culmination of a life's work, a lifetime of achievement, a room of my peers celebrating me as this year's champion of the artform. I had been thinking about the moment for the better half of my life, imagining what I would say, what I would do."

"And did it live up to it?"

"It did."

"What happened then?"

"I had been living in the future for so long, working towards my dream, that I didn't know what I was going to do once it was over. Every day that passed, every moment that the day came closer, added to the paradox of excitement and dread that was building inside me."

"What did you think was going to happen?"

"I had this recurring dream that I would wander the streets of Hollywood, naked and afraid, gripping my Oscar."

"And how do you think this fear transformed into your drug abuse?"

"Besides my wife kicking me out?"

"Unless you think your wife was the main reason?"

David crossed his arms and looked up at the ceiling, then, after some consideration, back at Dr. Brimage. "No, I think I probably would have gone in that direction anyway."

"Why?"

"Because, at the time, I wondered if there was any meaning in the world. I could get all the achievements I wanted, everything any man could ever desire, but at the end, it would always end up the same."

"How's that?"

"With death. My mom left me, and I would leave everyone else. There's no escaping it." He raised his shoulders. "What's the point?"

IT'S A LONG WAY DOWN

"Is that how you still feel?"

David shifted in his seat, the edges of the novel pressing into his underside. "I'm not sure what I think right now."

"Hm," she said, looking down at her notepad, scribbling furiously at the pages. She turned the page and continued, biting her lip and underlining large swaths of the page.

"So?" David said, breaking Tabitha's attention.

"So," she said, finishing her sentence, then looking up at David.

"Can you help me?"

"I certainly can't tell you the meaning of life," she said, smiling. "But, on top of my previous assignment, I'd like to recommend two books for you, which may help: The Myth of Sisyphus by Albert Camus and Viktor Frankl's Man's Search For Meaning."

"That's it?"

"Well, no. This is just day one. We're only getting started."

"What's next then?"

twenty four

HIS SHEET SOAKED through, gasping for air, David shot up from an unfamiliar bed. His surroundings were a series of wobbly concentric shapes. With an inability to process what was in front of him, he darted from wall to blurry wall. As he fumbled for his glasses on the side table, he realized where he was—the treatment facility. It was all alien to him, this new life, these sober mornings, like he was a foreigner in a strange, strange land, inhabiting a planet of pig people. Since he'd woken up in the hospital, mornings were the most difficult. Often, he would wake up, snatched from a dream where he'd given in, where he'd surrendered to the God sent end of a needle, and realize it was all a product of an addict's imagination, fighting to get it where it could, even if it was nothing more than an illusion.

It was day two, morning one, 6:32AM. He rolled out of bed, the open air cool on his sweaty legs, and stretched his arms away from his body. The pressure on his shoulders pushed out a squeak of air from his lungs. He released the tension and let his neck drop. There was a small, laminated paper on the ground. He picked it up and flipped it over. It was his weekly schedule, with the first block coming up in an hour: a half hour of meditation, taking place at the outdoor pagoda, behind the building.

He showered then brushed his teeth in front of the mirror, wiping the mist away with his hands, trying to get a better look at the man who was reflected back at him. Through the layered haze, he saw someone who was only tangentially related to the old David, the pre-cocaine David. The man looking back at him was partly the hit a day David, the mind's a maze David, the die in the street David, but there was a hint of another in there, too, the man who wanted to be here, the getting treatment David, the loves his wife David. He turned sideways and ran his fingertips down his stomach, following a line straight down, and not over his life-long grassy knoll, the hobbits home of a rolling mound. By the end of it all, the last dying days of a desperate addict, he rarely ate, and the only thing left was for his body to begin to eat itself.

"Not a diet I'd recommend," he said to the man in the mirror, "but I guess it worked for me."

He leaned over his sink, getting within a few inches of the now-dry mirror. His skin, after two weeks of sobriety, had regained its mostly-normal blood flow, moving from an ashy white to a grapefruit pink.

An alarm, sucking him away from his Narcissus fantasy, the microscopic evaluation of every pore and pimple on his face, went off in the distance. His own alarm joined it, and then, like a wildfire, the rest rang. They were pre-set and centrally controlled to go off at 7:00AM every morning. He put on one of his three pre-approved outfits: a labelless light grey t-shirt and grey sweats. The theory here was to eliminate the expenditure of mental energy on basic choices like clothing, reorganizing that energy into where it was aimed during their stay: self-discovery and self-control. According to the facility, every decision, however incremental it may seem, was a cup from a finite well, the limited resource of a damaged brain.

David, as if dodging through the groans and mutterings of his fellow inmates, the rustling of their rising bodies clear through the thin doors, tiptoed down the hallway, out into the back yard. The air was thick with dew, and the sky, like some God-child had dropped food colouring into it, and, while giggling maniacally, stirred it with a straw, was a swirling purple pink. In the distance, above the backyard fence, David spotted the top of the pagoda, its wooden point punctuated by a metal torch and a small flame billowing in the wind. He followed the edge of the yard, the fence taller than him, lined with rose bushes, to a break and a path. The path, which was lined with worn round stones encased in the ground, opened up to a larger expanse of greenery, the shared backyard before the ocean. Before the drop off to the beach, where grey sand and grass met, was the wooden hut. David wasn't the first to the pagoda, but was beaten by three others, their legs crossed, their arms folded, sitting peacefully amongst the sound of waves. Jamie sat at the front, facing David as he approached.

"Hello," David said from outside the pagoda.

"Hi, David," Mia said, turning to him, bright and eager.

"Glad you're with us this morning," Jamie said, his eyes closed.

The other woman, Donna, made no move to greet David, who looked to Jamie for instruction.

"There's a zafu in the corner," he said, opening his eyes, sensing David's still-standing position. "You can sit on it for the duration of the meditation or go without."

David found a mound of soft black pillows in the corner, picked one up, and found a seat beside Mia. He attempted to cross his legs, one over the other, as he'd seen self-proclaimed yogis do, but failed to get the left over the right.

"We'll be starting in," Jamie looked at his wristwatch, "about 15 minutes. We're waiting for three more to join us."

Adjusting her hips on the pillow, Mia leaned over and whispered to David. "How'd you sleep?"

"Poorly," he said, still fiddling with his shins.

"I keep having these nightmares that I'm using."

"I keep waking up and forgetting where I am."

"I hope my nightmares go away soon."

"They will," interjected Jamie, his eyes closed again.

David raised his eyebrows at Mia, who pulled the muscles in her face back. The group sat in silence, except for the momentary adjustments of bodies, until the next guest arrived.

"Hey," Mike said, stepping uneasily onto the pagoda floor. David and Mia exchanged their own hellos and Mike found a spot beside David.

"Kind of weird we're all together again, isn't it?" Mia said.

"What do you guys have next?" Mike asked.

"Yoga from eight to nine," David said.

"Same," the other two said simultaneously.

"Are we together the whole day?"

"Let me see your schedule," Mia said, as she snatched it out of David's hands. She held David's schedule up to her face, then her own. "Yup. They're exactly the same."

"Looks like we're in this thing together," Mike said.

The next two to arrive, Caden and Brixton, arrived together. Caden, a blonde-hair, blue-eyed all-American boy, was a recent high school graduate whose mom had caught him smoking weed in his bedroom. He said, in the first sharing, that he was there because he had to be, and while he was there, was going to treat it like a vacation.

Brixton, a trust-fund child, the son of a broker, was also there because he had to be, but he had to be there because he was a drug addict. He had a coppery mop that flopped as he walked, and big watery eyes perched atop sunken bags. He wasn't particular about what drug he used, as long as he was using. They sat behind the row of four and the class began.

"Close your eyes." Jamie's voice was understated, methodical, tempered. "Find that comfortable centre within yourself. Begin at your feet, wriggle your toes, move up to your knees, feel the hairs lining your thighs, and sit, and know you're sitting."

The ocean, and the crashing of the waves, the whisper of the wind, seemed to dampen in David's mind.

"Listen to my voice," Jamie said. "Feel how it travels through the air and vibrates through you. Truly experience every sound, every feeling. Lose yourself in the words. Now," he filled his lungs with air. "Relax." He breathed out. "Deep breath in," he said, following his own instructions. "And out. Let it fill every inch of your body, enveloping your lungs, removing the toxins from your blood and nourishing that underdeveloped part of your soul. Hold it. Hold it. And slowly out. All the way out."

David was hyper-aware of his breath and the air caught in his throat.

"And in again. Go slowly. Focus on it and nothing else. Rid your mind of all other thoughts. Forget my voice, the sound of the air, the salt on your skin, and the nagging in your bones. There is only your breath. If you find yourself wandering, re-organize your thoughts and bring them back to breathing. Now out."

David struggled to lose himself in anything but the overriding sensation that he could not breathe. It banged on his chest, exploded out from his skin, and demanded that he give it all up, that he open his eyes at once. He refused, and his mind screamed for oxygen; it screamed surrender. His breath, he decided, would never work as an object of focus. He was a lifelong smoker—his lungs could not be a source of strength. He shifted gears and thought of Alice's face, free floating in his mind. It was a bodiless apparition, the sculpted ivory face of an angel radiating infinite love in all directions. He made her blink, left then right. He extended her lips, curling them up, and down, and showing her teeth. He lost himself in her cheeks, swirling through them like a funhouse mirror. Soon, the world fell apart around her and there was only that face. It was everything. There was no him, no her, only his vision of her, glowing bright blue, an aura of the ages.

Is this what meditation is?

The meta-thought snapped him away from his own focus. He struggled to keep his eyes closed and his mind on task for the remainder of the session.

"Open your eyes," Jamie said, minutes later. His voice was a sweet escape from the nightmare of a raging mind. "How'd everyone like the sitting?"

"Little boring," Brixton said, using the back of his hand to cover his yawn.

"Boring?" Jamie squinted at the boy, but was otherwise emotionless. "Why was it boring?"

"You're just like, I don't know, sitting there. You aren't doing nothing."

"If you're doing nothing, Brixton, you're not meditating. Meditation is about focus. It's about controlling your mind. If you can control your thoughts and direct them on a single task, you can control your addiction."

"What do you focus on?"

"You can focus on anything, Brixton." Jamie closed his eyes, breathed in deeply, then out, and opened them again. "You see, everyone, there are two parts to our minds: the subconscious and the conscious. Your subconscious is made up of an infinite slideshow of hidden desires, wants, and needs. Your conscious mind, on the other hand, shuffles through the options, and gets to decide what actions to act upon. In an addict, the conscious mind is a slave to the subconscious. The subconscious is like a broken jukebox, playing whatever loud, incredibly distracting song that it feels like, seemingly at random, ignoring any inputs by the conscious mind. Our goal, in the 12 weeks you're here, is to retrain your subconscious mind, and to strengthen your conscious mind. Meditation is like a bicep curl for your brain. It's a moment to tell our brains what to do, instead of being led by every passing fancy or desire that strikes."

"And it works?" Mike said.

"Have you heard of Thich Quang Duc?"

"Who?"

"He was a buddhist monk made famous during the Vietnam War for self-immolation."

"I think I've seen the picture," David said, the billowing black-and-white flames from the photo still alive in his head.

"It's one of the most famous photographs of all time."

"It's eery," David said, chewing the inside of his lip.

"It was taken by an American journalist. Mr. Duc, according to witnesses, did not move a muscle or make a sound as he burned in front of an audience. That type of mastery over one's body can only be achieved through years of meditation. It's an achievement of the mind, a battering against his subconscious which surely screamed in pain. Does it work? There's examples of it working all over the world."

The group blinked in synchronicity, as if a light switch flipped in the outdoor room and all their bulbs, blinding as they were, were lit.

"Alright." Jamie clapped, snapping them away from his last lesson, and standing up. "Next up: yoga. Mastery of the mind and the body go hand-in-hand. Let's begin, nice and slow." He stood straight, lined his feet up, and pressed his palms together, elbows up, near his chest. "Follow along with me."

Despite the weight loss, David's body moved like a rusted chassis, cumbersome and creaking. The joints, stiff in their sockets, bled dry and burnt to the bone, still displaying the pock-marked scars of decaying junk, begged for lubrication. But, though he shook, and beads of sweat ran to wherever the force of gravity dictated, he grunted his way through the exercise, willing to give it his full commitment, and coming at it with the same avidity that he reached for a stick of needles. He was a man determined, focused on getting better, focused on, not just getting back to Alice, but getting back to her a new man, a better man.

They flowed through a repetitive series of movements enough times that David lost count, and every time he thought about giving up, right when he was at the brink, they would shift to another exercise, as if Jamie could read his mind, and knew the exact moment to change positions.

"Now move into a seating position, put your hands together, and repeat after me." Jamie sucked up the air around him and said a slow, but moving, "ohm."

Between each ohm, the only thought in David's mind was, "I hope this is the last one."

"Thank you, everyone," Jamie said, opening his eyes. "Thanks for sharing this space with me." He bent down and touched his forehead to the ground. "Namaste." He shot up from the ground, back straight, and smiled. "Right. Breakfast time."

David, Mike, and Mia, sharing the width of the path, walked back to the house together. In front of them, walking with Jamie, was Donna, taking two steps for every one that Jamie took. At the back of the pack was Brixton and Caden, their young-man's cackle rich in the air.

"Weird morning, man," Mike said. "Never thought I'd be up at 7AM doing yoga and meditation."

"No?"

"Don't get me wrong.. I couldn't be happier to be doing it, away from all that shit out there."

"I liked it," Mia said. The hop in her step, the bounce of

her ponytail, was a physical reassurance that she was telling the truth.

"I thought my bones were about to break during the last bit," David said.

"The yoga was pretty easy, but I couldn't find my focus during the meditation," Mike said.

"Neither could I, but I still thought the meditation was far easier than the yoga."

"It'll get easier," Mia said. "Give it time."

"What's next?"

"After breakfast?"

"Yeah."

"Group therapy," David said.

"I hate that shit, man."

"We'll be right there supporting each other." Mia looked up at Mike.

"Think there'll be a lot of people in the group?"

"Might just be the same six from this morning," David said.

"I hope so," Mike said. "Less is more, in my books."

David, who simply nodded at Mike, also believed the smaller the group, the better. In the last 24 hours, he'd shared enough for a lifetime. A man could only share so much of himself, without having to rip it from his soul.

In the dining room, waiting for them on tables lining the back of the room, the rest of the group having already returned from their own adventure and plated up, was a literal smorgasbord of vegetables, fruit, cheese, and bread. To the right of the selection was coffee, fruit juice, and water. David went straight for the coffee, stacked his plate full of food, then joined Mike and Mia at their same table.

"Are you married, David?"

"How'd you know?"

"Your ring, dummy."

"Right." He inspected his aged wedding band. It was an artifact of an old man that was as much a part of him as any other limb..

"How long?" she asked.

He counted in his head. "25 year—wait, no, 26 years. I have trouble remembering that the last year, my using year, existed."

"It's like—" she stopped and parsed her next words, then started again. "It's like coming out of a long dream, isn't it?"

"Exactly," David said.

"You re-enter life as if nothing happened, not really sure where you left off, or where people ended up. It's like some totally awful time travel machine that ruins friendships, your body, and your life, while jumping through time."

Mike stuffed watermelon chunks into his mouth. "I remember snapping out of it one day," he said, sliding more red cubes between his teeth, his cheeks puffed out like a chipmunk. "And I just sat there and wondered who I was." He swallowed. "I hope Mr. Hyde never comes out again."

"Look on the brightside," David said. "Both of you are young." He attempted to sip his coffee, but pulled back from the rim of the glass, the steam stabbing at his throat, and coughed. "Me, my body couldn't handle another go at the needle."

"We all have to look at this as our one shot," Mia said. "There's no other way to do it."

Addiction is a strange beast, thought David, as Mia continued. It levels everyone in its presence; everyone is equal under its thumb, squished down flat, slamming against the floor of humanity. He was glad he was surrounded by people who understood what it meant to not be your own keeper, to be guided by the pale spectre of narcotics, to be burnt out and broken.

The rest of the breakfast was punctuated by a kindness, a tender close-talking, between three lost souls sharing what it meant to be found again. So much so that, by the time breakfast was over, they thought anymore sharing would be an exercise in excess, not progress. But still, they put one foot after the other, and reluctantly guided their bodies to the sharing room.

In it, there were, once again, chairs in a circle, facing each other, seven in total: David, Caden, Brixton, Mike, Donna, and Mia. Dr. Brimage—who was already there when they arrived, sitting patiently, awaiting their arrival, notepad in hand, smiling to no one in particular—was leading the group.

"Welcome everyone." She opened her leather-bound notepad. "Today, we're going to start off light and low pressure. I'd like each of you to share the last time you used and what it was like. That way, we can start at the end, and work our way backwards. Anyone feeling particularly brave today and want to go first?"

Each face in the room, as if they were called on by a teacher for a question they should know the answer to, searched the others, while avoiding the steady gaze of Dr. Brimage. Everyone hoped another would sacrifice themselves to the room, for the greater good, but no one spoke up.

"Anyone?" she asked again.

The screaming silence, which consisted of the shuffling of feet, a far-off ocean breeze, chatter from another room, and the impossible act of hiding one's self within the same space, was deafening.

Dr. Brimage closed her notebook and calmed the room. "That's fine. I can start."

The fear in the room quickly dissipated and was replaced by incredulity, as the six of them tried to imagine the elderly woman, as small as a child in her chair, her feet barely reaching the floor, as an addict, just like them.

"My last time using was quite a while ago, before most of you were born, but not quite so long that it was before all of you were born." She winked at David, who recoiled away from her attention. "It was the late 50's and I, like some of my other psychology classmates, was a Freudian fanatic. I read everything and anything that included his name, was about him, or was written about him. While reading an early paper, "On Coca," I discovered his frequent cocaine use, or abuse. Being an impressionistic young woman in her early 20s, surrounded by competitive young men and feeling like an unwelcome outsider, I thought this might give me a leg up. It was, after all, a panacea to many of life's little and large problems, according to Freud. Of course, I knew, he soon found out how addictive it could be, but I, in my childlike naivety, my adolescent hubris, thought I was smarter, better prepared, more knowledgeable of the dangers of both addiction and cocaine.

Despite my habit, or, as I thought at the time, partly because of it—my dark secret, my backpocket performance enhancer—I graduated with high honours, and was accepted into a doctoral program. But that's when the floodgates opened, and I began to drown myself in the stuff, using every hour of every day. Some days the only thing I ran on was cocaine. I shed all my body fat, I stopped showing up for class, my friends eventually disappeared, and my grades plummeted. Three months into my first semester of graduate school, I realized my life had fallen apart. My family no longer recognized the skinny girl before them, the one wracked with paranoia, a loose jowl, and an empty bank account. I was, I had to admit to myself, an addict."

"How did you turn it around?" Mia said from the edge of her seat. "How did you beat it?"

"I didn't beat it, my dear. You never beat it. Somewhere in my mind it's still there, lurking beneath the shadows, waiting for the right opportunity to spring out and snatch freedom from my hands. But how did I stop? How did I stuff my demons in a sock drawer? Unfortunately, at the time, I didn't have the same resources that you all have here, but I took the next semester off for a 'medical leave,' as my parents referred to it, and locked myself in my room until I was better. After that, I dedicated my life to helping others get through it. I realized that if it could happen to me, someone who had, at the time, read all the appropriate literature, who had full knowledge of what they were doing, then it could happen to anyone. What I found is that we're all susceptible to it, but that susceptibility doesn't make us weak, nor does it make us any less human—it makes us nothing more than unlucky. Drugs crossed our paths and left us worse for wear. But, and here's the good news, I'm still here, as are all of you."

twenty five

DURING THE FOLLOWING stories, when they revealed the moment when their proverbial dams broke, when the final straw was pulled, the camel bent and twisted beneath the weight of addiction, David was struck by how similar their stories were to his. If they were not literally the same, spiritually, in his heart, they felt the same. Each had similar beats, similar ups and downs, the same sad sagas of irrationality, the same stupid self-hatred, or boredom, or fear of life and living, culminating in corresponding reasons for giving up, for disappearing from that life, and for finally ending their slow death, the now-clear cut case of poisoning their body. And as each of them shared, including David, they gave more of themselves back to the circle, spilled the beans, opened their soul, and went beyond the day's topic, deeper into their core. Even Caden, whose mother had forced him between those walls, bumping elbows with tried and true junkies, was showing signs of commitment—a movement towards the middle—to what the seven of them were doing. It was the rapturous wave of self-discovery, turned groupthink, at its core, devoid of John Hughes' director's touch, yet still the result of six (seven) flawed humans, enriched by the shared trials of their lives. A cause, a movement based on a shared sobriety, was forming in the air.

Their hearts full, their resolve steadfast, they broke for lunch, and, unlike this morning's relative quiet, as if they stepped into a high school lunchroom, there was a raucous chatter flowing outwards from each table. Wherever the other half of the people in this room was, whatever experience they just went through, they had that same energy that David held in his heart, that his shared circle moved from. It was a room of damaged souls, committed to making it to the other side.

After lunch, the entire program was dismissed, confined to their room, relegated to two hours of solitary self-discovery, tasked with a single objective: talk to the person you once were, the person who did drugs, and ask him why he wanted to start, and tell him why you want to quit.

David, pencil in hand, the wooden spindles of the chair stabbing into his back, blinked at a blank page. The silence in his small prison, the organic watch tower perched atop his body, was distracting. He didn't manage a single word yesterday. Not a single reason, other than Alice, came to mind. He tapped the end of the pencil against the palm of his hand.

"Just write something," he wrote. "Talk to me."

"Okay, let's talk," he wrote back, surprised by the movement of his hand.

"Why?" The elder wrote. "Why did you do this to us?"

"I told you before, 'why not?'"

"That's it? That's the best you have?"

"In twenty years, you'll be dead. I'll be dead. Why? Because there is no 'meaning of life'—it's a false cliche. Life is life, in all its good and bad moments, its ups and downs, and nothing happens because it should, but simply because it is, because it did, and nothing else. There's no great mystery, no hidden meaning lying in the shadows. You live, you die, then the last person who remembers your name dies too. After that, you are gone forever. A blink in an uncaring universe, a speck of stardust with a name. And do you think you found it now? You found something like meaning?"

"I don't know."

"You're kidding yourself, David."

"Maybe."

"Do you think you'll ever find it?"

"I don't know."

"Then why try? Why are you here? Why are you doing this?"

"Because I have to."

"Listen to yourself! 'You have to' — what reason is that to do anything? You are your own man, creating your own reality—"

"Maybe that's it."

"What?"

"That I can create my own."

"Go on. Tell me more. I've been waiting 56—57—years for this."

David put his pencil down and stared through the white wall in front of him, biting through the fingernails of his right hand, from pinky to thumb, then to his left hand. Halfway through the left, he abandoned the nail and picked up his pencil.

"Sure. Okay. Life is meaningless. Let's talk about that. Meaningless. Meaning. What is meaning? Meaning is something humans, ourselves, came up with. It's a subjective concept that before us, was itself, meaningless. Which gives us, humans, an unrestricted right to ascribe whatever meaning we choose to it. Life is meaningless, sure. You're not wrong. But a human's life, my life, while I am alive, is full of meaning—full of whatever I choose for myself, that gives me, as myself, meaning. And when I'm no longer here, when I'm gone, meaning disappears. You're not wrong. But while I am here, everything has meaning. All of it. The world is teeming with it. Every second of every day, meaning is coming out of my ears, bleeding on everything I touch, wandering the streets, wondering what it's going to eat in the morning. I am meaning. My life is meaningful. And it's my obligation, as a human, gifted with this short blink of consciousness, a moment in an uncaring universe, to fill it with as much meaning as I can, to give others meaning, to change the world positively. To waste away this gift of God or whatever, to throw it away, to smother it with black poison, is outrageous. It may have been meaningless before me, and after me, but while I am here, meaning exists, if that meaning is simply to ask "what is meaning?"—that's good enough for me. It's enough to survive on. I'll take it. I do take it. I am here saying I am meaning, from whence there was once no meaning. And that's marvellous—a spectacular wonder of creation. Who knows what any of this, everything, means, but that's not for me to decide. The only thing I get to decide is what my life means, to me, or to those around me, and beyond that, I cannot say, nor do I care to. Let me think about today, and let that be enough. It is enough."

"I don't think you need me, anymore, then," David the younger wrote.

"I don't think I do, either."

"Goodbye," he wrote, as both of them.

He put his pencil down and laboured through an exhale. His face was flush, but his limbs and his smile were loose and free. He shot up and the backs of his knees pushed his chair away. He walked in small circles, shaking his fists in front of his face. He pressed his right fist against his lips and stopped moving.

I've done it. I've had a breakthrough.

There was a knock at the door. "David?" The knob turned and the door opened. It was Mia. "Coming? We've got group exercise."

"I don't have much choice, do I?"

"About as much choice as I had in middle school gym class."

"Do I need to change?"

"You're wearing a sweatsuit already."

"Okay."

"Besides, we're late."

Outside, in the backyard, Jamie, his taut tanned skin, like a twelve hour turkey, stood shirtless beneath the late afternoon sun. Mia and David were the last to arrive. They quickly found a spot at the back of the group, hoping to hide from anything that sounded remotely close to the commands of a drill sergeant.

For a few minutes, David jogged confidently around the yard before lagging behind the group. His lungs burned and joints ached in their sockets as they grinded away the last remnants of junk hiding in the deep crevices of his body. After a series of jumping jacks, push-ups, squats, planks, he learned that being in shape was not the simple matter of shaving away the extraneous fat on your body. It reminded him that breakthroughs would happen, but success only came through the slow climb of will.

"Twenty more laps!" Jamie said, as he transitioned from a plank to his feet. "Let's finish strong!"

Stumbling through the run, David gripped his chest, hoping to transfer the energy from his palm to his heart. Sweat ran down his back like a small whitewater rapid. His body was a reminder of all the drugs—anything he could get his greedy hands on—he'd ingested in the last year and a half, all the times he went days without sleep, the recalcitrant attitude he had towards the need for food. The irony of it all, which he felt so plainly now, was that not once did death pass through his mind, not once did it knock on his mental doorstop, and whisper that he was around the corner, despite the very real fact that he was. But at that moment, as he put one foot after the other, as his heart worked overtime, he believed he was closer to death than he'd ever been before.

"Keep going!" Jamie said from the front of the pack, running backwards, gliding along at an easy pace, his shredded thighs glistening in the sun, his free flowing short shorts a testament to his devil may care state of mind.

David's legs buckling beneath his weight, he slowed to a walk, then stopped and bent over. Hands on his knees, he took in swallowing gulps of air.

"David!" Jamie said, circling around to the back of the pack.

His words came in short bursts between gasps. "I can't. Go on. I'm out. I tap. I give up."

Jamie jogged, knees up high, in a single spot, beside David. "You okay?"

David coughed up god knows what. "I think I might have pushed myself too hard."

"No way! You did great. Way to hustle!" He patted David on the back. "Catch your breath for a minute and do the rest of the exercise at your own pace. You can practically see the finishing line from here!"

No pace was the only pace David was capable of. He sat on the grass, cross-legged, and attempted to catch his breath. He snapped the strands of green off at the tips and watched the group struggle past him for another lap. Every time they passed him, he averted his eyes, focusing on anything else, unable to watch them head on, as he did nothing but mope around in the grass. As they ran out of sight of him, he threw the grass he had palmed and slammed his fist into the ground, which pushed him onto his feet. Slowly, he stumbled his way towards the group, or, depending on your perspective, they quickly caught up to him.

"That's the spirit!"

They ran around the yard twice more, then grouped up in their original spot and completed a final 100 countdown of jumping jacks, which David hoped signified a finish line.

He finished them with a sloppy mixture of determination, pride, and exhaustion.

"And we're done!" Jamie said, continuing to do laps around the group, as each person collapsed in succession. Everyone rolled over, giving each other sideways high fives. "You all did amazing," Jamie said, doing more jumping jacks. "Enjoy the next hour of free time."

The energy of anticipation, a bottled up desire to speak to the woman he loved, shocked David to his feet with renewed vigor. He glided towards the house, up the stairs, and into the games room, as if he had been running all his life. In one rapid movement, he slipped into the small room and closed the door.

"Hello?" her voice was sweet and searching.

"Hi," he said between near-drowning gulps of air.

"David! Oh darling! I've been thinking about you all day, hoping you would call. How are you? How was your first day? Are they feeding you enough? Have you made any friends? What are the other people like? What are the teachers like? What are they making you do? How's the food? Oh, I just have so many questions!"

"I can hear that." He stifled a guffaw. "Where do I begin?"

"Tell me what you've done so far today. I want to hear everything."

"We talked a lot. Like, I mean a lot. And you know I'm not the sharing type, but it's been good for me. Lots of talking."

"What else?"

"We did yoga first thing in the morning."

"Yoga!"

"Yup."

"How was it?"

"I'll just say I'm trying over here. I've exercised more in

the last 24 hours than I have in the last 24 years. I'm tired."

"You'll get used to it."

"But right now, I'm happy—happy to hear your voice."

"It feels like a dream sometimes." Her voice cracked, the sound of sadness breaking through the edges of her words.

"Talking to me is like a dream?"

"It is."

"Why?"

"The last year was so, so horrible, David. I thought I'd never see or hear from you again."

"I'm sorry."

"I know," she said, dragging the syllables out slowly, letting every sound resonate through the receiver.

"I would do anything to take back the last year."

"I think you're already doing it. That's why you're there."

"I'm going to come back to you the man you deserve."

"You don't need to come back as anyone but the David I know and love."

"I hope to do that and more."

There was only the sound of the both of them breathing, which moved back and forth through the receiver.

"David?"

"Yes?"

"Why did you do it?"

"Do what?"

"That night, the night of the Academy Awards. Why?"

David clenched down hard. "I was lost."

"Lost?"

"I was lost and I wanted to check out. I wanted to forget it all. I wanted to be destructive, so I was, and I made the biggest mistake of my life. I'll carry my regret close to my heart for the rest of my life. I'll carry it with me while I'm rotting in the ground."

"It's a wound we'll both carry forever, but it made me

stronger, and I hope it will make us stronger."

"It already has. Besides," he said, laughing, and shaking off the sadness. "You were already the strongest woman I ever knew."

"It's always been love, not strength."

"What brought you back to me?"

"It was always a matter of time."

"The last time we talked, before I woke up in the hospital, you told me you didn't want to see me ever again."

"Can you blame me? Out of nowhere, without saying a word to me, you broke into my house, high out of your mind, having a drink. Wounds need time to heal. Instead, I got an idiot who ripped a fresh scab off."

"I was an idiot wasn't I?"

She snickered under her breath. "Yeah."

There was a knock on the window, startling David. Caden was making a makeshift phone sign with his hand and holding it up to his ear.

"I've gotta go my little mouse. Someone needs the phone."

"Talk tomorrow?"

"Same time. I love you," David said.

"I love you too."

David savored his last few seconds of being connected to her, drinking in the rustling over the wires, sipping on the short breaths on the other line, linked up, ear to ear.

How could he have ever given this up?

Caden knocked again and David instinctively put the phone back.

twenty six

AN ORCHESTRA of songbirds were guided by mother nature's maestro somewhere in the distance. The repeating caw, a pleasant part of David's dreams, moving him through some quickly forgotten mission, gradually ripped him out of that very same dream. Wiping his eyes, he slipped on his glasses and adjusted to his once-foreign surroundings. He sat up and surveyed, for perhaps the final time, his room. It was the day he had been waiting for since he'd gotten here: the day he got to go home. He was ready. His mind was free and focused, clear of the clutter and cobwebs of a clunky, drug-burnt brain. His body, an external reflection of his internal health, was robust and powerful, hard and firm. And his soul, if such a thing existed, was a solid apparition, its holes and gaps sewn up in the early hours of each morning.

Alice would arrive to take him home within the hour. Instead of attending the farewell ceremony later that day, David, who could not imagine spending another unnecessary minute away from Alice, would make a quiet escape a few hours early, having said his goodbyes the night before. With his last hour, he chose to further cement the habits he'd learned over the last four months.

David pulled out his journal, the pages now thick with ever-improving handwriting, and turned to the first blank page. What sprung forth, focused through the habitual stroke of a pen, was an outpouring of appreciation for the last four months, a love of a positive routine. It was the complete absence of a separation between thoughts and written words—his hand having become an appendage of the mind, the final day's swan song. Then, as quickly as the wind of words started, they stopped. He closed his journal and unrolled his yoga mat. His body, like wet ink on paper, was loose and limber. He flowed through the motions with a lightness that hadn't touched his body since he was a child. The outside observer wouldn't be able to detect a hint of the physical struggle that plagued him during the first few weeks. His body was now an extension of the mind, a tool that stood at his beck and call, waiting for the steadfast captain to command its next movement. He reached for the sky, extending his limbs towards some heavenly purpose, one final time, before folding into himself and into a meditative position. As the rest of the earth fell away, the words "my actions are my own" moved, like the ocean's tide on a windless morning, through his mind.

When he opened his eyes, returning to the world with a gentle, smooth landing, it was time to go. He closed his journal, packed up his final few pieces of clothing, and rolled up his yoga mat. With everything in hand, he went for the doorknob, then stopped, and turned back. There was a longing to stay, to remain in his new home and bask in all he had achieved. But, he knew, that was the fear talking, telling him to hide from the real road ahead, to cower in the face of temptation. This was just the beginning of his life-long journey. Only when he died a sober man would he know he'd won. To think, as he sometimes did, that the battle was already won, to believe himself a changed man, was the first sign of an impending relapse. Vigilance was what he needed now.

He turned, opened the door, and walked out. With a small prance, a bobbling hop, culminating into a mild jog, he made his way towards the exit, purposefully avoiding a final goodbye with his fellow comrades. Outside, parked at the far end of the driveway, partially hidden by the statue, was the tail-end of Alice's idling car.

"Hey, stranger," she said, as he rounded the driveway. She leaned against the car, arms crossed at her chest, wearing a smile that grew with each step David took. She opened her arms to him.

"Hi," he said, his voice wobbling. He dropped his stuff and collapsed into her arms.

"You've finally come back to me." She gave him small, searching kisses, that travelled from his neck to his lips.

He drank her in, wrapping his lips around hers and pressed her body into his. They were like chimeras, eternally fused, two bodies buckling at the knees, folding beneath the earth shattering weight of their love.

She pushed his shoulders back and looked him up and down, then gripped his shoulders tighter. "You feel so strong. You look so young!"

"I can't remember ever feeling this good."

"I can't remember you looking this good," she said, laughing.

"You look beautiful, too."

"Shall we?" she asked.

"Please."

That night, in his own bed, the two of them made love and it was quick and hard and okay, because they went again, until the exertion of ecstasy made beads of sweat roll off his body onto hers and they collapsed in each other's arms, still hungry, yet exhausted, and just before sleep overtook him, he knew, finally, he was home.

twenty seven

THE RISING TIDES of the Pacific Ocean went in and out, the crescent moon, perched atop the sky, continued through its never-ending cycles, carcasses decayed and became food for new life, babies were born, old men died in their sleep, and six months passed in a single breath of a bursting star. There was no inherent logic, no graspable gradual gain, to this time jump. Sure, they say time moves faster every year, a product of perspective, perhaps, or the paradox of temporal subjectivity, but here was David, six months later, a man of the future, space boots and all.

But the David of the future was not the David of the past—he'd learned from his time in the clinic and had stuck by everything he'd learned—he was up at the gym every morning, worked with a dedicated nutritionist and personal chef, and still had time in the afternoon to practice yoga, and to meditate, while keeping up with his daily journaling. Every evening, at 9PM, he went to a narcotics meeting, where he saw both Mike and Mia, whose friendship had progressed to a more intimate bond. His own relationship with Alice was now the guiding light of his life, a beacon of strength, and any gulf between them had been conquered and diminished. Recently working again, he'd landed a supporting role in a PT Anderson film, and the table read was two weeks away. For the first time in years he was nervous to begin a film. He was stronger, but he was still human. He was worried his old, out-of-shape appearance was part of his mystique, and wondered if without it, he was still the same actor, but with equal measure, he was confident that he'd become an even better actor, channeling his demons into his craft. Finally, he'd invested a small fortune into camera equipment and was experimenting with his own brand of avant-garde films, while trying to master the editing software. After his next film, he hoped to direct a quasi-autobiographical film about his time away from Alice called "Drowning Above Water."

It was a Tuesday, around noon, and David was sitting at his kitchen table, momentarily lost in his head, currently in-between bites of a tuna sandwich, imagining a double-exposed shot of a flower growing and a building crumbling.

"David," Alice said, snapping him away from the scene. She was holding up a piece of mail lifted from a pile of similar looking envelopes. "Are you ever going to do anything about these?"

"They're from the apartment."

"I know."

"They're mortgage payments."

"Right."

"What should I do about them?"

"I meant you should do something about the apartment."

"Like what?" He took a bite of his sandwich. A small chunk of tuna rolled out from the back end and fell out onto his lap.

"Sell it?"

"I don't know if I'm there yet."

"What do you mean?"

"I'd have to go down there, see what state it's in, and talk to people from that time in my life. Even existing in the apartment, a place where I only existed high, scares me."

"You can hire someone to sell it, can't you? Do you even

have to step foot in it?"

"I can't imagine how I left it."

Alice cocked her head with a question mark.

"I wasn't exactly the cleaning type while I lived there."

"Well," she said, throwing the envelope back into the pile. "If you think you can handle it, then get rid of it, but if you aren't there yet, I understand."

The thought of his apartment, and the question about whether he was strong enough to return, was the general theme of his afternoon, and into his yoga session, creeping up in the background of his mediation, and seeping out the end of his pen and into his journal.

The cravings, he thought, were gone, and his cells no longer yearned the sweet release of the tar. His purpose, the direction of his movements, were gently guided, consciously, by decisions that would benefit himself in the long run. He had a rock in Alice, a woman who knew his inner struggle. With directing, he had a new goal to move towards. Nothing in his life resembled what propelled him to that life in the first place, and nothing in that apartment had any sort of hold over him. It would be in and out—a small price to pay to destroy the last living vestige of the old David. If anything, it would be cathartic, a right of passage, a proverbial and literal moving on.

"I'm going to sell it," he said over dinner.

"I'm glad," she said, needling a brussel sprout with her fork.

"I'm going to call a cleaning service in the morning."

"It's going to be that bad?"

"It'll be worse."

"Better them than you, I suppose," she said, giggling between bites. "But I guess that'll be a big burden off your shoulders."

"I can meet them there, hand them the keys, and then

give them to a realtor once it's clean. After that, I'm home free."

"Free of an extra home, actually."

"Exactly."

The next morning, after getting off the phone with the cleaning service, it was as if David's stomach, a twisted jumbled knot, had been put through a tumble dry cycle. The cleaners would be there in two hours, and he was already a mess. He pictured himself walking through an idyllic meadow, sun bearing down on his back, a light mist in the air, and into the hellfire of a melting apartment. While meditating, the image of his burning apartment, the floorboards spitting and crackling around him, crept into his thoughts, a spontaneous combustion, rising and falling towards the image. He stood on unsteady ground and wondered whether he was prepared to re-enter, even if for a moment, his old life. As a final act of discovery, one last wrestle with himself, he pulled out his journal and went over every act of strengthening he had done in the last ten months. They seemed to add up to one thing: he was ready, and he had the data to prove it.

This was a final test, the key to moving on with his life—if not now, when?

"Live by the sword, or die by it," he wrote in his journal, before closing the worn-leather cover. With his confidence restored, he showered and left the house without saying goodbye to Alice.

As his old apartment came into view, the sun bouncing off the red brick, David stiffened in his car seat and sucked his mouth dry. Parking the car out of view of Teddy's window, he walked towards the apartment, chest up and proud, imposing upon the block his presence. The simple posture adjustment, a fake-it-till-you-make-it attitude, filled David with a false sense of confidence, which was enough to get him to the front door. He pressed a healthy index finger into the doorbell.

Timothy, who'd gone through his own small transformation, having shaved his head bald, appeared, squinting at the intruder that stood at his door.

"Yes?" he asked, his expression dull.

"Tim?"

"Do I know you?"

"I live here. Can you let me in?"

"I'm sorry, sir. I would know you if you did."

"It's David, Timmy."

Timothy moved closer, squinting harder. "Smith?"

"That's the one."

Tim jumped back, scratched his exposed scalp, then came closer. It was if he'd seen a ghost, because in many ways he had. "Holy hell, David! You've changed."

"For the better, I hope."

"Absolutely!"

"I got clean."

The man held his hands up, as if he were accused of something. "I'm not here to judge, Mr. Smith."

"I know," he said, smirking out the side of his mouth. "You're here to let me in." David motioned to the door.

"Right, sorry." Tim opened the door and stood back for David. "Please, come in."

"Tim?"

"Yeah, Mr. Smith?"

"Do you still have a spare key for my place? I can't seem to find mine."

"I have a spare of everyone's."

"Perfect."

Tim disappeared into his office, then re-appeared with a key dangling from his finger. He held it out to David. "Just as you left it, 701."

"Thanks," David said, letting the key drop into his hand.

"I also have a cleaning service coming in a few minutes, could you let them in?"

"Got it. Anything else?"

David looked down at the key, then back at Tim. "It's good to see you again, Tim."

"And you, Mr. Smith."

David walked towards the elevators, then stopped a few feet before the doors, lingering in the lobby. He turned back. "One last thing."

Tim reared his head from the office. "Sure."

"Does Teddy still live across from me?"

"Indeed he does, sir."

David, from the inside out, shuddered. He turned away, without reply, and summoned the elevator. The doors opened a moment later and he stepped through. He pressed seven and the doors closed. He crossed his arms at his chest, pulling tight on his body, and clenched his fists, as if he could squeeze out the cold shake, the chattering of his teeth. By the seventh floor, through a series of repetitive mouthings of his mantra, David had stilled his body. The doors opened. He peered his head beyond the precipice and, seeing the halls empty, stepped calmly out of the elevator. He walked slow, yet confident, chest up, shoulders straight, one foot after the other, ignoring the creaks in the wood below, keeping his eyes straight, unflinching, until he reached his door, that same once-hazy 701, now clear in sobriety. He fumbled for his keys, the jangling hot in the air, as he felt the judging stare of 706 behind him. As panic set in, as if he were about to piss himself right there at his front door, hopping from one foot to the other, he slipped the key into the slot, turned, and slammed the door behind him. Eyes closed, leaning against the back of the door, out of breath, he was hit with a strong, pungent smell, something akin to a hundred burning diapers. David's face turned inwards and he pulled his shirt

247

up over it.

It was his former apartment, in all its glory. He stepped forward, light on his feet, creating small prints in the layer of dirt caked to the floor. In his kitchen, to-go containers and dishes had been overtaken, as if they were growing at the bottom floor of some deep forest, overrun with mold, mushrooms, and all sorts of bottom-feeding plant life. Oranges had grown what looked like smaller oranges, coming out of their sides, like some twisted nuclear experiment, mutated beyond recognition, and garbage was littered in every direction. He wandered beyond his kitchen, out into the birth of his apartment, where 100s of empty bottles were strewn about, which he stepped over with grace. Some of them were half full, some crammed full of cigarette butts, the combination of which formed a thick material that was attempting a climb out of each bottle. There was a corner of his couch that was nothing but cigarette butts, a firm ball of ash, and rotting tobacco. There were unidentifiable stains on the furniture, the walls, the floors, odd colours that he couldn't name, streaks of them, as if a degenerate Pollock rolled in, fists full of garbage, and splattered his apartment in uncharacteristically unartistic ways, signifying the desperate sadness of the man who lived inside. The only thing mysteriously missing were the bags he expected to find, perhaps licked clean, every last one, within his last week in this hellhole.

A knock at the door startled David, ripping him from his exploratory mission, followed by an accented "Hello?"

David hopscotched over the pockets of rotting garbage and opened the door, still holding his shirt to his mouth. Four women, three in their teens, one who looked to be around David's age, stood at the door, holding an entire aisle of cleaning supplies. Their smiles, large and genuine, turned foul once the smell of the apartment hit them. In unison, they moved the masks dangling from their necks to their faces. David, without having been here himself, hadn't effectively communicated the full disrepair of his apartment.

"Hello," he said, through the thin cotton of his t-shirt. They moved swiftly past him, inspecting the apartment like generals recounting the bodies of the fallen, the gory gruesome display of death and decay. They looked through drawers, opened cabinets, wandered through his bedroom, opened the washer and dryer, wiped an index finger across a counter and came away with something not of this world, searched high and low, dumped out garbages, opened and closed doors. The mess inspected, the damage monetized, the upcoming clean estimated, the eldest woman walked back to David.

"24 hours," she said, clicking her tongue.

"That's it?"

"Si."

"I'll come back in 24 hours?"

"Si."

"And you can handle this?"

"No problem. It'll be better."

"Okay," David said, feeling like he'd stumbled upon a cleaning-based ponzi scheme. Reluctantly, he handed her the keys. "I guess I'll see you in 24 hours."

She didn't reply, but stuffed the keys into one of her many teal coloured pockets.

David backed away from the scene, towards the door, as he watched the women start turning his already-upside down apartment right side up. He gripped the door handle, turned, and slipped out, before remembering the animal who lived next door. David walk-ran to the stairs, almost tearing the door off his hinges as he opened it. He ran down the stairs, out of the building, not stopping to say goodbye to Tim, and was out of the apartment, clear and free, on his way back home, to rejoin his new life untarnished. There was nothing left to do but grab the keys from the maid service tomorrow, then hand them to a realtor. His hands would be clean and soon this period would be the distant memory of another man.

The next morning, he sprung out of bed, light on his feet, and with calm in his heart. Today was his Christmas—a chance to to break free, stop looking back, and look to the future. In the autumn of his life, he would become a director, a break out hit, and before his time passes, be known as one of the greatest living actors, and directors, to have graced the world of film. It would be his new purpose, his new Mount Everest, waiting out there for him to climb, to master, and internalize. Today was the day his new journey actually began. Everything else was all just leading up to today. From here on out, the old David would be no more. There would only be his replacement, a man better, stronger, who was a force for love in the world.

Eager to begin, he threw some clothes on, brushed his teeth, and attempted to say goodbye to Alice, but he couldn't stir her. Instead, she rolled over, grumbled, and went back to sleep. Her body, a peaceful protest against the waking world, humming itself gently up and down, rose and fell with the tempo of David's heart.

How could he have ever let her go, he wondered. He whispered "I love you" in her direction before leaving.

Thirty minutes later, he'd returned to the David Thompson. Tim, his blue dress shirt unbuttoned uncomfortably low, greeted him at the door

"They still up there?"

"Far as I know they haven't left. Musta been 20 hours they've been working away."

He checked his watch. "A little less than 23 hours, actually."

"Musta been some mess."

"Musta been," David said, as he continued towards the elevator.

Inside, he, for the final time, pressed the circular seven. Only the top right corner, the area surrounding the angle in the number, glowed. A familiar song came from the elevator speakers. "Uno, dos, tres, quatro." It was Gil Scott-Heron's "The Bottle," Teddy's favourite.

Like a break in the dam, a blown gasket, a two buck Tuesday all you can eat buffet, a flood of memories, some bad, most good, of a man unfiltered, uncaring, and free, came back to him. He steadied himself against the wall, as if he were blown over by the rush of memories. The door opened as Gil sung, "He done quit his 9 to 5 to drink full time so now he's livin' in the bottle." David shuddered, but didn't move.

Who was that man who listened to it the last time? Who was the man who listened to it now?

Before the doors could close, David stuck a foot between them, and they once again opened. He left the elevator on unevening footing, but still chest up and confident. He knocked on his front door.

"Si?" a timid voice from inside said.

"It's Mr. Smith."

"Si. Come in, come in."

He opened the door and, as if they had declared war on his nostrils, was blasted by a mixture of pinewood and a wild earthy citrus. For a brief lapse, while his mind was scattered from the debilitating smell of pure cleanliness, he thought he'd stumbled into the wrong apartment. But there it was, sanitized of his existence, de-speckled of debauchery, punctuated by the unmistakable sparkle ringing in his ear. It was as if they had scrubbed clean his soul, and all the sins that went with it. This was an apartment reborn in the hellfire of lemon scented cleaning wear, and there was with little left for him to do but to take the keys and run.

"Wow," David said. He wandered slowly around the apartment, taking it in through every sensory input he could.

The older woman saddled up beside him, beaming but tired. "You like?"

"I love," he said.

She held the keys out to him. "Thank you, Mr. David."

He took them off her, while turning in small circles, trying to convince himself this was his old apartment.

"Anything more?"

"Just the bill, I guess."

"In the mail soon." She turned back to the other women and called out, "Vamonos!"

They appeared, hands full of garbage bags, pails, cleaning supplies, long-handled equipment, short-handled equipment, dirt stains on their hands, faces, and knees, laughing and chatting in Spanish, until leaving the apartment and closing the door behind them.

David wandered through his old walls, now new, an ear to ear grin painted on his face, skipping from leg to leg, rubbing a finger over his counters, inspecting the walls, opening and closing windows, and pulling out covers.

What kind of black magic occurred here, he wondered.

The burn holes in his furniture, the cracks in the paint, broken and bent blinds, they were all fixed by some elbow-grease based sorcery. Like a ghost examining a past life, retracing all the steps where he went wrong, only to wake up back in his bed, lessons learned, he rounded his apartment one final time, shrugged, and left.

twenty eight

As DAVID WAITED for the elevator, he began to giggle. At first a gentle cawing, then maniacally, a cackle that bounced off the walls. It was as if the tension he felt coming here released at once, coming through his lungs, in gasping hee-haws. But, like all good things in life, his laughter was cut short. A voice boomed from behind him.

"Good God, are my eyes tricking me?"

Every inch of blood flooded from David's surface, fighting its way to its core, turning him ghost-white, and leaving his stomach shattered, like a wrecking ball ran through it. His blood hardened, crunching down inch-by-inch, before bursting, then caving in on itself, like a collapsing black hole. Exclamation marks jumped from his body and ran out in every direction.

This was it. A dance with the devil, the final boss, after the final boss, one last cut scene, the red giant from across the hall, the bastard son of floor seven, the kingpin of pleasure in the flesh. Theodore. Teddy. Ted.

He took a deep breath and turned.

"Christ brother!" Teddy said, lumbering towards David, who took a step back. "We all thought you were dead."

David, the saliva having gone to whatever hell his blood fled to, tripped over his words. "Hi," he stammered out. The chime, signalling the elevator's arrival, went off behind him. He looked over his shoulder. "I—uh—can't talk. I gotta go."

"Not a chance, Davey-boy." Teddy put his baseball mitt

around David, pulling him in. "We've gotta catch up."

"Catch up?"

"Sure!"

David could feel the heat of Teddy's exhalation on his face—a combination of cigar, whiskey and decay.

"About what?"

"First of all." Teddy took a step back, holding David by the shoulders. "You've shrunk right down. You look fantastic. I miss you. I want to know what you've been doing. What's new? What happened?"

"A lot."

"No kidding, hey?."

"I really—"

"You really what? You gotta go?"

"Well—"

"We were friends, weren't we?"

"Sure."

"So why not talk to me a minute?"

"Why not?" David drew the words out in long syllables.

"I wanna know where you've been this whole time. You need to catch me up."

"That's really not necessary."

"It is to me. Don't you have any questions of your own?"

"I guess," he said, the words surprising himself.

"And don't you want answers?"

"I do."

"Perfect!" Teddy slipped an arm over David and pushed him forward.

"But I can't stay long." David looked back, the elevator doors closing.

As he walked into the apartment, he was struck by the power of time. An eternity of progress had passed between now and the last time he'd stepped foot in here, yet he couldn't trace the steps in between, how he got here, how long it really was, and if it were more than mere moments, spread out through eternity, a fractal re-emerging here and forever. Nothing was out of place. The sheets were still there, every trinket accounted for, the same sadness coming out from the floorboards.

David followed Teddy to the black leather couch with no legs. They sat, knees almost touching and no one spoke. David rocked slightly back and forth.

Teddy cleared his throat. "You clean?"

"Eight months."

"Hell of a job. You look damn fine."

"Thanks," he said, crossing and uncrossing his legs.

"Not everyone can beat the bug. Lord knows I've wrestled with it brother, but I always came back to her."

David tapped his front pocket, but nothing was there. "Wasn't easy," he said.

"But I learned to live with it. Probably a part of me as any other organ."

David looked past Teddy, around his apartment. His lip curled slightly. "Glad to be off it."

"And your wife?"

"Stronger than ever."

"Wow!" he slapped a mitt on David's thigh. "Looks like you've got it made."

"Couldn't be happier."

"You always talked highly of her. Tell her thanks, from me, for saving you. Glad we didn't lose you."

"So am I."

"But, I guess, in a way we did lose you."

"I guess."

"How'd it go down?"

"Getting clean?"

"Last I remember, we were getting pretty close. Good

friends, even, I'd reckon. Then you just disappeared. Thought I'd never see you again."

David eyed Teddy, his face contorting. "We were good friends?"

"I thought so? But you disappeared without even a good-bye."

"Is that how you remember it?"

"Am I wrong?"

"You stopped talking to me long before I left, Teddy."

"What?" Teddy snapped back, as if David's words were a swipe at his face.

"You cut me out of your life, dropped me like a sickness, like I didn't matter to you."

"Brother, you got it backwards. We drifted a bit near the end, sure, but you were the one who turned cold."

David shot out of his seat and walked away. "You're insane, Teddy."

"Tell me then. How'd it go down?"
He turned back. "You needed money. I gave you money. You disappeared."

"Money? Is that what you want?"

"What? No. I don't want anything from you."

"I'm shocked, here, Davey-boy. I had no idea you felt that way."

"Fuck you, Teddy," David said, throwing his index finger Teddy's way, as if he could push the insult into him further.

Teddy got out of his seat. "I can't believe I came off that way."

"Why do you say it like that? 'I came off that way.' That's what happened. You didn't come off in any other way than how you meant to. You knew what you were doing."

"What can I do? Let me make it up to you."

"There's nothing you can do."

"What do you want? Name it." Teddy looked frantically around his apartment.

"You don't have anything I want." David turned to the door.

"I could, uh…"

He put his hand on the doorknob.

"What about a lil' H?"

David paused, then looked back at Teddy. "I don't do that shit anymore."

"I know, but, for old time's sake. Just a taste."

"No."

"Remember all the good times we had in this apartment?"

"I remember a lot of bad times. A lot of low times."

"This would be a good one."

"It would be nothing but guilt. Black tar guilt."

"One last time."

"I've already had a last time."

"Then a final goodbye. A swan song, for good ol' Teddy."

"This is our goodbye."

David turned from the Red Giant, head high and proud, but as the door clicked behind him, he slumped in place and there was a small rumble in his chest. He sipped in short, choking breaths, all the way back to the elevator. The floor numbers folded onto themselves, changing from one to seven. The door opened and he got in. Gil Scott-Heron was still playing over the elevator radio.

He steadied himself, between floors two and three, against the wall. The pressure of the needle against his skin, the sweet pin prick, the smell of the bubbling tar twirling in the air, this and more flashed through his skin, buckling him. He craved to be a child again, to feel the ultimate surrender, a moment of uncaring, where he let the trials of the day slip away into the nothingness of a needle. The doors opened and his new life, the life he wanted, stood before him. He shook the desire. He had his life back. He belonged with Alice.

But she wouldn't know a thing. She would believe he was here, as he would be, taking care of the last roadblock to happiness. It would be a final so long, before he sold the apartment—a last goodbye, a simple taste, a dab of the tongue. He'd be back in the house, with no one the wiser, before dinner. And what about his tolerance? It was non-existent. Not a trace of the black tar ran through his cells, hitching a ride to heroin heaven. He was clean. Free of its grip. Which would make it all the sweeter. It would be pure ecstasy, like nothing he'd ever experienced. There was no way around it. He had to do it, if for nothing else but the uncharted territory of the high. Songs would be written, plays made, movies captured, paintings displayed, novels typed, word by joyous word, of the high. It would be poetic and pure and powerful. A true artist's paradise, here on earth.

The doors closed, forcing David into a non-reaction of a decision. He pressed seven and the elevator engines whirred, beginning his short ascent. He climbed up to seven and beyond, away from the apartment, through the thin brick roof, up into the rich blue sky, and into the atmosphere, soaring through the emptiness of space, until earth was a far off glimmer, a distant memory in a cold universe, never to be seen or heard from again.

about
the
author

Ian Canon was born in Edmonton, Alberta.
He received his B.A. in Philosophy at the University
of Alberta before spending time in the marketing
industry. Other works of his include "Madam, in
Eden, I'm Adam" and "Before Oblivion."

You can find him on:

facebook www.facebook.com/thisisallcanon
instagram @thisisallcanon
twitter @thisisallcanon
website www.thisisallcanon.com

www.ingramcontent.com/pod-product-compliance
Lightning Source LLC
Chambersburg PA
CBHW061955170626
46813CB00006B/2647